OFF THE RECORD

ANNMARIE BOYLE

DAHLIA
MEDIA

Edited by Jolene Perry

Cover design by Qamber Designs

Copyright © 2022 by Annmarie Boyle

ISBN: 978-1-7359351-9-5

ALSO BY ANNMARIE BOYLE

The Storyhill Musicians
Love Me Like a Love Song
Don't Let the Music Die

Storyhill Novellas
Friday at the Blue Note
Fine Tuned

"There are too many people in the world today who decide to live disappointed rather than risk feeling disappointment."

-Brene Brown, Atlas of the Heart

CHAPTER ONE

BRIDGET HAYES' PLANE LEFT IN EXACTLY TWO HUNDRED and eighteen minutes, and her suitcase sat open and empty on her bed. A giant black hole mocking her. It wasn't like she didn't know how to pack. Years on the road made her an expert. But this trip wasn't about a basketball game or a business development meeting. Nothing that simple.

"I have nothing to wear," Bridget mumbled. Hangers clattered into one another as she rejected every option.

"You have more clothes than the average New York City boutique in that massive closet," Kal said, laying across Bridget's bed, sorting through the romance novels on Bridget's nightstand.

Bridget deflated into the oversized reading chair tucked into the corner. "I give up."

Kalisha lifted her eyes and waved at the closet. "The red one is nice."

"The one in the back?" Bridget pushed her dark-rimmed glasses up her nose and squinted. "That's a dress."

Kal huffed and spun into a sitting position, flipping her long braids over her shoulder. "And you wear dresses."

"Not in front of my family," Bridget said, pulling her legs

underneath her. She absently ran her fingers over the scar that carved a deep red path from her thigh to her lower calf. If her family didn't see her scars, there was less to trigger their sympathy. Less sympathy from them meant fewer memories for her.

"Don't you think it's time to . . ."

Kal's question trailed off as Bridget's phone blared out its familiar ringtone. Without thinking, Bridget moved toward the dresser where it sat and reached for it. Kal slapped her fingers away. Even ten years after her bestie took home the Final Four award for Most Outstanding Player, her razor-sharp reflexes were still fully intact.

"Leave it," Kal admonished. "You're on vacay."

Bridget looked from her friend to the phone. She should leave it, but honestly, they both knew she'd never do that. "Hey Kristina," Bridget said, after hitting accept.

Kal rolled her eyes and Bridget spun, ignoring Kal's frown, and talked her assistant through downloading the financial information the Flames CEO requested. Guilt for taking the entire day off coiled in her belly. If the CEO needed budget information, it ought to come directly from her, not her assistant.

Kal picked up Bridget's alarm clock and shoved it within an inch of Bridget's nose. "Ticktock. The countdown is on. Wrap it up," she whispered with a twist of a manicured finger.

Son of a Brunson. Phone calls and wardrobe indecision shrunk the time from "seasoned traveler casually boarding the plane" to "they won't hold the plane for you, ma'am." She despised being late, but when duty called—

Kal pulled the phone from her. "Hey Kristina, it's Kal. Oh, yep, thanks. I'm glad you enjoyed it. We all good here? Your boss lady is in real danger of missing her plane." Kal laughed. "I know, right?"

Bridget attempted to wrench the phone back, but Kal

pivoted, said goodbye, and ended the call. "What if she needed something else?" Bridget said, unable to quiet the churn in her stomach.

"You're too available, Bri. They don't even think before they call you."

"It's my job, Kal." Bridget turned back to her closet, praying for something she hadn't already rejected to materialize. "Pre-season starts in two weeks. It's not the best time for me to take off."

"Bri, you're not getting your nails done. It's your *brother's wedding*. They can manage a day without you."

"Three days," Bridget reminded her.

Kal snorted. "Two of which are weekend days. Do not even get me started on your weekend work schedule."

Bridget tipped up her chin. "*You* work on the weekends."

Kal's eyes popped wide. "Because my contract requires me to. Can you say the same?"

"Sometimes," Bridget countered. Over the past ten years, Bridget had moved through the ranks from Communications Coordinator to President of Business Operations for New York's WNBA franchise, the Flames. An occasional league-wide trip took her away over a weekend and she attended most games, but Kal was right. Most of her job could be—or should be —handled during normal business hours.

"Fine," Bridget said, letting her shoulders fall forward. "No more work until Monday, I promise."

"Unlikely," Kal muttered, pushing off the bed and walking to Bridget's dresser, pulling open the top drawer. "Start here."

Bridget reached into the open drawer and pulled out a stack of underwear and two bras, carefully placing them in the top pocket of her carry-on. Kal added a lacy black thong and a nearly transparent matching bra.

3

"What are those for?" Bridget asked as Kal zipped the mesh pocket.

Kal lifted a shoulder, the corner of her mouth tugging up. "They're bored in the drawer. They need to get out occasionally. Party a little."

Bridget cocked an eyebrow. "And Andrew and Grace's wedding is the place to let them out?"

Kal strode to the closet, pulled the red dress off its hanger, folded it, and placed it in the empty suitcase. "I think it's the perfect place to clear out the dust and cobwebs."

"Dust and cobwebs, Kalisha? Seriously? It's not been that long since I've dated."

Kal tipped her head and stared at her with the intensity she historically saved for referees—an incredulous, you can't be serious glare. "It's been over two years since you broke it off with Steve, the boring have-you-seen-my-skyscraper engineer—"

"And that wasn't even a euphemism. He really wanted to show me the building his company had just completed." Bridget shook her head. Was it possible that she hadn't noticed not having sex in over twenty-four months? Maybe. Her job required her full attention. Especially since she'd launched two new community programs and set the goal of having the league's largest season ticket member base.

"I can hear you thinking, Bri. Busy is an excuse."

Bridget slid her favorite jumpsuit from its hanger and exchanged it for the red dress in her bag. "Wow. Where is all the tough love coming from today?"

Kal ignored her question. "Your brother's wedding is the perfect place to give your vajayjay some playtime. And you know exactly why it's perfect. Do not act like you don't know what I'm talking about."

An image materialized in Bridget's mind. A vision of the only thing she'd never been able to control. A crush that, no matter how old she got or how many people she dated, never fully subsided. And she hated that. She played by the rules, in control of every aspect of her life—except this one stupid thing. Plus . . .

Bridget lowered her voice as deep as it would go and said sternly, "One does not hook up with any member of Storyhill."

Kal rolled her eyes. "Is Andrew the boss of you?"

Bridget folded a pair of black leggings and a tunic and tucked them neatly on top of her jumpsuit. "No," she scoffed. "But it's likely still good advice." While her personal life was none of her big brother's business, she didn't need to go looking for trouble.

Kal held up a pair of shoes to the tunic and, evidently satisfied they matched, tucked them in Bridget's suitcase. "How would Andrew even know? He'll be far more interested in his own wedding night than anything you're doing."

Bridget dropped to the bed with a sigh. "Why are you not letting this go?"

Kal lightly tugged at the ends of Bridget's hair. "Because you've had this crush for YEARS. Maybe a good shag would get him out of your system."

Bridget rubbed at the tension gathering between her eyes. "And how do you propose I do that? Walk up to him at the rehearsal dinner, tap on his elbow, and say, 'My best friend thinks it'd be a good idea for us to sleep together. You in?'"

Kalisha laughed. "I would pay so much money to hear you say that."

Old Bridget might have done something like that, but today's Bridget? No way. Current Bridget understood that most risk was not worth the reward. "Yeah, well, that is not happening. For so many reasons. Not the least being, he's one of my brother's best friends."

"Aren't half the romance novels you read about a brother's or sister's best friend?" Kal said, gesturing to the stack of books on the bedside table.

"Yes, but my life is not a romance novel."

Kal snorted. "You can say that again."

"Enough," Bridget said, swatting her friend with an empty hanger. "Crush or not, it's not worth the drama."

"But . . ."

"No 'buts,' Kal. Help me pack. My ride will be here in a few minutes."

"Fine." Kal flipped through Bridget's garments. "Keep it simple. You need one outfit for the rehearsal dinner tonight, one for tomorrow, one for Sunday, and an extra. You've got two already in your bag. I'll pick out the other two."

"Um, why do you get to pick the other two?"

"Because you've been standing in front of the closet for like twenty minutes, stymied." She shooed Bridget away. "Go pack your other necessities."

"Okay," Bridget said, her shoulders sagging with a sigh. "But no dresses."

"While I disagree, you've made yourself clear." Kal tapped her chin. "Now, what to pack for a woman committed to hiding her amazing figure and miles long legs underneath pants?"

Bridget grabbed a pillow from her bed and pitched it at Kal. She skillfully batted it away while simultaneously pocketing Bridget's buzzing phone. "Defensive player of the year," she said. "Twice."

"Yeah, yeah," Bridget said, reaching toward Kal's back pocket. "Give me my phone, superstar."

Kal swiveled her hips away from Bridget. "You promised no more work stuff until Monday."

Anxiety propelled Bridget's heart into her ribcage. A buzzing phone was her kryptonite. An unhealthy attachment for sure, but one she'd address on a day that didn't include navigating family dynamics and unwanted crushes.

"What if it's Grace or Andrew?" she said, trying to conceal the anxiety racing across her nerve endings.

Kalisha sighed and pulled out the phone, eyeing the screen. "It's your mother."

Bridget's eyebrows rose. "My mother?" If she was a betting woman, which she wasn't, she'd have put all her money on the text being from her assistant.

Kal turned the screen toward Bridget. The name "Mom" filled the bubble on her lock screen, followed by three words: *Call me ASAP.*

Bridget pinched the bridge of her nose with one hand and waggled her fingers at Kal with the other. "Hand it over. You know she won't stop until I answer."

Bridget dropped into her seat, scanning the larger, comfier chairs in first class. Someday she'd splurge on a better ticket. But not today. Today she'd spend the three hours from JFK to Minneapolis in coach. She shifted in her seat, trying to settle her six-foot frame into the small space while extracting her laptop from the bag at her feet and balancing a 16 x 20 white bakery box on her lap.

A box of three dozen lemon cookies.

Apparently, her soon to be sister-in-law decided at the last minute that she wanted Curtis, Grace's best friend from childhood and one of NYC's most popular chefs, to make his "special" cookies for the rehearsal dinner. That's why her mother had called. To inform Bridget a courier was on his way to her apartment to deliver the baked goods. Sylvia Hayes, always the master of ceremonies—didn't matter that no one asked—explained Curtis's travel itinerary didn't allow time to make them in Minneapolis, and he was carrying another food item in his lap.

"Can I help you?" the man across the aisle asked, extending his hands.

Bridget turned with a smile. "That would be great. If you could hold this for a moment," she said, handing the cookies to him.

After she'd tucked her laptop in the seat pocket and stowed the bag under her seat, he handed the box back and said, "You look familiar." Or more accurately, *you look familya*—clearly a native, not a tourist.

She never knew if people meant that as a question or a statement and learned through the years to wait and see what they said next. As every year ticked by since her playing days, she got recognized less and less. And she was totally okay with that.

He snapped his fingers and pointed at her. "UConn," he said, smirking, clearly proud of himself.

She turned in her seat and smiled at him. If he remembered her from her college playing days, he was a genuine fan, and women's sports, at every level, needed every fan they could get. "That's right. I played for UConn and then briefly for the New York Flames." She'd prefer to leave the second part off, but as a representative of the team that had given her a job when her entire world fell apart, she owed them her loyalty—even if it came with painful memories.

He shook his head knowingly. "Too bad about your accident."

The air rushed out of her lungs, but she held her smile, even as it wavered at the corners. "Thank you."

Every time someone alluded to her career-ending accident, she wished for a better response. It never came. Probably because the minute someone mentioned it, the sights and sounds of shattering glass and bending steel hijacked her thoughts. In sports years, it qualified as ancient history, but the ache in her muscles and bones meant the memories lived just under her skin. Her wounds had healed, but the scars—visible *and* invisible—remained.

The man reached into the seat pocket in front of him and pulled out a small notebook. "Can I get your autograph?"

Bridget squirmed in her seat, forcing herself to maintain eye contact. The familiar cocktail of guilt and unease coiled through her chest. Refusing an autograph request wasn't professional, but scratching her name across a piece of paper felt synonymous with writing "Has Been." "I haven't played in years. My autograph isn't worth much these days."

"My girl, my oldest," he said, his voice softening, "she's an amazing athlete. At least I think so. Dribbles a ball like nobody's business, but she, ah," —the man rubbed a hand across the back of his neck— "she's got some confidence issues."

Bridget nodded. "Athletics are great in so many ways but can also be hard on self-esteem."

He nodded, his lips twisting in thought. "She's a point guard, and, just like you, kind of tall for the position. If you sign something for her, it would give me a reason to show her some old clips of your playing days. You know, how you switched so easily between point guard and shooting guard when the team needed it. How you were a master of the pick and roll. I think it'd help her believe in herself a little more."

Bridget's heart pinched, and nausea rolled through her at his past tense description. *Old* clips. *Were* a master . . . *Reign it back in, Bridget.* She grabbed the notebook and pen. "What's her name?"

A wide grin broke across the man's face. "Ruby. Like the beautiful gem she is."

Bridget matched his smile. Such a proud papa. Writing the girl's name across the top of the page, she wrote the only piece of advice that didn't make her feel like a fraud: *The only difference between a good player and a great player is time spent in the gym. Keep dribbling, throw up at least 50 shots a day, and you'll get there. Persistence and practice trump talent every time.*

She closed the cover and handed the notebook back as her phone rang. Bridget carefully wriggled it free from her pocket, causing a passing flight attendant to stop in her tracks. "Ma'am, we're three minutes from take-off. You need to stow your phone."

Bridget smiled. "It'll only take two. I promise." She understood the rules of flying, followed them without fail, meaning she would flip her phone to airplane mode the minute they pulled back from the gate, but not a second before.

The attendant raised her eyebrows but said nothing.

Bridget turned the phone in her hands, surprised to see Kalisha's name. "Everything okay?"

"Why is your phone still on?" Kal asked, irritation threading through her voice.

Bridget chuckled. "Are you testing me?"

"If I am, you clearly failed. And I know Bridget Hayes does not like to fail tests."

Bridget peered over her shoulder, searching the plane for the flight attendant. "I've already gotten the dreaded 'put your phone away' warning. What do you need?"

"Just to remind you—*again*—to not work this weekend and enjoy the wedding and all the other things we talked about." The tap, tap, tap of Kal straightening her papers echoed through the phone.

"I am not sleeping with one of Andrew's groomsmen," Bridget hissed into the phone.

"Fine," Kalisha huffed. "I secretly hope you forgot your phone charger."

Bridget gasped. "Do not even put that out into the universe, you evil woman."

Kalisha laughed. "Okay, but seriously, have some fun."

"Ma'am," the flight attendant said again, pointing at Bridget's phone, this time waiting and staring at Bridget.

"Gotta go, Kal. I'll talk to you when I get back."

"After your weekend of *F-U-N*. Love you."

"Love you too." Bridget placed her phone in airplane mode and dropped it into the seat pocket. The silver edge of her laptop winked at her over the top seam of the pouch. She could practically feel her inbox filling up. She should pull it out. But balancing it on top of the cookie box wouldn't be easy. And she didn't want to disappoint Grace with broken cookies. She snorted. Using baked goods as a reason not to work was a first. But, hey, whatever got results.

She pushed her knee against the laptop just hard enough to force it deeper into the pocket and out of sight. Popping in ear buds, she opened her audiobook app, let her head fall back, and her eyes droop shut. Kal wanted her to have a romance, and in Bridget's world, listening to a romance novel was a lot less risky than attempting a real one.

CHAPTER TWO

For Blake Kelly, weddings ranked up there with root canals and mushy peas. Thanks, but no thanks. He scanned the room as Grace's nuptial army scurried to reposition tables, drape tablecloths, and tie little gold bows on the back of every chair. It seemed there were at least two people for every job, making him feel more like set dressing than helping hands. If he stood still much longer, he risked someone tying a gold ribbon around him, too. He eyed the door. Wouldn't be hard to make a break for it.

But he wouldn't.

Andrew had requested his help and when one of his Storyhill brothers asked, he showed. From the day the five of them formed the band, they became his family. He wouldn't risk that, no matter how much he disliked weddings.

He had, however, hoped for at least one day to explore Minneapolis before the wedding madness began. But with Andrew and Grace's honeymoon bumping up against their next tour dates, they'd spent the entire week prepping for their upcoming concerts.

"You're next, you know," a voice said from behind him.

Blake turned to find Nick, Storyhill's baritone, standing beside him holding a tray overflowing with something that looked suspiciously like mini scrolls of sheet music tied with a, you guessed it, gold ribbon.

"Excuse me?" Blake said, snatching one of the miniature scrolls from the tray and unwinding it. Printed in curly script, between rows of music notes, was the first verse of "Love Me Like a Love Song"—the song Grace wrote for Andrew. It was adorable. If you liked that type of thing.

Nick gestured to the other band members, arms loaded down, weaving around the ladders being used to string Edison bulbs across the ceiling of the industrial space. "Joe and Matt are already married. And Andrew has" —Nick checked his watch— "twenty-eight hours left of bachelor freedom. That means you're next."

Blake turned his head to pin his buddy with a look. "What about you?"

"I'm already married," Nick answered in a flat monotone.

"About that . . ."

Nick readjusted his ball cap and crossed his arms over his plaid-covered barrel chest. "That subject is not open to discussion. Nope. Nada. Not going there. We're talking about you, not me. Stop trying to deflect, Casanova."

"Hey, hey," Blake said, holding his hands up in surrender. "Just because I enjoy taking a woman out to dinner occasionally does not mean I have any intention of getting married." Blake shook his head. "And I'm surprised you, of all people, are encouraging it."

A sadness passed behind Nick's eyes as he sat. "You shouldn't let my experience color yours."

Blake didn't need Nick to sour his opinion on commitment. His mother had accomplished that years ago. "I'm perfectly happy being single. Doing what I want when I want."

Nick scrubbed a hand over his beard and met Blake's eyes. "You think you're strong enough to resist it?"

"Nick!" Andrew called, crossing the room, saving Blake from having to answer Nick's question. Thankfully. There was only one scenario that came close to challenging his stance on long-term relationships. And he planned on keeping that nugget of information to himself. Especially in this crowd.

"Annie wants those favors right now." Andrew stopped in front of his two bandmates, surreptitiously glancing over his shoulder. "And we don't want to make Annie mad."

Nick stood with a shudder.

Grace's best friend, Annie, practiced law—and ball busting. Blake laughed and stretched his hands out, motioning for the tray. "I'll take them. I'm not afraid of Annie."

"No," Andrew said, and both men spun to face him. "Blake, I need you to pick up Bridget at the airport."

A shiver streaked down Blake's spine at the mention of Andrew's sister. And not the cold kind. The so-warm-if-you're-not-careful-you-might-get-burned kind. "You want *me* to pick up Bridget?" Andrew had spent years discouraging Blake's interaction with his sister.

"Not really." Andrew grimaced. "But everyone else already has an assigned task, and Grace promised to make our wedding night very boring if I let my little sister take an Uber."

"Little" was an interesting way to describe Bridget Hayes. At thirty-four years old, six feet tall, and one of the youngest basketball executives in the league, *little* would be the last word Blake would choose. Stunning or accomplished seemed better starting places.

Andrew tucked his hands in his back pockets. "Just remember—"

Blake blew out a breath. "Yeah, yeah, she's off limits. I heard you the first hundred times."

"I was going to say it takes her extra time to get from the gate to baggage claim. But," Andrew said, pushing a finger into Blake's chest, "what you said, too."

Nick picked up the tray of favors and chuckled. "Don't worry Andrew, gingers are very few people's cup of tea."

"I think you got some bad data, my friend." Blake ran a hand down his chest and winked. "Red heads are the world's unicorns and who couldn't use a little more magic in their life?"

"Wow, just wow," Nick said, shaking his head and striding off toward Annie.

"Those are exactly the type of lines you will not be laying on my sister," Andrew said, pulling his car keys from his pocket and pushing them into Blake's hand with a little more force than necessary.

Blake twirled the keys around his finger. "She knows to look for me?"

"She will when she turns her phone back on," he called over his shoulder, already heading back to his fiancée.

Blake paced in front of baggage carousel number three, his eyes darting to the monitor every ten seconds. Bridget's plane touched down sixteen minutes ago, and this remained the correct baggage claim. A bead of perspiration collected under his collar. Normally, he'd welcome any chance to get away from wedding bullshit, but this situation was more "active minefield" than "helpful errand." For so many reasons.

He circled the pleather chairs in front of the carousel for the third time, sunk onto the end seat, and dropped his head into his hands, trying to slow his racing pulse.

"Blake?" a soft voice asked just behind his right shoulder.

He lifted his head and turned, forcing himself to take a deep breath. It was always the same. Intense attraction held one end of the rope. On the other side, trepidation pulled with all its might. And neither side ever won. Somehow, both sides got pulled into the sludge, mixing and muddying the emotions and confusing the hell out of him. Slowly, he stood, bringing their eyes nearly level. From a distance, they were the color of expensive brandy. Up close, green and gold flecks formed delicate constellations around her pupils.

"Did you just get in too?" Bridget asked, balancing a big white box on her hip. "What are the chances?"

"Zero," he managed to utter. "Andrew sent me."

Her eyes widened. "Andrew sent you? Why?"

"I do know how to drive," he said dryly.

She rolled her eyes. "It's not that, it's just . . ."

Her gaze roved from his face to his shoes and back again and, if he wasn't mistaken, a small flush climbed from her neck to her cheeks. *Interesting.*

He shook his head, clearing his thoughts before they led him down a dangerous path. "Andrew said he texted you."

She pulled her phone from her back pocket and studied the screen. "Huh. I must not have heard it. I told him I'd take an Uber."

He smiled at her, his natural charm oozing back in, and winked. "You can pay me if you enjoy my services."

She laughed, the sound a little unsteady. "Probably better you don't say things like that in front of my big brother."

Blake forced himself to hold her gaze when all he wanted was to watch the way her full lips curled in a delicate smile. "I didn't take you for someone who's easily intimidated."

Bridget shrugged. "There's no reason to go looking for trouble."

The truth in that statement wasn't enough to distract his brain from conjuring all kinds of trouble—the tempting kind of trouble that included Bridget Hayes The quiet hum of passengers grew decidedly louder as people jockeyed for position near the baggage carousel. He knew it was imminent, but still jumped when the horn sounded, and the belt started moving.

Bridget dropped his gaze and stepped forward. "If you're willing to hold these" —she held the box out— "I'll grab my bag."

Blake took the nondescript box from her and tipped it side-to-side in his hands. "What exactly am I holding?"

A small gasp escaped her lips, and she placed a palm on top of the box, stilling it. "Cookies straight from Curtis Owens' kitchen. Do not tip them. Do not drop them." She waggled her finger at him just like Andrew had done thirty minutes ago. Genes, they were a powerful thing. "I did not carry them all the way from Manhattan for you to break them."

He slipped his finger under the lid, sliding it toward the tape holding it shut. "Maybe we should try one."

"No," she said, her voice rising above the airport din. "No sampling allowed."

The corner of his mouth curled up. "Do you think I'd get in more trouble for flirting with you or eating one of these cookies?"

Bridget Hayes, beautiful, powerful, and the consummate rule follower. He couldn't help it. The need to tease her was involuntary. He loved the way her eyes flashed and how pinpricks of pink popped on her cheeks.

Bridget's expression flattened, and she shook her head. "Flirting will make Andrew angry, but if you eat a cookie, you'll make Andrew *and* Grace unhappy."

"Okay, we agree. Flirting is the less dangerous option."

Bridget spun and placed both hands on her hips. "We do not agree."

Blake swallowed a chuckle. He needed to stop this—remind himself of what was important. His friendship with Andrew.

Harmony in the band. If only . . . No. No "if only's." He wrenched his gaze from her, focusing on a spot over her shoulder. "The bags are arriving," he said, pointing to where the first few suitcases slid down the chute.

Bridget stepped up to the carousel, and Blake released a breath he didn't realize he'd been holding. Why was she so tempting? He only saw her a handful of times a year, and each time he expected the attraction to have faded. But it never did. Maybe all of Andrew's warnings challenged the rule breaker in him. Maybe she was like his mother's liquor cabinet when he was a teenager—only tempting because he'd been told to stay away from it.

That sounded right. A solid, simple explanation. A quick reminder of that and everything would be fine.

He drew in a fortifying breath and stepped up behind her, catching her mumbling to herself. "Care to share?" he whispered, lowering his head next to her ear.

She jumped, her hand flying to her heart, but her eyes remained pinned to the rotating belt. "Sorry, I talk to myself. Bad habit."

"So, what's the issue?"

"Pardon?"

Blake stepped back. The smell of her perfume tickled his nose—and other parts that had no business being tickled. "I'm pretty sure I caught a couple of curse words. Well, the Bridget Hayes version of curse words. Is there a problem?"

She pointed at the nearly empty carousel. "It's been two minutes since any new bags arrived. I'll be really unhappy if the airline 'misplaced'" —she raised her fingers in air quotes— "my bag. Those cookies thwarted my plans to carry it on."

He smirked. "Because your phone charger is in that bag?"

She snorted. "You sound just like Kal."

His stomach pinched. "Who's Cal?" Neither Grace nor Andrew had mentioned a boyfriend or a plus one.

Before she could answer, her bag bumped down the chute. It rolled and a flash of silver glinted as it landed with a thud, popping open. She ran to get it, but it continued moving, the spilled contents following behind.

He carefully set the lemon cookies on an abandoned luggage cart and went to help her. She manically grabbed shirts and bottles, throwing them at the open suitcase. A comment about her basketball skills hung on his lips when something caught his attention.

"Are these yours?" He meant the question to be playful, but his voice caught, the words rasping out.

She turned and gasped at the items in his hands—a black lace thong and a sleeve of condoms.

Heat rushed up her neck, crimson pooling in her cheeks.

"Just what do you have planned for this weekend, Ms. Hayes?" He slowly folded the condom sleeve into a single square, holding her gaze. "*Six* condoms?"

"I'm going to kill Kal," she muttered.

Cal again. Why would her boyfriend pack condoms in *her* suitcase? "Is Cal meeting you here?" He wanted to bite back the words. He shouldn't care what—or who—she did.

"No," she said, two lines forming between her eyes before she ripped the condoms and underwear from his grasp, stuffing the items in the outside pocket of her bag. "Can we go now?" She snapped up the handle on her bag and pivoted toward the doors, wincing as the knee on her left leg locked. "Where did you park?"

"Let me help you," Blake said, reaching for the handle of her suitcase.

"I'm fine," she said, pulling the bag back.

"But your leg—"

"Grab the cookies," she said, pointing at the luggage cart. She dropped his gaze and surreptitiously placed a hand on her hamstring, nudging her leg forward.

Bridget Hayes handled embarrassment about as well as the rest of the Hayes. That is, not at all. He needed to distract her. "You're going to be here for two nights, right?"

"Yes," she said, suspicion lacing her voice.

"I guess needing three condoms per night isn't unheard of." Yep. His distraction involved bringing up the condoms. Because he was stupid. "I should applaud Cal's stamina." Why dip your toe in the stupid waters when you can jump in headfirst?

A confused look danced across her face before morphing into irritation. "Drop it, Kelly."

"Or?" Seriously, he was brilliant at this distraction thing or about to get punched.

"Or I tell Andrew you were manhandling my underwear at the airport. How do you think he'll react when I tell him you picked up a pair, brought them to your face, and sniffed?"

Blake raised his hands, palms out, in surrender. "Wow. Who'd have guessed that stick-to-the-rules-Hayes could play dirty?"

Her lips pursed and her eyebrows rose, challenging him. "Sometimes the rules call for drastic action."

A smile tugged at his lips, and he immediately bit it back. Distraction complete. Defiance replaced the discomfort. Mission accomplished. "Car's outside door five," he said, pointing at the farthest exit sign. "Lead the way."

She stomped forward without a glance back to see if he followed.

CHAPTER THREE

BRIDGET PEEKED INSIDE THE COOKIE BOX AS BLAKE PULLED her brother's car up to the hotel valet. How was it that staring at delicious buttery, scallop-edged, lemony scented cookies proved far less tempting than sneaking a glance at the man sitting twelve inches to her left?

Because cookies didn't stand in the middle of the airport, looking hot as hell, holding condoms and her panties while smiling big enough so that their dimples carved half-moons into their cheeks.

"When is Cal arriving?" Blake asked, pulling her back to the present.

Why did he keep asking about Kal? She scoured her memory. Had Blake met Kal? She couldn't remember it happening, but they all lived in Manhattan, so it was possible.

"Arriving where?" she asked, giving voice to her confusion.

"Um, here?" He gestured toward the hotel. "I assume the guy who packed the condoms is your plus one."

Realization dawned, and a burst of laughter erupted from her throat. "Kal's not my plus one."

"No?" He dropped her gaze and ran his fingers through his hair.

"No." She bit back a smile. "Kal is short for *Kalisha*, not Calvin, and she's not my plus one—she's my best friend. You might have heard of her? Kalisha Harris? Played at UConn with me, now a big deal commentator for the Sports Network?"

A red flush climbed up his neck, flirting with his jawline. "Oh. Yeah. The Harris part of Harris & Hayes."

She turned in her seat, shifting the cookie box to look at him. "How do you know about Harris & Hayes?"

He squirmed in his seat and swept his hands over the steering wheel, the tint in his cheeks inching toward scarlet. "I follow basketball," he said with a small shrug. "And Andrew talks about you. Tells us what you're up to."

Her eyes narrowed. "Harris & Hayes hasn't been a thing for over ten years. I'm surprised you remember."

His shoulder dipped as he reached under the dashboard and popped the trunk. "You're pretty memorable," he said under his breath, just soft enough that Bridget wondered if she'd misheard. Blake Kelly calling her "memorable?" Not likely. I mean, yes, he never missed an opportunity to flirt with her, but flirting was as essential to him as breathing. He liked women. She was a woman. So naturally, he flirted with her. Simple as that.

But. Had she also imagined the jealousy that colored his questions about Kal? She shook the ridiculous thought from her mind. Blake Kelly was not jealous. Curious maybe, but not jealous. His proximity and her silly crush were messing with her, making her imagine things.

"I didn't catch that," she said, immediately wanting the words back. What was she doing? The goal was to get over this crush, not add fuel to the fire.

Something resembling panic crossed his face but disappeared in a blink. He turned his face up to the car roof and sighed. "I said, you, Bridget Hayes, All-American point guard, first-round pick, and executive extraordinaire, are *memorable*."

Her mouth dropped open as he slipped effortlessly from the car without another glance her way and handed the keys to the valet. Reciting her resume wasn't all that impressive, but that *he* knew it? Her heartbeat ratcheted up and fluttered in her windpipe.

In desperate need of air, she wrapped her fingers around the door handle. She swiveled in the seat and the muscles in her thigh clenched, sending a spasm cascading down her leg. Wrenching her attention from the man outside the windshield, she dug her fingers into the soft tissue behind her knee and breathed in and out through the pain, just like her physical therapist taught her, and massaged down her calf while holding the cookie box steady. Squeezing her eyes shut, she willed the muscles to relax.

A knock sounded on the glass next to her ear and she jumped, jostling the cookies. Playing cookie sherpa, riding with Blake Kelly, and leg pain from sitting too long was too much. She threw back the box lid, grabbed a cookie, and shoved it in her mouth. Blake's lips parted as he opened the door. She thrust the box into his abdomen, and it nearly bounced back into her lap. Her brain immediately offered an unhelpful image of magnificent abdominal muscles concealed just under a starched shirt. *Bad brain.*

Time to play some defense.

She stood, willing her leg to cooperate, and put her finger under his chin, closing his mouth. "See, Blake Kelly, I can break the rules."

And I'm going to break all kinds of them if I don't get away from him.

"Take those to Grace," she said, pointing at the box, snapping the handle of her suitcase up, and rolling it toward the hotel entrance.

"Bridget," Blake called after her.

"Please," she said, throwing the word over her shoulder, not daring to look back. She blamed her beating heart and churning stomach on Kal. If she hadn't made all those suggestions—if she hadn't packed condoms—Bridget's thoughts wouldn't be a confusing cocktail of presumed jealousy, dimples, and rock-hard abs. She'd still be in control and her simmering crush would still be on the back burner instead of boiling over after a measly twenty minutes with the man. Yep. This breath-snatching, chest-constricting queasiness was one hundred percent Kal's fault.

Letting the hotel room door drop behind her, Bridget kicked off her shoes and sent up a silent thank you for making it through the lobby and check-in without running into her family. She needed a moment, or ten, and a shower before the rehearsal. Unzipping her suitcase, she picked through the pile of twisted and matted clothing, hung up the pieces that would wrinkle, and shot a text off to Kal.

Bridget: *Thanks for the condoms.*

The three dots jumped immediately.

Kalisha: *You found them already?*

Bridget: *They made themselves known when my suitcase popped open on the baggage carousel. Spilling everywhere. In front of the guy Andrew sent to pick me up.*

Kalisha: *OMG. LMAO.*

Bridget: *Not funny.*

Kalisha: *Yes, it is. So funny. WAIT. A guy or THE guy?*

Bridget: *<eye roll> What do you think?*

Kalisha: *Condoms jumped out at the guy you've been*

crushing on for forever? IT'S A GD SIGN, BRI!!!!!!!!

Bridget: It is not.

Kalisha: All the experts agree. Flying condoms are the universal sign for "take me now." What did he do?

Bridget paced to the window, staring at the Minneapolis skyline rather than allow her mind to replay the scene at the airport.

Bridget: He picked them up . . . along with a black lacy thong . . . which I also did. not. pack. Kalisha: This is TOO GOOD. What did he say????

Bridget: He wondered why my boyfriend CAL had packed the condoms in MY suitcase . . .

Bridget's screen went quiet. No text, no jumping dots. She closed the curtains and pulled the cosmetic bag from the mess that was her suitcase and walked to the bathroom just as her phone pinged.

Kalisha: Just snort laughed my soda. Did you correct him? Bridget Asher Hayes, tell me you corrected him!

Bridget: I did. Because I'm a decent human being. Not for any other reason. I have to go. Rehearsal is in less than an hour and I need a shower.

Kalisha: WEAR THE BLACK THONG.

Bridget: Wow, Calvin, most boyfriends would not encourage this kind of behavior.

Kalisha: I'm special.

Bridget: Maybe not the word I would choose. Talk later.

Kalisha: Text me if you have something juicy. Otherwise STAY OFF YOUR PHONE.

Bridget typed "OK," threw the phone on the bed, and stared at herself in the standard-issue hotel mirror. It reflected all the typical hotel room mainstays: requisite black-and-white photo of an iconic local landmark—this one featured a giant cherry fountain in the middle of an even larger spoon—two linear nondescript lamps flanking the bed, and a coverlet made of something that felt like it was forged in a foundry instead of sewn in a factory. *And* it cast back the face of a woman who really needed to get her sh—*Sheryl Swoopes* together. If ever there was an appropriate time to use real curse words again, this qualified.

A knock on the door brought her hand to her chest. For a woman who prided herself on a "no surprises" lifestyle, her heart was getting a workout today. The knock came a second time, and Bridget stared at the door. No one knew she'd arrived except Blake. She threw her shoulders back, pasted on a smile, and strode to the door.

"If you're looking for condoms—" she blurted, throwing the door open and halting. It wasn't Blake. It was Andrew.

"Gotten into a new line of business, Bridgie?" her brother asked, an eyebrow arched.

She propped the door with her hip and motioned for him to enter. "How did you know I'd arrived?" she asked, ignoring his question.

"Heard you ate a cookie," Andrew said, amusement lacing his voice. "But I didn't believe my law-abiding sister would do such a thing, so I came to check."

Bridget pressed a fist into her palm. "Blake ate it," she lied.

"That sounds more likely." Andrew swiveled, opening his arms. "Give your big brother a hug?"

She stepped into his arms. Despite being overprotective and overbearing, he was still one of her favorite people. "Are you my entire welcoming committee?" she asked, retreating from his embrace and musing his hair.

"Just me and whoever was looking for condoms," he said, pulling the end of her ponytail. "Care to explain that?"

She lifted her head and pinned Andrew with a stare—the kind she'd learned to employ with corporate partners—crossed her arms over her chest and said, "No."

Andrew's lips pressed flat. "No?"

She didn't blink, refusing to offer one of the many excuses and explanations running through her mind. "No." She turned and pulled another garment from her suitcase and hung it in the miniature closet. "Where are the rest of the Hayes?"

Andrew's eyes narrowed, but let his question drop. "Mom, Dad, and Colin are all helping Grace with wedding stuff. I hope you're not too disappointed that it's just me."

Bridget's expression finally broke, her lips curving into a grin. "Based on the conversation I had with Mom this morning —she sounded like an audio book on triple speed—I should thank you. Hope she's not driving you and Grace too batty."

"No more than expected," he said, chuckling. "But I promise I'll keep your room number confidential so she can't rope you into one of her harebrained ideas."

"Thank—" Bridget stopped mid-word. "How did *you* know my room number?"

Andrew slid his hands into his front pockets and shrugged. "When Blake returned, I asked at the front desk."

Bridget stopped unpacking and turned to him. "I didn't think they gave out that information."

Andrew winked, and the corners of his mouth turned up.

"Oh my god, Andrew Hayes, you're flirting the day before you get married?"

He chuckled. "Only because I wanted to see my little sister. And to make sure it was really you. Bridget Hayes outside of New York City is a rare sight."

She slapped him playfully on the chest. "I'm home every Christmas and there was that time in London."

Andrew rolled his eyes. "That time in London that coincided with a work trip?"

The fatigue of the day spiraled around her and squeezed. She sank to the bed and pushed a finger into her temple. "Fine.

Fine. I work a lot. I get it. Now, I'm assuming you didn't flirt your way to my room number just to harass me. What do you want?"

Andrew held a hand against his chest, mocking indignation. "I really wanted to make sure you got in okay. I know travel can be hard for you."

She sighed. "Andy, since I started playing traveling ball at thirteen, travel is the one constant in my life."

He shifted from one foot to the other. "But that was before—"

She cut him off, dipping her head and peering over the top of her glasses. "And after, Andy. You know that. Which leads me to wonder if there isn't some other reason you're here."

Andrew sighed and fisted a hand in his hair. "Blake treat you okay?"

"There it is," she said with a shake of her head.

"Well, did he?" He leaned back against the console holding the television.

"I know you don't want me dating any of the Storyhill guys. You've made that clear. But a ride from the airport isn't a date" —even if it's the most action her panties had seen in years— "so it makes me think this is about Blake, specifically. What's your deal with him?"

"He's the only single one left . . ." Andrew said, backing toward the door.

"And?" She stepped up into his space. Her playing days might be over, but she still had moves.

"I don't want him to take advantage of you."

She inched closer, locking her gaze with his. "You don't want him playing with me because I'm fragile?"

"Yes, that's right," Andrew uttered, nodding, his shoulders dropping as if Bridget agreed with him.

His eyes grew wide when Bridget sucked in an audible

breath. "No, Bridgie, no. That's not what I meant. It's just I love you and I can't stand to see you hurt again."

One more step. She'd forgotten how good it felt to back down a defender. "I'm a big girl, Andy."

Andrew grimaced and stepped back, pressing his back against the door. "I know," he said, "it's just that after the accident—"

"Andrew Charles Hayes, don't you dare go there. I broke my leg, not the ability to make my own choices. And the accident was a long time ago."

"I know," he repeated, holding up a hand, palm out.

Weak defense, big brother.

"I'm not sure you do. You do realize that I'm old enough to 'play' with as many boys as I want, right?"

He squeezed his eyes shut. *Victory!* Bridget Hayes for the win at the buzzer. Want your brother to shut his mouth? Mention sex. Works every time.

She pushed a finger into his chest as her phone blared out the ring tone associated with her assistant. She grabbed the phone, turning it over in her hand. "Saved by the bell. It's work," she said, "I have to get it."

"Of course you do," Andrew said dryly.

Ugh. He was *really* getting on her nerves. "Doesn't Grace need you?"

Panic flared in his eyes, and he rotated his wrist, checking the time on his watch. "I better go."

Bridget nodded. "Sounds like an excellent idea." She hit Accept on the call as Andrew tapped her on the arm. "Kristina," she said into the phone, "hold on a moment."

She covered the speaker with her hand, sucked in a calming breath, and lifted her eyes to her brother. "Yes?"

Andrew nibbled on his bottom lip. "Grace rented a bus to

take everyone to the wedding venue tonight. Meet us in the lobby at 5:30."

5:30? That gave her less than half an hour. So much for that shower. "Fine," she said, waving him out the door. "I'll be there."

"Don't be late."

"Andy," she growled.

"It's just I know how you can lose track of time . . ."

Her free hand balled into a fist. "Andy, I love you. And you should go before I forget why." She turned her back to him and lifted the phone to her ear. "Thanks for waiting, Kristina," she said after the door closed. "You have an older brother, right?"

"Um, yes," Kristina answered, confused.

Bridget placed the phone on speaker, stripping off her jeans and exchanging them for the leggings in her suitcase. "Is he a giant pain in the ass?"

Her assistant laughed. "Pretty sure they give them a manual on how to be irritating along with their first I'm a Big Brother! t-shirt."

Digging through her cosmetic bag, she extracted a brush and redid her ponytail. With no time for a shower, this would have to suffice. "It's six pm there, Kay. Why are you still at the office?" Bridget might be a workaholic, but she didn't expect the same of her staff.

"I'm sorry. I know you're on vacation. I tried to solve it myself."

Ugh. She should have taken a later flight. Gone into the office for a little while this morning. She pressed a hand against her abdomen. "What's the problem?" she said, trying to sound casual.

"Niomi Rohn called about an hour ago, saying she hadn't received the updated version of their sponsorship contract. She needs it for a meeting on Monday morning. I tried to pull it up, and I've looked everywhere. It's not anywhere on the shared drive. Not that I can find."

She blew out a breath. This she could handle. She never created a file she didn't back up—multiple times. "No worries," she said, reassuring her assistant. "I'll email you the copy I have on my hard drive." She popped the lid of her laptop and searched for the file. Nothing. Time to pivot.

"I can't seem to find my copy, either. Did you check for the paper copy?" Maybe not the most environmentally wise choice, but Bridget printed out key documents for just this reason.

"Paper copy?"

Bridget eyed the clock on the bedside table. 5:15. She needed to hustle. She was not about to be late and prove Andrew right. "Go to my office." The sound of Kristina pushing back her chair and walking down the hall echoed through the phone.

"Third file cabinet from the left, in the—"

"Found it!" Kristina exclaimed. "I'll scan it and email it right away. Emergency averted."

It didn't quite qualify as an emergency, though someone needed to tell that to the cortisol flowing through Bridget's veins. "Anything else?"

"Nope. That was it."

"Great. Thanks for all your work, Kay. Now, get out of there. Go enjoy your weekend."

"Thanks, boss. You too. Remember to have some fun."

Another person reminding her to have fun. Did she need to worry that to her work was fun and having fun felt like work? Her mother, the psychotherapist, would likely have plenty to say about that. All things she didn't have the time, or desire, to unpack. She ended the call with Kristina and exchanged her long sleeve t-shirt for a tunic.

"Bridgie," a voice yelled through the door. "Bus is leaving in ten minutes."

She quickly padded over to the door, pulling it open. "Hi Daddy."

"Hello, Sugarplum. You ready?"

She motioned for him to come inside. "Almost."

Charles Hayes strode into the room, strong, tall, and at the age where a few more gray hairs appeared at his temples every time Bridget saw him. She straightened his collar underneath his classic navy jacket. Andrew wouldn't want to hear it, but it wouldn't be long before her big brother looked just like their father.

"Am I dressed okay?" she asked, digging through her suitcase for the shoes Kal selected for this outfit.

Charles nodded. "Grace keeps saying it's a 'casual affair'— though I've seen no evidence to back up that claim."

Bridget chuckled. She was pretty sure Grace's idea of casual did not match her father's definition. "Mom's not with you?"

He grunted and lifted his eyes to the ceiling. "She's downstairs marshaling the troops."

Bridget swiped a deep red lipstick across her lips. "And they sent you to marshal me?"

Charles scratched the top of his head and squinted behind his glasses. "Andrew thought maybe you'd gotten caught up in a work call—"

Bridget's spine stiffened. "I've just about had it with that—"

"Now, Bridgie, before you go getting all mad at him, he told me your room number instead of telling your mother." Charles chuckled. "God knows I love that woman with all my heart, but she is in full 'Sylvia Cyclone' mode today."

"Then we'd better go," Bridget said with a smile, grabbing her handbag, "before Andrew cracks and tells her where to find us."

"You always were the smartest among us, Sugarplum."

CHAPTER FOUR

Bridget gripped the metal railing and gingerly maneuvered the bus's stairs, careful to step forward with her right leg each time. Puddles dotted the pavement and a damp breeze coiled around her, blowing the end of her ponytail against her cheek. She scanned the sidewalk, instinctively mapping the driest path to the entrance.

Dramatic iron gates and mammoth copper urns flanked soaring glass entry doors. A woman in a green apron rhythmically snipped stems and ringed towering topiaries with plate-sized peonies. A halo of blush pink popping against the verdant leaves, like a sunrise breaking through the boughs of an evergreen forest.

Topiaries and peonies might not qualify as juicy, but Kal needed to see this. Bridget reached into her back pocket. No phone. Right pocket? No. Left pocket? No. Panic gathered at the base of her neck. She'd promised no more work, but let's not get crazy. She needed her phone.

"Looking for this?" Her phone appeared in front of her face, held by long, masculine fingers.

She'd like to say it was the crisp cuff of an expensive button-down that identified the person holding her phone, but it was the distinct smell of cedar and bergamot that provided the unmistakable sensory calling card. He'd worn the same cologne since she'd first met him—sixteen years ago.

She'd skipped afternoon classes and driven the hour and a half from UConn to Boston for a Storyhill concert. Andrew had invited her backstage after the show and slung a protective arm around her shoulder as he introduced her to his bandmates for the first time. Twenty years old, Blake had looked nothing like the lanky eighteen-year-old boys in her classes, and he was *traveling the US* with a *band*. Didn't matter that her brother was doing the same thing. Andrew would always be just her annoying brother. Blake was a *man*. And in the flash of a single smile, she was completely smitten.

Standing backstage that night, she'd never have imagined that a decade and a half later she'd still harbor the same crush. It was maddening. When she dated other people, thoughts of him waned, but the second she was single, his face reappeared in her dreams. And if they were in the same room? She stood about the same chances as an ice cream cone in an August heatwave. She accepted everyone had their weaknesses, but why couldn't hers be Snickers or M&M's instead of a giant piece of ginger man candy?

She willed the image of licking a bergamot flavored lollipop from her mind, extracted the phone from his fingers, and turned to him, attempting a casual smile. "I didn't know pick-pocketing was among your many skills, Mr. Kelly."

Blake stepped around her, opening the glass door and motioning for her to enter. He leaned in as she passed. "Even I'm not stupid enough to put my hand near your ass with Andrew nearby."

And if Andrew wasn't here?

That it took every ounce of her willpower not to ask was

reason enough to keep her distance. The only time she ever felt like playing with fire was around Blake Kelly. And Bridget Hayes no longer played with fire. No matter how tempting.

She cleared her throat, burying her impulses. "Where did you find it?"

"On your seat on the b—" he said, whirling toward her as she gasped.

"Are you okay?" he said, scanning her from head to toe.

Her eyes bounced from the industrial brick walls to the soaring glass vases filled with the same peonies used outside to a suspended floral arrangement at the end of a white silk aisle runner. "Sorry," she said. "It's not like I expected Grace to do anything less than spectacular, but this exceeds my expectations."

Blake chuckled and knocked his shoulder into hers. "The only less than spectacular thing Grace has ever done is to agree to marry your brother."

Bridget rolled her eyes and smirked. "And speaking of my brother, I know he called Storyhill into service. Which part did you do?" she asked, motioning to the room.

"I can't take credit for any of this. I had off-site duties," he said, a smirk pulling at the corners of his lips.

Lips she had no business looking at.

"Like picking up flowers?" she said, forcing her gaze back up to his eyes. Not that his emerald eyes, dancing with his own personal brand of mischief, were a safer option.

"No. Like picking up sisters." He leaned closer and whispered next to her ear. "And condoms and panties."

Heat roared up her neck, pooling in her cheeks. "We agreed not to speak of that," she hissed.

"Agreeing to something like that sounds completely out of character for me." He sucked his bottom lip under his teeth and winked at her. Slowly.

Great. Now all the heat sped in a completely different direction.

"Hello, my almost sister," a voice said from behind her, causing Bridget to stumble as she wrenched her gaze from Blake and spun toward the voice. Blake subtlety wrapped a hand around her elbow, steadying her.

"It's so good to see you," Grace said, yanking Bridget into a hug and squeezing hard. "I'm sorry I wasn't around to greet you when you arrived."

Bridget laughed, happy to think about something other than the spicy ginger groomsman to her left. "You might have a few other things on your mind. This space is amazing, by the way."

Grace nodded shakily, tears welling up in her eyes.

Bridget wrapped her fingers around Grace's arm. "It's not amazing?"

Grace rubbed a finger under her lashes. "Sorry. I've been blubbering on and off all day."

"I'd cry too if I had to marry Andrew," Blake said.

Grace playfully slapped him on the chest. "I've traveled with Storyhill. I know how deeply you care for each other."

Blake's hands flew up, palms out. "Care, yes. But live with? No thanks." He looked right to left and leaned toward Grace, whispering, "You know he never picks up his socks, right?"

Grace laughs. "I do, but I'm also familiar with his finer qualities, too," she said, wiggling her eyebrows.

"Ew. No. Just no." Bridget pulled her lips down and tapped her fingers against her chest. "Sister here. Too much information. Brain can't handle it."

Grace tipped her head. "And yet, Andrew told me you offered him condoms earlier today. Want to tell me about that?"

Blake snorted, and Bridget willed herself not to look at him. "Condoms? I don't think so. Clearly, he misheard. He doesn't pick up his socks and is already hard of hearing? Are you absolutely sure you want to marry him, Grace?" Diversion and subterfuge while maintaining a straight face? Yep. Bridget prided herself on the skills she'd honed in the boardroom—and wasn't above using them outside of work.

Grace's smile fell and, with a blink, two fat tears streaked down her cheeks.

"Grace, no," Bridget said, reaching out for her soon-to-be sister-in-law. "I'm kidding."

Grace swiped at the tears with the back of her hand. "I know." She wiped her wet fingers down the front of her tailored ebony pants. "I'm just so grateful. After Jax died . . ." Her words drifted off and her eyes darted to Andrew, currently across the room in deep conversation with a man behind an elaborate DJ set-up. "I really didn't think this would happen for me again." She pulled in a breath. "I know I already said it, but I'm so glad you're here." She reached out and placed a hand on Blake's forearm. "Both of you."

Bridget smiled and chanced another brief glance at Blake. "Of course. Where else would we be?"

Grace strung her arm through Bridget's. "I know it's hard for you to get away from work."

Bridget started to protest, but Grace continued, "And that one" —she pointed at Blake— "has never made it a secret that weddings aren't his thing."

Bridget spun toward him. This was news to her. "You don't like weddings?"

Blake shuffled his feet, pushed his hands into his pockets, and shrugged. "I'm shit at buying gifts," he said, not meeting Bridget's gaze.

Grace laughed, all traces of tears gone. "Oh, it's about the gifts, is it?"

"Just wait until you see what I got you. You'll doubt no more."

Blake didn't like weddings. Huh. Curiosity piqued, Bridget opened her mouth with a follow-up question, but a diminutive man, dressed smartly in a matching checked vest and bowtie, rapped a pen against a formidable clipboard, cutting her off.

"I need the wedding party, front and center, please," he thundered, the sound bouncing through the cavernous space.

Grace tugged on Bridget's arm. "We don't want to keep Bernard waiting," she whispered. "He's equally organized and terrifying. One icy glare could level a man twice his size."

"But I'm assuming he's responsible for all of this," Bridget said as Grace led them over to the dozen people assembling in the space in front of the rows and rows of Chiavari chairs.

"He is. Can't argue with his results." Grace stopped in front of the wedding party. "I think everyone knows everyone else, right?"

Bridget nodded as she scanned the gathered friends and family. The four other members of Storyhill would serve as Andrew's groomsmen while Grace's attendants included Annie, Curtis, Megan, and Bridget. The bride and groom's brothers—Ben and Colin—would act as ushers.

The wedding planner—Bernard—skimmed a bony finger over a rainbow of tabs protruding from his clipboard, stopping at the blue one. "Attendants, you'll follow Grace's niece and nephew—the flower pal and ring bearer—down the aisle. You'll walk from tallest to shortest."

Bridget's stomach flipped. Blake was the tallest groomsman. She sized up Curtis, hoping—praying—he had an inch or two on her. Otherwise . . .

"Blake and Bridget, you're up first," Grace said, her words confirming Bridget's fears.

Bridget stayed rooted to her spot. "Isn't Curtis taller than me?" she squeaked, attempting a last-ditch effort.

Bernard looked over the top of his half-moon glasses,

assessing Curtis before pinning Bridget with his withering gaze. "Are you planning on wearing heels tomorrow?" he drawled.

Pairing her white sneakers with the gorgeous dress Grace had chosen would not be a good look. Her shoulders sagged. "Yes."

"Then you're up," he said impatiently, pointing to the space next to Blake. She trudged to the spot.

"My, my, don't you two make a handsome couple," the planner said, nudging Bridget a step closer to Blake. A couple of catcalls and whistles tore through the air.

"Do not encourage him," Andrew barked out and everyone laughed.

Blake offered her his arm. She stared at it, unmoving.

"Afraid of my cooties?"

Bridget pulled an expression of outrage. "Wait. You have cooties and you didn't tell me? Rude," she said, crossing her arms over her chest.

"They're not contagious," he said, a smile tugging up the corners of his lips.

"How can you be certain?" she asked, dragging out the interchange. Anything was better than acknowledging what the simplest of his touches did to her.

"I had them tested."

The tension in her chest released, and she laughed. "I wasn't aware there was a test for that."

He nodded sagely. "It's expensive, but I'm all about protecting those closest to me."

Something green and hungry bloomed inside her. "You mean all the women?"

His eyes passed over her body, and he winked. "Maybe."

The heat in his gaze curled around her like wisps of smoke. Or maybe the smoke was coming from her. Didn't matter. His shameless flirting was another reminder that she needed to squash this crush. Immediately.

"Chop, chop," Bernard said, pointing at her. "I'm not getting any younger."

She grunted and strung her arm through Blake's, and the wedding planner nodded approvingly.

"Next, we have . . ." Bernard continued, but Bridget didn't catch a single word on account of the fire exploding from the spot where her arm rested against Blake's.

She jumped when the first strains of "Love Me Like a Love Song" started playing. She wrenched her gaze from Blake and turned to the wedding planner. "Should we start down the aisle?"

He *tsk*-ed and a muscle in his jaw twitched. "I'll signal you when it's time."

"Just tell me the cue. How many bars into the song?" They really needed to get this show on the road. The faster she made it to the end of the aisle, the faster she could get away from Blake.

The wedding planner gave her an exasperated sigh. "Kids go on six. You go on eight."

"She doesn't know how not to be in charge," Blake said to the man.

Bridget opened her mouth and closed it. What could she say? He spoke the truth. She settled for an epic eye roll and a tiny shake of her head.

Four bars in Blake whispered, "How's the leg?"

She wanted to scream. Her accident happened ten years ago. After a decade of physical therapy and a regimented workout schedule, a slight, nearly undetectable limp was the only sign the accident had happened at all. "Why?" she hissed.

He dipped his head in her direction but stayed looking forward. "I noticed it gets stiff if you stand or sit too long."

She searched his face. How was it that someone who only saw her a few times a year caught a detail most people missed?

Her face must have given away her surprise because he said, "What? I notice things."

"Like?" She wanted to slap herself. How hard was it to keep her mouth shut until they finished walking the plank? She shook her head. Walking the *aisle*.

He scrubbed a hand through the front of his hair. Of course, it fell back into place perfectly..

"Like . . . how you always wear pants," he said, his gaze dropping to the floor. "Or how you slip your fingers under your thigh before standing up."

How was she supposed to get rid of this infatuation when he said things like that?

"And how you live your entire life in nine-point Times New Roman."

And, just like that, the crush-o-meter ticked down from ten to eight. "Did you just compare me to a *font*? What the *Havlicek* does that even mean?"

"Maybe not the best metaphor." He shrugged. "But you could stand to let loose a little more often. Have some fun."

Could this day get any stranger? It started with Kal giving voice to Bridget's lingerie, and now she was a font?

His comment dug under her skin. "I have fun."

He patted the hand resting on his arm. "Okay."

"Blake. Bridget. Go." The wedding planner tapped his pen against his clipboard. She stepped forward, pulling Blake with her. "Slowly," the planner chided.

"No, not 'okay,'" Bridget said from the corner of her mouth, trying to match her steps to the slow ballad. "My job comes with a lot of responsibility. We can't all go through life all Comic Sans style."

Blake barked out a laugh, earning him a disapproving glare

from the wedding planner, who seemed to be everywhere at once. "Don't knock Comic Sans until you've tried it," he whispered, his breath floating over the shell of her ear. Tingles shot down her spine. *Her body not caring, even a little, that he'd just insulted her.*

Or inconveniently hit her with the truth.

Laughter commingled with the sounds of forks striking plates. Bridget smiled, looking at the family and friends gathered around the table set for twenty. Perfect. Intimate. Relaxed.

Except for the roller coaster ride happening in her belly.

Blake had left her at the altar . . . wait, that didn't sound right. Blake had followed the rest of the wedding party to the table and lowered himself into a chair near her parents, while she had sped walked to the other end and plopped into a chair next to Nick. Better not to tempt fate. With Blake Kelly, proximity was enemy number one.

He'd accused her of being buttoned up and stuffy and still her crush showed no signs of abating. It was annoying. And it made her feel out of control. And there was nothing she hated more.

She glanced at the end of the table—because she couldn't stop herself. His head was tipped back in laughter, dimples on full display. Heat pooled in her belly as a sudden desire to run her tongue down the column of his exposed neck blocked every shred of common sense she possessed. She squeezed her thighs together, trying to ease the building pressure. Seriously. She needed to get a grip.

Her hands twisted in her lap. Kalisha's words mixed with Andrew's, making her slightly nauseous.

Break the rules. Follow the rules.

Quench your crush. Don't do anything that might jeopardize Andrew's dreams.

A mental tilt-a-whirl.

Andrew clinked his knife against his glass. Bridget looked up, grateful for the reprieve from her swirling—and unproductive—thoughts.

"Thanks for coming. Grace and I" —Andrew gazed lovingly at his fiancée— "wanted some time with the people we love the most. To us, you're family." He lifted his glass. "We couldn't imagine doing this without you. Cheers."

Crystal stemware pinged and pealed as everyone at the table lifted their glasses in honor of the bride and groom. Blake caught her eye, tipped his champagne flute toward her, and offered a small smile. And her little crush turned into a pulping. What was happening to her? She always felt off-kilter around him, but this was significantly more intense than usual. Must be the wedding vibes.

"Finish your desserts. We've got work to do," her mother said, rubbing her hands together and standing. The assembled group groaned as Sylvia produced a clipboard from under the table and tapped her manicured nails on the thin board.

"There's enough of us. Think we can overthrow her?" Nick whispered, leaning toward Bridget.

She laughed. "You'll need more than a champagne-fueled amateur coup to unseat Sylvia Hayes," Bridget whispered.

Nick smirked behind his well-trimmed beard. "In that case, it's every person for themselves." He pushed back his chair and stood. "Grace, Andrew, I look forward to celebrating with you tomorrow, but right now I need to get back to my son. His grandma's been on duty all day."

"Chicken," Bridget hissed out.

Nick laughed. "It's not a lie."

"The chicken part or the son part?"

He straightened the gold bow on the back of his chair and pushed it in. "Yes."

"Go on," Bridget said, biting back a smile and gesturing to the door. "Save yourself."

Bridget stared at Nick's retreating form and searched her own mind for a reason to leave. She loved her brother and Grace, but it had been a long and strange day. Maybe she could . . .

"Bridget," her mother called.

Too late. She sucked in a fortifying breath and turned toward her mother, reassuring herself that the sooner she helped, the sooner she'd be back in her hotel room. Alone.

"I'd like you and Blake—"

Seriously? This had officially turned into "Bridget Hayes Cannot Catch a Break Day." She picked up the champagne bottle in front of her, peering inside. Empty. But there was one lemon cookie left on the plate in the center of the table. She snatched it and stuffed it into her mouth, a throaty groan escaping her lips as the butter and sugar melted on her tongue. The one she'd inhaled earlier was an act of defiance. This one was pure pleasurable coping mechanism. Her eyes fluttered shut and her tongue darted out to catch any crumbs dangling from her lips. Not one morsel of something this good should go to waste. Must remember to thank Grace for requesting this culinary sorcery. Humming, she licked lemon sugar from the tip of each finger. She opened her eyes to scan the table for remaining cookies, but only found empty trays— and Blake staring at her, his lips parted, pupils blown.

"*Bridget*," her mother called a second time, dousing whatever had just happened between her, that cookie, and the man who apparently watched her eat it with lustful abandon. Fortified with cookie power, Bridget stood and walked to the end of the table, where her mother hovered across from Blake.

Sylvia glanced up, absently picking a stray crumb from the front of Bridget's tunic and rolled it in her fingers. "I couldn't imagine why Grace was so insistent about transporting those cookies all the way from Brooklyn, but I get it now. They're amazing, don't you think?"

Bridget smirked, turning her gaze on Blake. "Downright sinful. Would you agree, Blake?" She was playing with fire. *Again.* But it felt good. Empowering even. If Kal could see her now, she'd be so proud.

"What do you need, Mrs. Hayes?" Blake rasped, his voice less steady than usual.

Sylvia pointed to a table loaded down with votives and tea lights. "Each table in the lounge area needs three candles. I'd like you and Blake to put a candle in each votive and set them on the tables."

"The venue isn't handling that?" Bridget said, empowerment seeping out of her more quickly than air from a punctured balloon.

Sylvia spoke to the clipboard, her finger sliding down the list. "I told the site manager that we could do a few things and she could send her staff home."

She supposed that was nice—or a way for her mother to exert more control over the situation. *Hello pot, meet kettle*, a little voice whispered. Had she become her mother? No. Their situations were entirely different. Before the annoying little voice offered another opinion on that subject, she said, "Seems simple enough, Mom. I can do that myself. Blake can help with something else."

"Nonsense," Sylvia waved Bridget off. "It'll go quicker with the two of you doing it." Her mother made an exaggerated check next to the item on her list. "Now, Joe and Julia," Sylvia called, walking off, the matter settled in her mind.

"Trying to get away from me?" Blake asked, rising to his full height and meeting her gaze.

Her girl parts sighed "yum" as her brain yelled, "warning."

"No," she lied. "Just striving for efficiency."

"How very Times New Roman of you," he said, amusement dancing in his eyes.

"A girl's got to go with her strengths," she said, unwilling to let him see how much that comment got under her skin.

"Not to worry, I like a woman who's in charge," he said, waggling his eyebrows.

Correction. That comment was far more unsettling.

CHAPTER FIVE

BRIDGET SMOOTHED HER HANDS DOWN THE DEEP PURPLE dress and twirled in front of the full-length mirror. While all the bridesmaids would wear the same color, Grace selected each dress for their different body types. Her dress hit the floor, hiding her leg, but the front dipped into her cleavage and a single over the shoulder strap crossed over her mostly bare back. And after a morning spent with Grace's stylist, Bridget's normally straight hair hung in loose curls over her shoulder, and she'd opted for contacts instead of glasses.

She hadn't felt this sexy in . . . well, maybe ever. Years of warm-up pants and jerseys had given way to an overflowing closet of stylish yet conservative business suits. Even though this dress was outside her comfort zone, it felt good. She snapped a selfie in the mirror, showing the front and back of the dress, and texted it to Kal.

Bridget: Juicy enough for you?

The three dots jumped immediately. During the NBA and WNBA seasons, Kal spent Saturday afternoons at the studio preparing for that evening's game, her phone never more than an arm's reach away.

Kal: Who is this? My phone says it's Bridget Hayes, but it can't be.

Bridget: Because?

Kal: Because the Bridget Hayes I know would not be showing back AND boobs.

Bridget: It's a Grace O'Connor mandated dress. And there are no boobs, just a little cleavage.

Kal: This is one time following the rules is going to help you break them.

Bridget: ????

Kal: You look drool worthy and I'm not the only one who's going to notice.

Bridget: I have no idea what you're talking about.

Kal: Tall, ginger, smile that drips naughtiness, sings like an angel. Ring any bells?

Bridget's gaze flashed to the mirror. What *would* Blake think about this dress? She pointed a finger at her reflection and muttered, "Stop it." Returning to her room last night, she'd promised herself no more wondering, no more fishing, no more flirting. She sighed. That lasted like, what, eighteen hours?

"Bridgie," a male voice called through her door, with several sharp raps. "You ready?"

Bridget pulled open the door and waved her younger brother, Colin, into the room. "Nearly," she said, giving him a quick hug. "Did Mom or Andrew send you?"

Colin laughed. "Both."

Bridget lifted her eyes to the ceiling before returning her attention to her phone.

"Work on a Saturday?" Colin asked, pointing at her phone.

"Why does everyone assume it's work?" Her brother's expression was answer enough. "Never mind. But for the record, it's Kalisha, not work."

Bridget quickly thumbed a response. *Gotta run. Colin's here to collect me. You covering the Celtics game tonight?*

Kal: Ignoring my question, I see. But I'll let you off the hook. For now.

Bridget: xoxo

She flipped her ringer to silent and dropped her phone into her clutch. "Lead on, baby brother," she said, grabbing her key card and pointing at the door.

"Hey Bridgie," he said, his hand stilling on the doorknob.

"Yeah?"

"You look freaking amazing."

Bridget sucked in a tiny breath. Colin never said things like that to her. "Thanks," she said, waiting for the brotherly tease that inevitably followed a compliment.

"What?" he said, opening the door and holding it.

She rolled her hand. "Get on with it."

Confusion crinkled his forehead. "With what?"

"The insult. The joke. The adult version of pulling my pigtails."

"I got nothing, Bridgie. You clean up real good." He rolled his eyes. "You know, for a sister."

And with that moment from the Twilight Zone, Bridget stepped around him and walked to the elevator.

Bridget accepted a bouquet of white ranunculus and blush pink Juliet Roses from Annie. Stunning flowers befitting a stunning venue. She peeked around the bride's privacy curtain. The last of the guests were taking their seats, lit only by strings of overhead lights, and a few carefully placed up lights casting pink hues up the bricked walls. The only word that adequately captured the scene was "magic."

"Bridget," Bernard whispered, "please take your place."

She nodded, drawing in a fortifying breath. The word "President" appeared on her business card. She regularly negotiated contracts with the likes of Nike and Google. She could manage five minutes arm-in-arm with Blake Kelly. Stepping up behind Grace's niece, who was being sternly reminded that she should not throw the flower petals until she was walking toward Uncle Andrew, she lightly tapped Blake's arm. He turned at the touch and his dimpled smile fell. His gaze moved from the hem of her dress to her hair. Her body tingled as his eyes perused.

She squirmed under his focused attention, readjusting the fall of her skirt and fiddling with the shoulder straps. "Is something wrong? Do I have something on my face?" She ran a finger under her lower lip, checking for lipstick.

"No," he breathed out. Clearing his throat, he added, "I just can't remember the last time I saw you without glasses."

She touched her temple. "Oh. Yeah. I don't really like contacts, but I keep some around for occasions like this."

A hand touched her elbow and she nearly jumped out of her skin.

"It's time for you to go," Megan whispered from behind her.

She nodded, and Blake offered her his arm. He took a small step and waited for her to match his step. He was doing it again —understanding her needs without calling attention to her limitations.

"We good?" he whispered.

"All in working order," she said. There was no reason to pretend she didn't understand his question.

"Try not to outshine the bride," Blake whispered in her ear as they came to the end of the aisle.

She turned to him, confusion knitting her brow.

He shrugged a shoulder. "You didn't get the memo that bridesmaids aren't supposed to be more beautiful than the bride?"

She dropped his arm and moved to her designated spot. It sounded like a line, but it didn't feel like one. She glanced over at him, but his gaze followed the remaining attendants walking down the aisle.

An audible gasp from her brother pulled Bridget's attention from Blake. Grace's simple ivory sheath dress shimmered under the lights and her lips curved in a small smile. Despite being anchored to her father's arm, she appeared to be floating, as if Andrew pulled her magnetically down the aisle.

Emotion clogged Bridget's throat. Happiness for her brother. Gratitude for her soon-to-be new sister. Seeing their dreams come true was everything she wanted for her family.

Bridget tipped back her second glass of champagne, draining it. The low hum of muted chatter swirled around her as she scanned the room. Grace and Andrew mingled with their guests, smiles gleaming. Grace's father gesticulated widely as he told Bridget's parents what appeared to be a very entertaining story.

"A little help here," Nick said, returning to the wedding party's table, expertly balancing five drinks in his hands. Matt jumped up and passed the drinks around the table, knowing, without asking, which drink belonged to which person. He set a dark beer in front of Blake, who was casually leaning back in his chair, tux coat unbuttoned, his attention focused across the room.

Bridget followed his line of sight, her eyes landing on a striking blonde seated at a table in the far corner. An angry green monster stirred, raising its fists.

She slid over to the empty chair separating them. Because she was a glutton for punishment. "See something you like?" she asked.

He shifted, leaning toward her. "This reception is a veritable who's who of the music industry. Did you see who's over there?" He inconspicuously pointed toward the place he'd been staring.

"Who is she?" Bridget didn't recognize the woman.

"She?" Blake's brow furrowed in confusion. "No, the guy. I think that's Adam Hewson."

She leaned toward Blake to get a better look. "From The Red Project?" He was certifiable rock royalty.

Blake nodded. "Yeah. I'm not normally star-struck, but he'll do it."

"His date is gorgeous, don't you think?" Bridget asked, because clearly, she was a masochist.

"I hadn't noticed."

Her head whipped around, her hair following and flipping over her shoulder. "You didn't notice?"

He brushed her long curls back, his hand skimming her bare shoulder, and every one of her nerve endings stood up and danced a jig.

His eyes floated over her face, lingering on her lips. "No."

"I find that hard to believe," Bridget said shakily, trying to block out the sensation running through her. "Your reputation suggests you notice all women."

He knocked his knuckles on the table, watching his hand. "Reputations are often exaggerated."

Bridget snorted. "I've been at bars with you. I've seen it firsthand."

He blinked several times and gave his head an almost imperceptible shake. "Why do I smell cake?" he asked, ignoring her statement. He scanned the room, ostensibly looking for the wedding cake.

"I think it's me," she said.

Blake smirked. "You smell like cake? That might make you the perfect woman."

Her cheeks flooded with heat. "Not exactly," she stammered. "I use vanilla scented body wash and shampoo. That's probably what you're smelling."

He leaned in, just inches from her body, and drew in a slow breath. When did being sniffed become sexy? Apparently, when Blake Kelly did it.

An all too familiar tapping noise sounded next to Bridget's ear. She didn't dare turn to see if it was her mother or Bernard holding the clipboard. Both were equally frightening.

"The first dance begins in a few minutes," the wedding planner announced to the table, answering Bridget's question. "At the start of the second song, the bride and groom requested the wedding party join them."

Blake winked at Bridget. "Looks like it's you and me, TNR."

She groaned inwardly. He's already turned the font reference into an acronym. She shook off the irritation. "Why is it you and me?"

Blake pointed around the table. "Everyone else is legally bound to their dance partner."

Bridget tipped up her chin. "What about Nick?"

"On kid duty," Nick answered. Unhelpfully.

"Doesn't matter. Bridget doesn't dance," said a deep bass voice. Andrew had returned to the table.

Bridget peered at her brother from the corner of her eye. She was in the perfect position to make his wedding night unpleasant. It'd only take one quick jab with her elbow. It's what she would have done when they were kids.

But as she was no longer that little girl sandwiched between two annoying brothers, words would have to do. She really didn't want to dance with Blake, but Andrew didn't get to make that decision for her. "Excuse me, I dance."

Her words pulled Andrew's gaze from Blake's face. "But your leg—"

Irritation flared in her chest, and in her practiced way, she pushed it back down before she said something she'd regret. Instead, she sucked in a clarifying breath and stood up, ignoring the stiffness in her leg. She wouldn't grimace and give Andrew more ammunition. She stepped closer to her brother. Her modest heels brought them eye-to-eye. "Thank you for your concern, Andy," she gritted out. "But I am more than capable of taking a few slow spins around the dance floor."

Andrew huffed. "I don't want you to get hurt."

"So, this is about dancing in general, not about dancing with *Blake*?" She stabbed a finger in the air, connecting with Blake's shoulder.

"Ow," Blake said, rubbing his shoulder.

Andrew's gaze flashed to Blake and his mouth dropped open to answer her.

"Think before you answer, Andy. I appreciate your care, big brother, I do, but lying to me is a step too far." Bridget pinned him with a stare she normally saved for men denigrating women's sports.

"Andrew, we're needed on the dance floor," Grace said, wrapping an arm around Andrew's waist. Her eyes flashed between Bridget and Andrew. "Whoa," she said. "I don't know what's going on here, but I'm only allowing positive vibes tonight. Tell her you're sorry, Andrew."

His eyes flew to his new wife. "How do you know it's my fault?"

"Was it?" Grace asked, raising an eyebrow.

Before Andrew could answer, Bridget wrapped her new sister-in-law in a hug. "Welcome to the family, Grace. The Hayes family is now three women, three men. Mom and I no longer have to play zone against the boys."

Grace laughed. "I'm honored to be on your team, Bridget."

"Basketball analogies," Andrew mumbled.

Bridget pointed her finger at him. "Don't push it." She tried hard not to rock the boat with her family, but even she had limits.

"Sorry, Bridgie," Andrew grumbled. "I can't turn off my protector gene when it comes to you. Or you," he added, turning his attention to his new bride.

"I don't need a protector, Cowboy," Grace said, using the nickname that stuck after their disastrous first songwriting session. "But I could use a dance partner."

Andrew's expression softened and he grabbed Grace's hand. "Holding the most beautiful woman in the room while my favorite music plays? You'll get no complaints from me." They stepped onto the parquet dance floor to the opening notes of a song they'd co-written.

Blake stood, moving to stand behind Bridget. "Is dancing really okay?"

Bridget pulled her eyes from the couple commanding the dance floor, tilting her head toward Blake. "Promise not to tell Andrew?"

Blake smirked, making an X motion over his heart.

"It's not the easiest, but only when I step back or to the side with my left foot."

He nodded, his expression growing serious. "I have an idea." The song changed and he held out his hand to her. "But you're going to have to let me lead."

"You mean 'give up control?'"

"Think you can manage?"

She placed her hand in his and allowed him to lead her to the dance floor. "Maybe for five or six minutes," she said, trying to focus on anything other than the electricity pulsing in her fingers. Like how her constant need to be in control felt utterly exhausting in this moment. Or how the idea of letting Blake lead, if only for a single dance, suddenly felt liberating.

Blake wrapped an arm around her waist, his warm hand resting on her bare skin. "Do you know how to waltz?"

She nodded. "Do you?" she asked, surprised.

"I do. If you follow me, I'll move us around the floor, turning you so you can mostly lead with your right foot."

He took a half box step forward. Then a step to her right. A half box backward. Where did he learn to waltz so skillfully? Nights at home alone watching Dancing with the Stars? Hah. Not likely.

"My mother dragged me to a lot of charity events as a kid. Dancing lessons became a requirement. So I wouldn't embarrass her."

Magic Johnson. Had she said that out loud?

He swiveled his hips, brushing against the front of her dress. "But I might have picked up a couple of rumba moves from DWTS."

Searching for a clever response, her brain offered comebacks like "holy hips batman" and "hubbadahubbada." Yep, better just to nod and keep her mouth shut.

With his fingers pressed into her back, he guided her. Each step, each turn, designed to keep her comfortable. The tenuous threads locking her crush down frayed dangerously and her lungs went on strike.

Great.

She was going to pass out and her overprotective family would call the EMTs and when they asked what happened, the charming Blake Kelly would answer, with a casual shrug, "I think I killed her with a waltz."

"You okay?" he asked.

"Just a little out of breath."

He pulled her into his chest. "You want to stand on my feet?"

"Hey Kelly, it looks like you're manhandling my sister," Andrew bit out as he twirled Grace around them.

Something in Bridget snapped. Her family treating her like she was a fragile piece of glass. Andrew's overprotectiveness. The never-ending comments about her workaholic tendencies. A crush that no matter what she did, she couldn't shake. Her practiced restraint reshaped into something volatile. She slid her fingers up Blake's chest, cupping his cheeks, and before reason doused the fire in her belly, she leaned in and brushed her lips over his, letting one hand fall to his ass. When she forced herself to pull away, she had to bite her lip to not to giggle at Blake's wide cartoon eyes.

"No, big brother, he's been the perfect gentleman. I'm *woman*-handling him."

"Bridget," Andrew said, a touch of warning in his voice.

"Grace," Bridget said, not dropping Blake's gaze.

"Got it," Grace said, pulling Andrew in the opposite direction.

"What was that?" Blake breathed out when Andrew was out of earshot.

Bridget lifted a single shoulder. "Years of pent-up frustration."

"With Andrew?"

"Yes." Her gaze fell to his lips, and back up to his eyes. "And no."

"No?"

This was it. She either stuffed everything back inside and left the dance floor, frustrated but safe, or gave in to the adrenaline pumping through her veins.

She inched closer to him, snaking an arm around his neck,

and whispered in his ear, "I'm really feeling like trying some Comic Sans living. And I'd like you to show me."

Adrenaline for the win.

He pulled back, eyes wide again, and he tapped a finger to his chest. "You want *me* to show you?"

"Yes."

The song ended and another, faster song started, while the DJ invited everyone else to the dance floor.

He held her gaze as people moved around them. "Are you sober?"

She touched her index finger to her nose. "Yep. You?"

Blake nodded. "Just the one beer . . . and the champagne toast."

"So are you in? Are you ready to get all Comic Sans with me?" Warning bells reverberated in her head, but she wanted to forget all about the rules. For one night.

"What do you have in mind? Comic Sans living encompasses a lot." He searched her expression, his eyes darting over her face. "You want to do tequila shots? Or go get some super spicy tacos? Or . . ."

She shook her head and, with the hand still resting on his ass, she squeezed and cocked an eyebrow.

He cleared his throat. "Really?"

She slid her fingers under his tux jacket and dipped a single finger just under the waistband of his pants, moving it ever so slightly back and forth. If Kal could see her now, her brain would explode.

He squeezed his eyes shut and took a deep breath before opening them. "Are you doing this just to piss off Andrew?"

"I have zero intention of telling Andrew."

He dipped his head, meeting her eyes. Something that looked like vulnerability passed over them. "That didn't answer my question."

A trickle of doubt coiled in her belly. If she wanted this, it had to start now. Before she talked herself out of it. Before she gave up this chance.

She squared her shoulders and tipped up her chin. "I'm going to tell my parents that my leg is tired and that I'm going back to the hotel. Then I'll listen to the 'I-told-you-so's' and, when my mother insists I not travel to the hotel alone, I'm going to say you generously agreed to escort me."

She moved away, letting her hips glide side-to-side, and threw a look over her shoulder at Blake, where he stood rooted to the spot. She didn't know how to do this. She had a lot of skills, but seductress wasn't one of them.

But there was only one time Bridget Hayes didn't finish something she started. And she had no plans to make this time number two.

CHAPTER SIX

HOLY SHIT. HAD THE ONLY WOMAN EVER TO SHAKE HIM OFF his axis just propositioned him? He received his fair share of offers—some he accepted, most he didn't—but he never thought one would come from Bridget freaking Hayes.

"She finally get enough of your stiff moves?" Matt asked with a chuckle, his wife Avery in his arms.

Blake startled, realizing he was still standing in the middle of the dance floor. Alone. Looking like an idiot. "Couldn't keep up with me," he threw back, praying his attempt at a smile was more "cool cat" than "deer in the headlights."

He stepped off the dance floor, his gaze moving from one bandmate to the next. Matt and Joe dancing with their wives. Andrew and Grace across the candlelit room, deep in conversation with yet another famous guest. Nick sitting alone at a table eating the remnants of a double fudge cupcake, his son draped over his shoulder, asleep. Bandmates. Best friends. Brothers.

As a lonely kid with a mother who was always working and grandparents that lived states away, this was what he'd craved. This was the family he'd always wanted.

Was the chance to feel Bridget Hayes in his arms after years of denying his attraction worth the risk of angering Andrew and driving a wedge in the band?

He turned and watched Bridget exchange pleasantries with her parents. If he went with her, it's not like his bandmates would suspect a thing. Escorting her back to the hotel *was* the perfect cover.

The irony wasn't lost on him. Risk-averse Bridget Hayes looked to him to shake her out of her routine, yet here he stood, normally a jump-first, ask questions later kind of guy, conflicted about what to do next.

She tossed her long brown waves over her shoulder and a voice whispered, *you might never get this chance again.* Bridget turned, pinning him with a look, and damn if his cock didn't twitch. Her smile widened, and every excuse, every argument, vanished. With a mind of their own, his feet closed the distance between them. He doubted that anything could stop the magnetic force pulling him to this beautiful woman—not even Andrew stepping in front of him.

Sylvia turned when he stopped inches from Bridget. "Thanks for escorting her to the hotel, Blake. I know she's capable, but I feel better knowing she won't be alone."

He swallowed the growing lump in his throat and flashed Sylvia his trained, never-failed-with-women-of-any-age smile. "Wait. *I'm* protecting *her*? I'm pretty sure it's the other way around."

Sylvia smiled and playfully swatted his arm. "Funny."

Was it? Right now, he was so far outside his comfort zone, he wondered if he might need a little protection.

"Say goodbye to your brother and Grace," Sylvia said, waving toward the newlyweds.

Blake's spine stiffened. That was possibly the worst idea ever.

Bridget calmly leaned down and placed a kiss on Sylvia's

temple. "He's enjoying his guests. No need to interrupt. I'll see him tomorrow morning at brunch."

Blake's stomach unclenched, grateful for Bridget's quick thinking.

She turned to him. "I ordered an Uber. It should be here in a couple of minutes. You ready?"

The honest answer ran the gamut from "not even a little" to "I've been ready since Andrew first uttered the words, 'Meet my sister.'" He nodded, not trusting himself with words.

"Bye, Mom," Bridget said, her dress swishing around Blake's legs as she stepped away from the table. "Bye, Daddy."

Charles Hayes peered over his old fashioned and pointed a finger at his daughter. "This better not be an excuse to go back to the hotel and work, Sugarplum."

"Don't worry, I have *no* intention of working tonight." She snuck a hand behind her and gave Blake's thigh a little squeeze.

"Good night, all. Enjoy the rest of the party," Blake said, praying his cheeks didn't mirror the heat erupting in the rest of his body.

"From what I understand," Charles said, smirking at Blake, "this might be the earliest you've ever left a party."

"D-d-duty calls," he said, his heart pushing against his ribcage as a tempest of thoughts roared through his mind. Bridget Hayes. Long-time crush. Most beautiful woman in the room. And Andrew's sister . . .

Bridget, clearly sensing his hesitation, squeezed the tips of his fingers. "You can stay. I'm sure I can find someone else to accompany me back to the hotel."

Something surged through his body. Something unfamiliar. A little green monster pounding on his temples at the idea of "someone else."

"No," he said more harshly than intended, and her eyes

widened. He pulled a breath from deep in his chest. "I said I would take you."

"Take me," she mouthed, and then blinked rapidly, like she'd surprised herself with her boldness. She gestured to a small open space behind the bar. "Let's exit that way. Andrew is on the other side of the room, but no reason to tempt fate."

"Good idea," he said, following her lead. He wiped his palms on his pants. Had a woman ever made him this nervous? Maybe his mother. But for entirely different reasons.

Huh. Would you look at that? One thought about Bette Kelly and the growing heat in his body cooled.

Bridget pushed open the door and the early April breeze hit his face, cooling him further. Mist hung heavy around the lamps dotting the street. An Uber idled at the curb, its engine sputtering every few seconds. A Kia Soul. Electric blue with "I (heart) Spam" and "There's a little hippie in all of us" bumper stickers. A dent in the back door suspiciously shaped like the side of a grocery cart. Hollywood couldn't have designed a better set for their clandestine departure.

He opened the door, and Bridget gathered the fabric of her dress, sliding inside.

"Hi kids!" a woman in a tie-dye shirt with tight gray curls peeking out of a Minnesota Twins baseball cap bubbled. A faint smell of weed hung in the air, which explained both the hippie bumper sticker and her love of Spam. "If I had to guess, you're escaping a wedding."

"We are," Bridget said, matching the driver's cheery tone.

She pulled away from the curb, signaling into the nearly deserted street. "There's only two reasons young folks leave a reception early."

"Is that so?" Bridget asked.

"Yep," she nodded, making a left without hitting her brakes.

"It's either a bridezilla situation or the whole romantic vibe made ya horny."

Blake nearly choked on his tongue when Bridget looked at him, winked, and said, "The bride is lovely."

Gladys—her name supplied by a tag hanging from her rearview mirror—chuckled and depressed the gas pedal, causing Bridget to tumble toward him. "Well then, let's get you to that hotel."

"Thanks for the ride, Gladys," Bridget said, as the Kia Soul came to an abrupt stop outside the W Hotel, two tires up on the curb.

"You're welcome, honey. This might be my Saturday nights now, but I remember what it was like to be young."

They slipped out of the car, and with a beep and a wave, Gladys sped off.

"I gave her a *giant* tip," Bridget said, giggling.

"You know she's just going to spend it on weed," he said. "Is that the behavior you want to encourage, Ms. Hayes?"

"Is smoking weed part of Comic Sans living?" Bridget asked as the hotel concierge held the door open for them.

He followed her across the black-and-white marble foyer, stopping in front of the elevators. "Nope. No way."

She raised an eyebrow, punching the up button.

"Not for former professional athletes." He raised his hands in a 'what can you do' motion. "It's in the manual. Subsection 4.37B. Under the title, 'It's Dribble and Dunk, not Dribble and Drunk.'"

She rolled her eyes, smirking. "I'll take your word for it."

They rode the elevator in silence, words no competition for the unexplored waves of heat and electricity pulsing through the small space.

"Bridget," he said, winding his fingers around her wrist when they arrived at the alcove in front of her door. "You're absolutely sure about this? The chance of this going sideways is a very real possibility."

"Sideways, back-ways, front-ways, whatever works for you," she said, giving her shoulders a shake.

He dropped her wrist and scrubbed a hand through his hair. "See? Comments like that make me wonder if you've thought this through."

She sighed and her shoulders slumped. "I'm terrible at this whole seduction thing. Most Times New Romans are. Or so I've heard. But I know what I want, Blake."

"And that is?"

"I want one night to be someone other than Bridget always-plays-by-the-rules Hayes. Something to drown out all the 'shoulds' that are constantly jockeying for space in my mind." She slid a hand up his chest. "Haven't you ever wanted to escape your life—if only for a little while?"

He stared at her. Hell yes, he'd wanted to escape his life. Not for a long time, but he still remembered the feeling.

"Too honest?" she asked, searching his face. Her expression was wary for the first time since she'd propositioned him on the dance floor.

"No, nothing is sexier than honesty."

"But?"

"But you're sure it's *me* you want to 'escape' with?"

"You're pretty much the Yoda of Comic Sans living. So who better?"

He shifted his weight from one foot to the other. He needed more. For the first time in a long time, he didn't want to be just another carnival ride. He didn't want to be just a means to an end. Not with her. This might be a night for her to forget, but he knew it'd be a night he'd always remember. He needed to know she wanted *him*, not just a warm body. "That's it?"

"Yes." She pushed her back against the door and slowly shook her head. "No."

"Which is it?" The next words out of her mouth would determine whose bed he slept in tonight.

She grasped the door handle behind her, nervously twisting it up and down. "Can what happens in Minneapolis stay in Minneapolis?"

God, he hoped so. "Yes."

She squeezed her eyes shut and sucked in a breath that did amazing things to her chest. "Okay, here goes." Another deep breath. "I've kinda, for a little while, had a teeny weenie" —she pinched her thumb and forefinger together— "crush on you." The last words rushed past her lips.

Relief flooded through his veins, and he stepped into her space, holding her gaze, one corner of his mouth quirking up. "Do not use the words 'teeny weenie' in front of me."

A choked laugh gurgled from Bridget's throat. "And there he is. The Blake Kelly we all know and love."

"Love, huh?" His lips stretched into a full smile.

"Not like that," she said, rolling her eyes.

"You might change your mind after I show you my not-so teeny weenie."

Her eyes dropped and pink crept into her cheeks. "This is one night, remember? Anything else is too complicated."

He knew that once he got a taste of her, he'd crave more. But faced with the choice of one night or nothing, he'd take tonight, knowing she was right—anything more was unrealistic.

He pressed her up against the door, hands on either side of her head. Woman with a plan? Sexy. Woman with everything to lose and still honest? Incredibly sexy. "What's a little while?"

She blinked a few times. "Sorry?"

He ran a finger from her temple to her cheek, tucking a curl behind her ear. "You said you've had a crush on me for 'a little while.' How long, Bridget?"

She grimaced. "Um . . . since the first night I came backstage?"

"Same," he said, stepping forward, leaving less than a hair's width between them.

"W-w-what?"

"Boston," he said, letting his finger fall to her chin, giving it a tender pinch. "Your first year at UConn. Already setting records—assists, I believe. You had on jeans, a red sweater and your hair pulled back in a ponytail. No glasses that night either."

"You had a crush on *me*?" she asked again, as if that was the most implausible thing she'd ever heard.

"Not had, Bridget. *Have*." He snaked an arm around her waist. "Open the door, Bridget." Her—*their*—confessions muting every clanging warning bell.

She waved the key card in front of the sensor, pushed the door open with her backside and grabbed him by the lapels, dragging him into the room. "We're clear that this is just for tonight? And no one breathes a word to Andrew?"

He nodded. He'd agree to about anything right now. Though . . . "Six condoms for one night? Feels like a bit of stretch, TNR."

She laughed. "You're obsessed with those condoms."

"Maybe it's not the condoms, but the woman in possession of them."

Bridget released a nervous laugh and ran her hand over his short beard, tentatively tracing his bottom lip with a single finger. Desperate to feel her lips pressed against his, he held himself in check and let her explore. He'd imagined kissing her so many times. Too many times. The kiss on the dance floor didn't count. That was a sister egging on her brother. But here, just the two of them . . .

He brushed his nose against hers and kissed her cheeks, her chin, before letting his lips sink into hers. She hummed in response, the small vibration coursing through his lips, down his neck, and settling in a spot in his chest he refused to acknowledge.

His lips sought the long column of her neck, softly nipping and biting until his mouth arrived at the rise of her collarbone. He nudged the shoulder strap over, hungry for more of her velvety skin.

As it slipped down her arm, she placed a hand on his chest, creating a space between them. She held his gaze, but stepped back, flipping on the small bedside lamp, lowering it to its lowest setting and turning off the overhead light.

"Ambience?" he said, his voice low and raspy, even to his own ears.

Something he didn't recognize passed over her face. "Something like that," she said, backing up to the bed. She sat and crossed her legs, and then uncrossed them and stood again.

He loosened his tie, slipped it from his collar, and tucked it into his tux jacket. "I'm nervous too, Bridget."

Her eyes flashed to his. "Really?"

He nodded. "When you've imagined something for so long . . ."

"Isn't it strange?" she said, walking toward him. "That you've imagined, and I've imagined, yet we've never . . ." She pointed to the bed. "I guess because . . ."

"The stakes are high," he said, finishing her sentence. And it wasn't just about harmony in the band or his place in the Story-hill family, it was also what walking away from her once they crossed this line would do to his heart.

"Have you changed your mind?" he said, slipping his hands into his pockets.

She answered him with a bruising kiss, sliding her fingers under his coat, pushing it off his shoulders. "Once I make a decision, I don't retreat."

He slipped his coat the rest of the way off and threw it across the chair beside the bed. "And that's me?" He still couldn't quite believe it.

She slowly unbuttoned his shirt, kissing lower on his chest as each button dropped open. "Did Michael Jordan win ten NBA scoring titles?" She pushed off his shirt in one fluid movement. It dropped to the floor with a hiss.

She popped his belt buckle and stilled her hand. "I think it's time for you to catch up." He slid his hands up her spine. "This thing have a zipper?"

Her lips curved into a smile, and she turned her back to him. With a quick shoulder shimmy, the dress pooled at her feet. Leaving her only in the black lacy thong. It looked a hell of a lot better on her than in his hands in the middle of an airport.

His lungs seized, a rush of air pushing up and out. "Turn around," he asked, his voice low and raspy. "Let me see you."

She smiled over her shoulder, but didn't turn, sliding between the sheets and scooching to the far side of the bed.

"Shy?" he asked, surprised.

She hummed and shook her head.

Awareness shot through him. "Bridget, you don't need to hide your scars from me."

"You gonna lose those pants?" she said, a small smile curving her mouth, but not reaching her eyes.

"Bridget."

"I'm not here for therapy. I'm here for Comic Sans tutoring,"

"But—"

"No buts, Blake. Blocking out my normal life, remember?" She gave him a hard look before repositioning and letting the sheet fall to her waist. And damn if her nipples didn't harden under his stare.

He was pretty sure he'd never shucked a pair of pants quicker. "You play dirty, Hayes."

"I prefer to call it 'strategic.'"

"Okay, then," he said, climbing onto the bed next to her. "What's your next move?"

She pushed his shoulders into the mattress and flipped a leg over his waist. A tiny grimace passed over her face as she positioned herself on top of him.

"If this hurts you—"

She silenced him by circling her hips, the scrap of lace between her legs rubbing against the length of him. "I'm a former world-class athlete. I think I can handle this."

"But—"

She ground down on him, and his hips bucked. "I told you. No buts."

"Bridget," he said, reversing their positions, flipping her under him. "You keep doing that and this will be over way too quickly. And I'm a firm believer in 'ladies first.'"

She held his gaze, her breath already coming hard and fast.

He traced concentric circles around her breast until his fingers met her nipple. He wanted to draw it into his mouth and suck it until she started panting his name. But first things first. "Tell me where to find that stack of condoms you flashed at the airport."

"Outside pocket," she said, pointing at the bag sitting atop the hotel luggage rack. He rolled out of the bed and the heat of her gaze followed him.

He tore one off the sleeve and tucked it under his pillow. Sliding into the bed, he pulled her close, relishing the feel of her skin pressing against his. "Remind me to thank Kal for packing those when I meet her."

Bridget stiffened, pushing a hand against his chest.

He wrapped his fingers around hers. "I'm kidding. I know tonight is off the record. First rule of *Fight Club* and all that."

"Blake—"

He laughed against her skin. "Too much talking?"

"Yep."

He nipped the soft spot under her ear and kissed down her jaw, her neck, her cleavage, giving her nipple a flick with his tongue and sucking it into his mouth while rolling the other one in his fingers. Her back arched and she groaned. The sound sent a lightning bolt crashing down his spine, making him impossibly hard.

She reached for his erection, but he stopped her, wrapping his fingers around her wrist.

Her brow crinkled. "Boo. Ten yards for illegal use of your hands."

He brought her hand to his mouth, kissing her palm. "I thought your game was basketball, not football."

"Fine. Flagrant foul on number . . ." —she ran a hand down his back— "you seem to have lost your jersey. Might have to add a delay of game violation for not being properly dressed."

He propped himself up on one elbow. "A flagrant and a delay of game call? You sure, ref? I think the combination would get me kicked out of the game."

She blew out a dramatic breath. "Fine, just the flagrant. But if I were you, I'd quit complaining about the calls and keep the game moving."

"Message received, ref." He dragged his fingers down her torso, following every touch with his lips, trying to memorize every curve, every dip, every inch. If this was his only chance, he wanted to remember everything, catalogue every sight and sound.

He left a trail of kisses over her belly, and reaching her upper thigh, sucked a patch of skin into his mouth. He'd never once felt the urge to mark a woman before, but tonight was full of surprises. He lightly ran a finger over her crease, and she whimpered, tunneling her fingers in his hair. "So wet," he murmured into the junction of her thigh and center.

She wiggled, trying to move his mouth. "Blake, *please*," she gritted out.

"Why, Bridget Hayes, are you begging?" he teased, moving his mouth to her other thigh.

"No." She gave the roots of his hair a tug and electric impulses shot through him.

She squirmed again, but he stilled her hips. "Comic Sans living requires *asking* for what you want. Tell me what you want, Bridget."

"Do it," she said, the words hoarse and rough. "Please."

"Do what?"

She groaned. "You know."

"I can't be sure unless you tell me." He teased her with his fingers, dipping inside her folds. He pulled back to watch her expression. It was clear she was fighting to maintain control. "I'm guessing you're very specific in the boardroom, Bridget. Do it here. Tell me exactly what you want."

A growl fell from her lips. "Fuck me with your mouth, Blake." With the words still hanging in the air, her hand flew to her mouth and her eyes popped wide.

He laughed softly. "Well, well, well, Bridget Hayes, did you just use a curse word? Correction, did you just *yell* a curse word? I might be legally obligated to tell Andrew that you finally lost the bet."

Clearly over the shock, Bridget propped herself up on her

elbows. "Please tell me you did not choose this moment to bring up my brother."

Blake grimaced. *Shit.* Way to invite the elephant into the room. A trickle of panic dripped into his belly, and he forced himself to concentrate on the beautiful—naked—woman splayed out in front of him. "Can we rewind thirty seconds and forget I said that?"

A whisper of a smile danced across her lips as she slid her hand down her belly, his gaze locking on her fingers, following their path. "I don't know. Can you remember exactly where you were and what you were doing?"

"I might recall." He pushed her legs wider and lowered his mouth to her center, giving her what she'd asked for before his ill-timed statement, listening to what drew the loudest sounds from her and repeating those things. When her hips rose off the bed, he slid a finger inside her, aiming for the spot that would drive her over the edge.

One stroke. Two strokes. She tugged on his hair again, his name escaping her mouth in a whispered scream. He stayed with her while she rode out her orgasm. When her breathing slowed, she bit out, "Condom. Now."

He sheathed himself and put a hand under her right knee, pushing it up and seating himself between her legs. She reached for him, placing him at her entrance. He slid into her in one fluid motion and the warmth of her had him seeing stars. He hovered over her, slowly pressing into her again and again, his body demanding more speed, his brain wanting to savor every moment. Wanting her to come again along with him.

She dragged a single finger down his spine. "I've had mine. Take yours."

"But—"

"Did you enjoy watching me come, Blake?"

"Hell yes." It was one of the best things he'd ever seen.

"I'd like the same chance."

His restraint snapped and he thrust into her, sensation building at the base of his spine, lost in the feeling of her wrapped around him. His release came fast and hard, and he collapsed on top of her. His heart thumped against her chest as he kissed the side of her neck, tasting salt and vanilla. He needed to move, to stop crushing her, and he'd do that as soon as the room stopped spinning. After a few breaths and a persuasive conversation with his noodle-like muscles and bones, he kissed her on the tip of her nose and rolled off the bed to take care of the condom. "I'll be back shortly. Don't move."

She hummed. "Don't think I could even if I wanted to."

In the bathroom, he leaned on the counter, catching his breath, and studying himself in the mirror. Desire, consequences, guilt, and what-ifs jockeyed for position in his mind. Bridget deserved better than sneaking around. She deserved a man who knew how to commit, a man who didn't run from relationships.

He stepped back into the room and Bridget had rolled over, soft snoring noises whistling from her nose. Her expression was peaceful, a softer version of the one she carried while awake. Another memory to pack away in his mental Bridget file.

Like the night they first met backstage.

Or the time she sang karaoke and proved, beyond any doubt, that Andrew got all the musical talent in the family.

And sitting at the bar, smiling at him over the top of her glasses, as all of Grace's bridesmaids chimed in on wedding plans.

He thought nothing would top the memory of her face as he stood at the airport holding her condoms and panties. But this did. And he'd trade all the other memories combined for this one. Longing tore through him, razor-sharp. He rubbed his thumb over his sternum. If only he could have her *and* the band. If only he had any idea how to do anything more than casual.

But he couldn't. And didn't.

Crawling into bed, he pulled her back to his front, grateful to hold her. If only for a few hours. He wouldn't get another night with her, but he had tonight. He'd keep her until he couldn't.

CHAPTER SEVEN

BRIDGET ROLLED OVER AND RAN INTO A BRICK WALL. A warm, muscly brick wall. Her eyes traced the ridges and valleys of his chest and the way his hair contrasted with the white pillow. Her fingers itched to touch him, but if she didn't move, she could pretend this was a dream, a figment of her imagination. After all, it wouldn't be the first time she'd conjured him in the middle of the night. It would, however, be the first time his warm breath swept across her face.

Holy Hakeem Olajuwon. Apparently, when she finally broke the rules, she went all in.

Maybe not so surprising. What was that saying? That a person's greatest strength is also their greatest flaw. Two sides of the same coin and all that.

There had only been one time in Bridget's life where she'd set her mind on something and didn't get it. But this might be the first time she'd gone all in knowing the proverbial pot at the end of the rainbow was all smoke and mirrors. What happened last night wasn't the first step toward attaining a goal. It was impulsive and shortsighted.

Careful not to disturb him, she inched over, reaching for her phone. How long had they been asleep? A few minutes maybe? She tapped the screen to life and bolted upright. Four am. They'd been out for hours.

"Blake," she said, jiggling his shoulder. "Blake, wake up."

He smirked, his eyes still closed. "You ready for round two?"

Yes, her body yelled. "No."

His lids popped open at her emphatic response.

She wrapped the sheet around her torso. "It's four am. You need to go back to your room before anyone sees you doing the walk of shame."

His brows knitted together. "There is nothing shameful about two consenting adults enjoying themselves."

She waved her hand in the air. "It's just an expression."

He scrubbed a hand down his face, scratching his beard. "One I've always hated."

"Noted. Now get dressed." She placed her hands flat on his chest (not one of her wiser decisions) and pushed.

He captured her fingers. "Everyone had a late night. No one will be up for several hours." He ran a finger down her bare arm and her traitorous body shivered in approval. "You sure you want me to go? Your body seems to have a different opinion."

He turned her hand over and placed a soft kiss on her palm. She inhaled a deep breath, searching for her missing willpower. She placed a light kiss on his lips—because she wasn't superhuman. The man she'd dreamed about for years was naked in her bed. Yet . . .

"Don't you think it's best?"

He pulled her into his chest and again her body ignored reason and she snuggled up to him. He wrapped his arms around her and there was no denying his arousal. Tucking her hand under the covers, she ran a finger along his erection. Because, again, not superhuman.

"Someone's not playing fair," he said, but didn't remove her hand.

"You're probably right about everyone sleeping in and we did only use one condom. Seems a shame to bring them all the way to Minneapolis just to take them back home."

"It does. And," he said, his eyes flashing to the small opening in the curtains, "it's still dark, so this still qualifies as one *night*."

"Mmm," she hummed, her fingers tracing the trail of hair up his abdomen. "I like your logic. But the deal still stands. This is it."

If she didn't know better, it looked like something resembling disappointment crossed his face. But, no, they'd both agreed to one night.

"Off the record," he said. "But, fair warning, if you get a second taste of all this" —his hand floated over his many, many pack abs— "you might develop cravings for more."

"I'll take my chances. I have world class willpower." Clearly a big fat lie.

His smile drooped and he studied her face with such intensity it felt heavy on her skin. She waited for his quick-witted response, but he drew her in and kissed her with a ferocity that stole her breath—and emptied her mind of every worry, every excuse, every thought but him.

Bridget leaned against the bathroom doorjamb, wrapped only in a towel, watching as he buckled his belt and stepped into his shoes. "Once more" had included sharing a shower and a third orgasm. When she'd come so hard her leg threatened to buckle under her, he'd held her steady, almost reverently. She pushed the image from her mind. She couldn't think about that right now. She needed to get him out of the room so she could . . . could what?

"See you at brunch," he said, breaking into her thoughts.

"Brunch," she said, nodding. She glanced at the clock. In three hours. Was that enough time to douse the giant neon sign that hung over her head blinking, "Look at me, I've just had the three best orgasms of my life?"

"And Blake—"

He cupped her cheek and kissed her forehead. "I'll make sure no one sees me. Though when I get back to the room, Nick will probably have some questions."

Bridget gasped and backed away from him. "You're sharing a room with Nick and didn't think to mention it?"

He laughed. "Just yanking your chain."

She picked up one of the throw pillows she'd hastily flung on the floor last night and chucked it at him. "That was mean."

He caught the pillow in mid-air and tossed it on the bed as he stepped up to her. His smile faded and he ran his finger along the top of the towel. His expression was so soft, so tender, she had to look away. "Thanks for an amazing night. And morning."

She nodded like some sex-sated bobblehead. "Yep. You too," she squeaked out.

He pulled her into a hug, resting his chin on her shoulder. "There *are* three more condoms."

"Go," she said with a laugh, pointing at the door. "And if you get to brunch before me, friends save friends mimosas."

"Is that what we are? Friends?" He slipped into his jacket and placed a hand on the door handle.

Yes. No. Maybe. And every other complicated, nuanced answer. She settled for, "I hope so."

Blake's eyes flashed to the bed and back to her, something inscrutable passing over his expression. "Would it be okay if I kissed you goodbye? Do friends do that?"

She threaded her fingers through his. If the ache inside her was any indication, another kiss was a bad idea. But it would wrap things up nicely. Seal the deal and all that. Wow, she was an impressive excuse manufacturing machine. "Maybe the 'friends' part starts at brunch?"

"Perfectly reasonable," he said, reeling her in. He placed his hands on her jaw, his thumbs caressing her cheeks. His lips covered hers, his breath warm on her skin. Simple and sweet, not pushing for more. "Goodbye, Bridget," he said, the words close enough to send vibrations across her lips.

It wasn't a "goodbye until brunch." It was a final goodbye. And exactly what she said she wanted. Why then did it feel like her heart had dropped into her stomach?

He stepped back and a classic Blake Kelly smile broke across his face. In this moment, she hated that practiced smile. She wanted the one that curved his lips last night as he hovered above her. *You asked for one night, Bridget. Snap out of it.*

He opened the door, peered side-to-side exaggeratedly, checking the hallway, making her laugh. "Coast is clear, Agent Hayes." He flashed her another quick grin and slipped out.

She collapsed onto the bed. What had she done?

Given in to her crush? Yep.

Acted completely out of character? Yep.

Had mind-numbing, toe-curling sex? With one of her brother's best friends? Yep, and yep.

Her fingers dug into the skin at the base of her neck. A futile attempt to stop the boa constrictor of panic coiling in her stomach, slithering upward, squeezing the breath from her esophagus. Her lungs sat inside her chest like flat balloons, no matter how many breaths she inhaled.

She exercised caution with everything in her life. Until last night. When standing in his arms, in the middle of the dance floor, she couldn't muster a shred of that caution. In that moment, it didn't matter that he was cavalier and carefree, and she craved a structured, controlled, neat life.

It needed to matter now. For her life to work properly. And for Andrew. She'd kept her crush quiet, never acted on it because she knew it would cause issues in the band. The band was Andrew's dream. She knew what it was like to have a dream ripped away, and she wouldn't jeopardize someone else's.

Why had she acted so recklessly? She slapped her hands against the bed, palms stinging at the impact.

Rap. Rap. Rap.

She sat straight up, jolted out of her panic spiral.

"Bridget!"

Her mother. Bridget's eyes flashed to the clock. How long had Blake been gone? Had her mother seen him leaving?

"Mom," she called through the door. "Just a second. I just got out of the shower." She pulled the towel tighter, swept the condom wrappers into the drawer—next to the Bible—and yanked the bedding up. "You alone?"

"Yes," her mother called back.

Bridget opened the door a crack, and Sylvia Hayes pushed through it.

"Hi, honey, I'm wondering if you—" Sylvia's words stuttered to a stop, turning to face Bridget. "Are you okay?"

Some parts are very okay. Other parts, not so much.

She pulled a quick breath in through her nose. "Why do you ask?" Bridget said, praying her voice sounded normal.

"The bed's a mess." Her mother pointed at the jumble of bedding. Sylvia stepped closer to her daughter. "Something keep you up last night?'

Panic paralyzed her. *Julius Erving.* Think Bridget, think.

Her mother pulled the coverlet taut. "Was it leg pain or bad dreams?"

Bridget could've fallen to the floor in relief. Either option was a logical excuse for the state of the room. The "dreams" her mother referenced were nightmares that started almost immediately after the accident and haunted her for years. She'd either be inside that crumpling car, brakes screeching, or immobilized in a hospital bed while the doctor, who, in the dream, bore a striking resemblance to her college coach, repeated "never walk again" over and over. She'd wake up with the covers twisted around her and covered in sweat.

Just like last night, but for very different reasons.

"Bridget?"

She turned back to her mother. "Nightmare," she lied.

"Do you want to talk about it?" her mother asked.

"Thank you," she said, "but I'm good."

"You're sure?" Sylvia said.

Bridget nodded. "When you came to the room, it sounded like you wanted something?" she asked, redirecting her mother's attention.

"Right" — she gestured to her slipper covered feet— "I broke the heel off my shoe last night and since we wear the same size, I'm hoping you have a pair I could borrow. I'll return them after brunch."

"Sure, sure," she said, heading toward her suitcase, but not before noticing Blake's tie at the foot of the bed. "How was the rest of the reception?" she asked, kicking it under the bedspread.

"Lovely. Grace really knows how to throw a party. Too bad you had to leave early." She continued, something about Curtis and Nick and karaoke, but Bridget only caught random words as she scanned the room for further evidence of her . . . indiscretion. Satisfied the only other clothes strewn around the room were hers, she held up the pair of black wedges she'd worn under her bridesmaid dress.

"How about these?" she asked, realizing she had no idea if she was interrupting her mother or not. "They're Eileen Fisher." Sylvia Hayes loved a pair of designer shoes.

Her mother nodded approvingly. "Do you have a pair to wear if I take these?"

"After yesterday's festivities, I'd prefer flats," she said, pointing to the pair sitting next to her suitcase.

She grabbed her mother's elbow and steered her toward the door. "See you at brunch? I'm getting cold in this towel. I should get dressed."

Sylvia stood at the door and assessed her daughter again. "You're absolutely sure you're okay?"

Bridget pulled the towel tighter around her. "Yep. Just a little tired from a long time on my feet yesterday. And you know, the bad dream," she added, wincing at the repeated lie. She didn't want her family focusing on her leg or the accident and now here she was, using both to cover the truth.

"Very well," Sylvia said.

Did she hear suspicion in her mother's voice? Wasn't the best sex of your life supposed to be relaxing, not paranoia inducing? She needed a moment alone, or the minefield otherwise known as "brunch" would be her undoing.

"See you soon, Mom," Bridget said, walking to the closet, extracting the outfit she'd planned to wear today. "You better make sure Dad is ready—you know what happens when he's left alone."

"You're right. He's probably sitting in his boxers watching CNN. That man and his news." She blew Bridget a kiss and stepped out of the room.

Bridget eyed the mini fridge. Was it too early for tequila?

"Mimosa, *friend*?" Blake said, meeting her at the entrance of the hotel reception room, two long-stemmed glasses in his fingers.

She took the full glass and tipped it back, downing it in one gulp.

"Long night?" he asked, his expression flat.

She took the half-full mimosa from his other hand and sipped. "My mother came to my room shortly after you left."

He grabbed a bloody mary from the passing server. "I saw no one between your room and mine," he responded, anticipating her question.

"You left your tie."

The color drained from his face. "Shit. It must have fallen out of my coat pocket. Did she see it?"

"I don't think so."

He scrubbed a hand down his face. "I'm sorry. I'm usually more careful than that."

A reminder that while she hadn't had sex in two years, this was a regular occurrence for him. And another example of their stark differences.

"Thanks for escorting my girl back last night," Bridget's father said, placing a hand on Blake's shoulder, causing them both to startle.

"Of course," Blake said with a forced chuckle. "I hate to think about the trouble she could have gotten into."

"Like answering emails at midnight?" Colin said, sliding into the conversation.

Blake laughed along with her father and brother while she glared at him over her glasses.

"Bridget," Andrew said, materializing as if from thin air, "please tell me you did not leave my wedding early to work."

Bridget tipped back the second mimosa. The end of this brunch could not come fast enough. "No, big brother, no work. I went straight to bed. Kept my leg elevated for *hours*."

Blake coughed, spurting tomato juice back into his glass.

Andrew pounded him between his shoulder blades. "You okay, man?"

Blake nodded, wiping his lips with a cocktail napkin. "Just a little spicier than I expected," he said, lifting his glass.

"Sorry," Andrew said. "Grace has an affinity for Tabasco."

"Not very midwestern of me, is it?" Grace said, stepping up, sliding her arm around Andrew's waist. "Are you feeling better this morning, Bridget?"

Bridget nodded. "I was just telling Andrew I got exactly what I needed last night."

Blake coughed again and the three Hayes men swiveled toward him. He pounded a palm against his chest. "Sorry, thought I was prepared for a second sip. Apparently not."

Grace's gaze flashed from Bridget to Blake and back to Bridget, her eyes widening. This was the worst possible time for her highly perceptive sister-in-law to catch on.

"Grace," Bridget said, scrambling for something, anything, to distract her. "Have you gotten any preliminary photos from last night? I'd love to see them. The venue was so beautiful, I bet it made a stunning backdrop." The words flew from her lips. Cyclone Sylvia had nothing on Bridget right now.

"The photographer sent over a few to play during brunch." Grace pointed at the large flat screen on the far wall. "I can give you a preview, if you'd like."

"That would be great," Bridget said, trying to slow her words.

"She got some excellent shots of you and Blake," Grace said, a knowing smile dancing at the corners of her mouth.

Heat crept up Bridget's neck and she fought the urge to run from the room. "Lead the way, new sister," she said, digging deep for her "I've got everything under control" voice. She grabbed Grace's elbow, guiding her toward the laptop attached to the hotel's audio-visual system.

"If I had to guess, the bloody marys aren't the only spicy thing Blake sampled in the last twenty-four hours," Grace whispered in Bridget's ear as they walked away from her father, brothers, and Blake.

Bridget opened her mouth, but not a single word formed. Was it too much to ask for a giant sinkhole to open in the floor and suck her in?

Grace stopped at the laptop and double clicked the thumb drive icon on the home screen.

Undoubtedly, Bridget was being punished for her reckless behavior because the file opened to a photo of her and Blake standing at the edge of the aisle runner and no one with any sense would label the smile they shared as "we're just two buddies hanging out."

"You look good together," Grace said in the year's biggest understatement.

"Thanks to you. Your taste in dresses and tuxes is exquisite."

"The clothes are great, but we both know that's not what I meant," Grace said, bumping her shoulder into Bridget's.

Bridget squeezed the bridge of her nose. "Please don't say anything to Andrew," she whispered, studying her shoes.

"I knew it!" Grace did a little shimmy, her smile growing wide. "It might take Andrew a little while to come around, but I like you together."

Bridget's head popped up. "No, Grace. No. It was a one-night thing. Promise you won't say anything. To anyone."

Grace's smile fell. "If you want me to keep it to myself, I will. But can I ask why?"

"Like I said," Bridget said. "It was a one-time thing. A wedding indiscretion. Nothing that merits mentioning." *Holy Lisa Leslie*, why couldn't she stop the babbling?

"Nope. Not buying it." Grace wrapped her fingers around Bridget's wrist. "You're both single. Successful. Live in the same city. If you're attracted to each other, why not explore it?"

"I don't want to cause any issues in the band," Bridget recited. A practiced response. A half-truth.

"And that would happen how?"

Bridget searched Grace's face. Why wouldn't she drop it? "Andrew's so overprotective of me. If he knew, he'd treat Blake differently. I can't be Yoko. I can't do that to Andrew."

Grace pursed her lips and cocked an eyebrow. "Yoko?"

"What if this thing" —she waved at the screen— "broke up the band? This band is Andrew's dream. I can't take that away from him."

"They're grown men. They'd figure it out," Grace said, reeling Bridget into a hug. She smoothed her hand over Bridget's hair. "You have to live for yourself, not Andrew."

She couldn't tell Grace that it wasn't only about Andrew. If a person had a dream, she'd do whatever she could to help them protect it. Save them from her fate any way she could.

"Are the pictures that bad?" Blake asked, causing Bridget to jump.

Grace pulled back, giving Bridget's hand a squeeze. "I'll let you see for yourself. Bridget can show you."

Bridget grabbed for Grace's arm like someone floundering in the ocean lurches for a life preserver. "They're your photos, Grace. You should stay and show them to Blake."

Grace's smile returned. "He's in excellent hands," she said with a wink.

"What was that all about?" Blake asked, his gaze following Grace's retreating form.

"You know Grace, she's a hugger," she said with a shrug. "Happy. Sad. New wedding photos. All reasons to hug in Grace's book."

He dipped his head to look at their picture and she stilled, waiting for him to call her out.

"I should wear a tux more often. I look damn good."

A laugh of pure relief tumbled out of her. "You ready for another mimosa, friend?"

"So ready," he said, catching her gaze. "I'd hate for Grace and Andrew to pay for all of this and it go to waste."

"Truth. It's not like you can recap an open bottle of champagne. Drinking it is an act of service."

He winked and placed his hands on her shoulders, turning her toward the bar. "Time to do our duty, TNR."

CHAPTER EIGHT

BRIDGET PULLED HER GLASSES OFF, UNCEREMONIOUSLY dropping them onto her desk, the dark frames stark against the black and white balance sheet and statement of cash flow. Dollar signs swam in front of her eyes, numbers bounced between the lines of tiny text. She needed another cup of coffee. Or a decent night's sleep.

She'd been back in Manhattan for three days and she hadn't slept more than a couple of hours. Her mind kept flipping through the weekend like an old-time slideshow. Blake standing at the baggage carousel holding her underwear. Blake taking off her underwear. Dancing. Playful winks. Knowing smiles. So much for scratching an itch, satisfying her curiosity, and getting him out of her system.

She rubbed her temples, trying to stave off the headache gathering steam at the base of her neck. She was exhausted and, worse, unproductive. Buried in work tasks was usually the one place she could block out everything else. It took her complete attention, and she let it. But not this week. One hundred percent confirming that playing by the rules and staying in her comfort zone was far more favorable to coloring outside the lines.

Lesson learned.

She'd give herself today to shake this off. Tell Kal. Get it off her chest and out of her mind. And then, no more. Out of sight, out of mind. And every other relevant cliché. Sure, yes, he lived across the park from her, but in all the years she'd called New York home, they'd only ever crossed paths at Storyhill-related things. And if memory served, the band wasn't returning to the city for another year.

A notification slid across her screen, blessedly interrupting her thoughts. A text from her marketing manager.

Tricia: Are you available to meet right now?

Huh. Bridget rarely got ASAP requests from Tricia. She had an amazing staff, each person hand-picked for efficiency and their attention to detail. And of all the people who reported to Bridget, Tricia's drama quotient was near the bottom. She rarely used words like "right now." Bridget rolled her shoulders, chiding herself. This is what happened with too much coffee and not enough sleep, nerves fired for no good reason.

Bridget: I'm headed out in a few minutes. I'll stop by your office on my way out.

She slid the financials into a folder, finished an email detailing the President's Circle to a potential new member, hit send, and levered herself out of her chair, giving her leg plenty of time to acclimate to the change in position. She groaned and dug her fingers into her thigh. You'd think all the "relaxing" baths she'd taken since her return from Minneapolis would help with the stiffness, but apparently not. Her physical therapist was a big proponent of the connection between pain and stress. Bridget had always denied the relationship, believing mobility was simply mind over matter. But the last few days were changing her perspective.

She grabbed her handbag, changed from modest heels to flats, and headed toward the marketing manager's office. She knocked softly on the doorframe. Tricia looked up, the fatigue Bridget felt mirrored in the gray rimming Tricia's eyes.

"Sorry for the summoning. Normally I'd come to you, but circumstances being what they are . . ." Tricia trailed off, sliding a piece of paper into the folder topping a large stack.

Bridget nodded. "No worries. But these circumstances you speak of, please tell me it's not an emergency."

Tricia drummed her fingers on her desk. "It's not an emergency."

"It is," a male voice said.

Bridget jumped and spun, discovering Tricia's husband, Scott, sitting in the chair tucked beside the office door.

Tricia rolled her eyes. "My husband is being melodramatic."

"I am not. Her doctor ordered bed rest," Scott said.

Concern trickled down Bridget's spine as his words sunk in. She might work all the time, but she encouraged her team to set boundaries and create sustainable work schedules. And as much as she told them that, she knew her example said something else entirely. "Are you and the baby okay?"

Tricia's lips curved into a tired smile. "Baby's good. Mama just needs to watch her blood pressure. And it's not bed rest. The doc just wants me to take it easy until the baby comes."

Bridget paced in front of Tricia's desk. "Okay, so you're about thirty-six weeks, right? So, you're adding four-ish weeks to your maternity leave?"

"I'm impressed you remember" —Tricia's eyes flashed to her husband— "I'm not sure Scott could even tell you how far along I am."

"Hey now," Scott said with a soft chuckle.

Anything that affected Bridget's team affected her. She strived to be an empathetic boss, but honestly, keeping track of as many things as possible meant fewer surprises. Something she could do without.

"What do you need me to do?" Bridget mentally checked her calendar for time she could free up. Maybe her insomnia would come in handy after all. Right now, she had two to four am open every day.

"I had an early morning meeting with my team, and they're prepped to start their maternity leave duties a little earlier than planned." Tricia pulled a face. "There's one thing I haven't been able to farm out. I hate to ask you. You're so busy."

Bridget ignored the churn of anxiety filling her belly. She schooled her features and pulled out her "it's fine" smile. "Whatever you need."

Tricia pulled a thin blue file folder from the bottom of the stack on her desk. "I volunteered to co-chair a charity event, using the Flames name to bring exposure to the event. They've got a quick turnaround time, with most of the work happening in the next month. My plan was to knock out my assigned duties before I went on maternity leave. But you know what they say about the best-laid plans." She shrugged and rubbed a hand over her belly.

Bridget knew far too well about plans changing in an instant. She blinked away the memories, refocusing on Tricia.

Tricia tapped the folder against her desk. "I don't like to pull out of things once I've committed."

That's why they worked well together. They agreed about the team's image in the community and the importance of protecting the Flames brand. The thought of not doing so made Bridget's palms sweat.

"I don't think you'll have to do too much," Tricia continued, clearly feeling like she had to sell Bridget on the idea. "The other co-chair is a longtime volunteer, and according to the staff, has helped with many events over the years."

Bridget didn't need to be sold. The Flames offered her a job when her entire life went pear-shaped, and since that day, she promised to do whatever needed to be done. "Shoot me an email with all the information."

Tricia held the file folder aloft. "Everything I have about the event is in this folder. There's just one more thing."

Bridget didn't like the expression on Tricia's face. "And that is?"

"The first meeting is today." She winced. "At three."

"Wow. Okay." It wasn't her favorite thing to do, but she could be flexible. She tapped a finger on the file folder. "Address is in here?"

"Yes." Tricia rounded her desk, hugging Bridget. "Thank you so much. I owe you."

Bridget squeezed the woman's shoulders. "You can thank me by having a healthy baby."

Bridget leaned against the side of the building and texted Kristina, letting her know she'd be out of the office for the remainder of the day. She might be a New Yorker, but she didn't text and walk. That's the way people got hurt. Hitting send, she turned toward Kal's favorite vegan lunch place three blocks away.

Scanning the restaurant and, not seeing Kalisha, Bridget picked a table and opened her email. Scrolling the list of messages, the words could have been in Sanskrit for as much as she absorbed. She flipped the phone over. This was ridiculous. She was one of the most focused people she knew. She needed to put the weekend out of her mind. You'd think having a new project dropped in her lap minutes ago would be distraction enough, but no. Given a moment of free thought, her brain bolted back to that hotel room, Blake's hands exploring her body, the look on his face when . . .

"Earth to Bridget." The voice came from miles away. A hand slapped the table in front of her. Okay, not miles away. Right next to her.

Kal dropped into the chair across the table. "I said your name three times. Where were you?"

Wrapped in the arms of the last man I should be.

Bridget motioned to her phone. "My marketing manager needs to go on maternity leave four weeks early and I need to pick up an off-site project. Was just trying to figure out how to work it into my schedule."

Kal hummed, her eyes narrowing. "Neither your email nor calendar app are open, Bri."

"Rearranging things in my mind."

Kal pulled the plastic-coated menu from behind the napkin holder and gave Bridget the side eye. "Really?"

"No," Bridget admitted with a heavy sigh. "I was thinking about the wedding."

Kal rubbed her hands together. "What about the wedding? Did you flirt with Mr. Multi-Year Crush?"

Bridget frowned and nodded slowly.

"You did?" Kal slapped the table. "Good for you."

Bridget nibbled the edge of her thumbnail. "Was it?"

"Wasn't it?" Kal searched Bridget's face. "Wait. You did more than flirt, didn't you?"

Bridget squeezed her eyes shut and nodded again. She thought telling Kal would help settle her thoughts, but there was nothing settled about the internal calisthenics currently happening in her body.

Kal leaned forward, grabbing Bridget's hands. "Did you sleep with him?"

"What can I get for you, ladies?" the server asked, giving Bridget a much-needed minute of reprieve.

"I want a number eight, no pickles. She'll have a number ten, extra vegan mayo. And two ice teas, please," Kal rattled off, not dropping Bridget's gaze.

When the server walked away, Kal waved her beautifully manicured fingers in front of Bridget's face. "You don't need to answer that question. It's written all over your face. You do, however, need to tell me why you didn't text me. I said I wanted *all* the juicy details."

Bridget fiddled with the button on her jacket. "My sex sluggish brain could only manage one thing at a time, and that was to make sure no one found out."

"How was it?" Kal leaned in and whispered, "Was it everything you imagined?"

Bridget rubbed her forehead with a single finger. "I'd like nothing more than to tell you it didn't measure up to my dreams, but Kal, it was *so* good."

Kal's eyes widened.

"What? You encouraged it. And you said you wanted the juicy details."

"I did. I do. It's just . . ." —Kal peeled the wrapper from her straw, dropping it into her iced tea— "a bit out of character for you."

"Because I'm a buttoned up nine-point Times New Roman," Bridget mumbled.

"What?" Confusion creased Kal's smooth forehead.

"Nothing. Apparently, put me on a plane to the middle of the country and I do all kinds of things—and people—I normally wouldn't."

Kal chuckled. "I never thought I'd see this day."

Bridget cocked her head and peered at Kal over the top of her glasses. "I wasn't planning on never having sex again, Kal."

"That's not what I meant, Bri. I know I encouraged it, but I guess I assumed that all your rules around this particular guy would always trump your feelings."

"It's a whole new me," Bridget said dryly.

Kal curled her lips in, biting back a smile. "Things could be worse."

Bridget rubbed the heels of her hands into her eye sockets. "Really? I just had the best sex of my life, with a zero chance at a repeat performance. And the season starts in less than two weeks and this whole *thing*" —she waved a hand in the air— "has scrambled my brain."

"Who says you can't do it again? If you want to see him again, do it. Doesn't he live here in New York?"

"We agreed it was a one-time thing."

"Un-agree."

"It's not that simple, Kal."

"Isn't it?"

"You know it's not." Bridget held up a hand, halting Kal's next pronouncement. "If Andrew finds out, it could cause issues within the band. The bond those guys have is amazing, and I don't want to be the reason that changes."

"And you're certain that would happen?"

Bridget sighed. No, she wasn't certain, but she couldn't risk it. There was too much at stake for Andrew—and Blake. Bridget laid her head in her hands. "This is why I don't break the rules anymore, Kal. Every time I do, bad things happen."

"Bri, honey," Kal said softly, next to Bridget's ear. "We've talked about this. So many times. The accident was not your fault."

Bridget looked up, meeting Kal's eyes. "I got in a car when I knew better. And it changed my life. Forever."

"And holding yourself to some ridiculously high standards and stifling rules because of one decision won't change it back."

"Maybe not, but it will keep more bad things from happening."

"This is not the same," Kal said, wiggling her eyebrows. "It sounds like some very good things happened this weekend."

Bridget took a long sip of her iced tea, wishing it was something stronger. "It's over and done. We've both lived in this city for over ten years and never once run into each other. And it's not like there's some Hayes family requirement to attend Storyhill concerts."

Kal snapped a chip in half, fixing her dark eyes on Bridget. "So that's it? You had amazing sex with the dude you've been crushing on for nearly half of your life, and your answer is to lock the memories away and avoid him from now on?"

Bridget barked out a tired laugh, a few drops of iced tea dribbling down her chin. "What? That doesn't sound healthy to you?"

"Just promise me you're not going to close up shop down there" —Kal waved a hand in front of her lap— "and make it some sort of mummified shrine to your singular night of extraordinary sex."

Bridget tapped a finger on her chin. "That hadn't occurred to me, but it seems efficient. Cross 'Have Exceptional Sex' off my bucket list and move on to the next item."

Kal laughed. "You and your damn lists." She shook her head. "Now, seriously, Bri, how did you leave it with him?"

Bridget grimaced and lifted her eyes to the ceiling.

"Oh no," Kal groaned, "what did you say?"

"That I'd see him at the next Storyhill wedding. And he reminded me he's the only member who's not married."

Kal bit her bottom lip. "Awkward."

"Right?"

"So, what are you going to do?"

Bridget tossed her napkin on her half-eaten portobello sandwich and pushed the plate to the middle of the table. "Keep busy until the memories fade."

"Busy-*er*? Is that even possible?"

"Yes, actually. There's that off-site project I mentioned. It's co-chairing a charity event." Bridget flipped over her phone and gave it a tap. "And I have to be there in less than two hours."

Kalisha left for an interview in Midtown, and as Bridget was too early for the charity meeting but didn't have enough time to go back to the office, she moved to the coffeehouse side of the restaurant, ordered a vanilla latte, and snuggled into an oversized chair saturated in the afternoon sun.

She opened Tricia's folder and skimmed the documents. Animal charity. A pleasant change of pace from the athletic programs that usually sought their help. A volunteer-driven rescue, Woof Watchers, found foster homes for dogs until they could place them in a forever home. A large influx of dogs had created the need for additional donations to cover veterinary costs and foster care support kits. They'd quickly put together a fundraiser and that's where the Flames entered the picture. Tricia had secured permission for the organization to use the Flames arena for a basketball themed event—in eight weeks. A tight timeline, but no worries, action and organization were Bridget's key skills.

Navigating to their website, Bridget located the names of the five staff, including the fundraising manager and volunteer coordinator she'd be meeting with today.

Her phone pinged with the meeting reminder, and she closed the open windows, suddenly feeling a lot lighter. An opportunity to give back while still promoting the Flames was exactly what she needed. And most of all, it gave her something to think about other than . . . that thing she was no longer thinking about.

Six blocks and two flights of stairs later, she pushed open the door to Woof Watchers. An enthusiastic chihuahua and a lumbering Newfoundland greeted her, the little guy prancing around her feet while his big buddy rubbed against her black pants, leaving a trail of hair and drool.

"I'm so sorry," a young woman said, grabbing the Newfie by the collar. "Charlotte and Archie are the self-appointed welcoming committee." She ripped off a piece of paper towel from the roll sitting on the counter and handed it to Bridget. "For the drool."

"Not to worry," Bridget said with a laugh, blotting her pants. "It's nice to be greeted so enthusiastically."

"Are you here to apply to be a foster or perhaps interested in adopting?"

Bridget bent to pet the tiny dog, who'd sat down on her foot. "While both sound intriguing, I'm here for a meeting with Lucy and Camila. I'm Bridget Hayes from the New York Flames."

"Oh yes," she said, her smile still wide. "I'm Lucy. Tricia emailed saying you'd be taking her place. Thank you so much for doing this." She let go of Charlotte's collar and scooped up Archie. "Follow me. Everyone else is already here."

Bridget nodded. "Tricia mentioned a co-chair. Are there other volunteers?"

"No," Lucy said, apologetically. "Because of our tight time-line and our need for more foster homes, it's just the two of you. And of course, me and Camila."

"That's fine," Bridget said. "Sometimes it's easier with a smaller team. Better control."

"Thanks for understanding," Lucy said, stepping into a room that looked like a cross between a conference room, a doggy playground, and supply storage. Covered in bright green

AstroTurf, dog toys of every shape and color dotted the floor. Across from a wall of windows, floor-to-ceiling industrial steel shelving held collars, leashes, and bags and bags of dog food. It was a color explosion, and it took Bridget a minute to notice the other two people in the room: a petite Latin woman in her early twenties—Camila, she guessed—and a tall, gorgeous man . . . with a shock of thick auburn hair.

CHAPTER NINE

"Bridget?" he said, rising from his chair.

"Blake?" Bridget whispered.

"You two know each other?" Lucy said, placing Archie in a small wire pen in the room's corner. "That's fantastic. It will make the tight timeline easier."

They stared at each other, Bridget's mouth hanging open, mirroring the shock coursing through him. In a split second, he watched her expression shifted from dazed and confused to practiced calm and confident. He was going to need a little more time.

Camila and Lucy told him they'd recruited someone from the Flames to help with the event. He assumed it would be a player, or a marketing person, not the President of Business Operations.

"Isn't co-chairing a small charity event a little below your pay grade?" It was a rude question—for all three of the women. But his brain was too busy performing a risk assessment on the rapidly mounting pressure in his chest to pay any attention to what came out of his mouth.

"Of course not," she said to Camila and Lucy with an apologetic smile.

He snorted. Because again, line from brain to mouth severed.

She flashed him a look of warning. "We're team players at Flames HQ. When Tricia needed to start her maternity leave early, I was more than happy to step in."

"O-kay," Camila said slowly, her gaze flashing between them. It was the same voice she used with spooked animals. "Will working together be a problem?"

"No," they said in unison.

"It's just surprising," Bridget said with a brittle laugh. "As I'm sure you know, Blake is a member of Storyhill. My brother is also a member of the band, and he got married last weekend. Normally, we go months, maybe even a year, without seeing each other—me and Blake, not me and my brother—and now it's been twice in just a few days. What are the chances?"

The number of words and the rate they were falling from her mouth slowed his pulse a little. This had thrown her too, and somehow that made him feel better. Still, he needed to steer this ship, and quickly, before the mental film of their time together booted up and crowded out his ability to think of anything else.

It had only been three days. He could still feel the softness of her skin against his own. Still taste her. Still hear the sounds she made when . . . He shook his head, knocking the image from his mind.

Blake rubbed his knuckles against his short beard. "Yep. Surprising." Damn, this cave dweller vocabulary was not a good look.

"Right," Lucy said, her gaze bouncing from his face to Bridget's. "I want to respect everyone's time, so let's get started." She passed out a packet of papers just as Charlotte scratched at the door.

"I'm so sorry," Camila said, rising from her chair. "Senior dog. Inconvenient bladder. I'll be right back."

"And I just realized I left a document on the printer," Lucy added, rising and slipping from the room.

"I think we scared them away," Blake said, finally finding his words.

"Yep, awkward party of two," she said, her eyes flashing to his and down to the papers in front of her.

He knocked a knuckle on the table until she looked up and met his gaze. "Doesn't have to be."

Bridget nodded, absently flipping through the papers. "Of course. We're grown adults. We can move on from this. We agreed to be friends," she mumbled, sounding more like she was giving herself a pep talk rather than answering him. "Did you have a good flight home?"

His flight? That was what she was leading with? Like they'd just been introduced at a cocktail party instead of having their tongues down each other's throats a few days ago? But if that's what she wanted, he'd play along. His mother was a master of small talk and networking, and he'd picked up plenty. "Yes. You?"

She pushed her glasses up her nose, pink coloring the triangle of skin revealed by her open neckline. "Fine," she said, the tiny catch in her voice belying her calm exterior.

"Got them," Lucy said a little too cheerfully, reentering the room, handing an additional document to each of them.

"So," she said, turning to Bridget, "I'm not sure how much Tricia shared with you."

"She gave me the basics," Bridget said, motioning toward the folder on the table in front of her. Her tone was completely business-like, any hint of tremor gone. "Eight-week timeline.

Basketball themed. Small volunteer team." Her eyes flashed to him before she returned her attention to Lucy. "The only thing that wasn't clear from Tricia's notes is where you are in the planning and execution process. I'll need to be brought up to speed on that."

She was talking as if he wasn't in the room. As if he hadn't worked with this organization for years. He was about to say that when Charlotte lumbered back in and walked over to Bridget, dropping her enormous head on Bridget's leg, and staring up at her adoringly.

He could relate. No matter how many times he recited all the reasons to keep his distance from her, he'd always felt like a lovesick puppy around her. Not that he did love, but it didn't stop him from being pulled into her orbit whenever she was near. All the more reason, that when she propositioned him last weekend, he should have politely declined.

"Charlotte," Camila chided. "Ms. Hayes does not need your slobber all over her pants."

Bridget patted Charlotte and laughed. "It's okay. I haven't had a dog in a long time. I didn't realize how much I missed it."

Oh god, the laughter. Bridget was beautiful, but when she smiled and laughed, it was magnetic. See? Pulled into her orbit. His resolve lasted exactly 9.7 seconds.

"At least take this." Camila pulled a towel from the metal shelves. "Lay it over your leg. She'll eventually tire of staring lovingly at you and flop to the floor. But fair warning, she's a dramatic flopper and it's loud when she hits the floor."

"Noted," Bridget said, scratching her fingers over the top of the dog's head once more, conjuring an image in Blake's mind that had no business in this meeting. The memory of her hands buried in his hair, her nails biting into his scalp, moaning softly . . .

"Blake, what ideas do you have?"

"What?" He blinked several times and cleared his throat, trying to shake off the memory. "Zoned out for a minute. My apologies. I haven't been getting a lot of sleep. Can you please repeat the question?"

"Ideas for the event," Lucy said. "What are yours?"

He had a few. He just needed a second to collect his thoughts. But, apparently, a second was too long as Bridget jumped in, taking charge. Like always.

"What if we followed the format of the NBA Skills Challenge at the All-Star game? A dribbling contest. A dunk contest. Wrapping up with a three-on-three celebrity, or pro-am, tournament."

"All that in one day? Seems like a lot," Blake said.

Bridget turned to him, looking over the top of her glasses in that naughty teacher's way of hers. "Afraid of a challenge, Mr. Kelly?"

He raised an eyebrow. "I think we both know that I'm up for most anything."

Her cheeks flared scarlet, but she ignored the statement, turning to Camila and Lucy and saying, "If we give each event a time or scoring limit, fitting it into a reasonable timeframe shouldn't be a problem."

"I like it," Camila said. "Sounds fun and active. Do you think the arena would allow us to bring some adoptable dogs in?"

Bridget tapped a finger to her chin. "If we had a cordoned off area, it should be okay. I'll confirm with Facilities and get back to you."

Worried about letting Woof Watchers down when he headed back out of the road, he'd agreed to help with the event only after Lucy mentioned a co-chair. Working with another volunteer, he could assist remotely. Now, he wondered, watching Bridget commandeer the meeting if he was needed at all. Maybe he should graciously back out? It would make his life easier. No event meant no Bridget.

His gaze flicked to Archie, currently in the center of his pen dismantling a plush green and orange dragon. This wasn't about him or Bridget, this was about dogs in desperate need of homes. He might suck at committing to another person, but this? Committing to this organization? He excelled at this and wouldn't let a little—okay, *a lot*—of confused feelings about his co-chair change that. He turned his attention back to Lucy when she asked, "We need a name for the event. Any ideas?"

He straightened in his chair, the perfect name popping into his head. "How about Dribble and Dunk?" he asked, skewering Bridget with his gaze.

The pink that he was quickly becoming addicted to crept into her cheeks.

"I like it," Camila said. "Dribble and Dunk. Dribble and Dunk for Dogs. Straightforward. Clear. Will make the marketing easier."

Bridget opened her mouth, but instead of words coming out, she gasped and jumped, her hand flying to her chest when Charlotte dropped to the floor. "*Charles Barkley.* You warned me it'd be loud, but I wasn't ready."

"Charles *Bark*ley?" Lucy asked with a giggle. "Is that a dog pun?"

"No," Blake said with a laugh. "Bridget's brother bet her she couldn't go a year without swearing, so she substitutes pro ball player's names in for curse words."

"That's funny," Camila chimed in. "How much longer do you have to go?"

Blake laced his fingers together and leaned forward on his elbows, biting back a smile. "He bet her when she was twenty years old."

"Oh," Lucy and Camila said simultaneously.

"Yep, when Bridget decides to do something, don't stand in her way."

"My brother pushes me to do crazy things." Bridget gave him a quelling look. "Things I don't always think through." She turned her gaze back to the two women in the room. "I don't have it in me to let him win," she said with a laugh.

"Around here, we're big fans of women who get things done," Lucy said with a nervous laugh. "And speaking of getting things done, Bridget, do you really think you could get people to play on such short notice?"

Bridget tapped her phone a few times and nodded. "The Flames season will have started so if we pick a date near a home game, they'll be in town. I know we have some dog lovers on the team. And I can reach out to the men's side. And my best friend, Kal—"

"You best friend *Calvin?*" It was like they were playing some weird mental game of chicken and, passive-aggressive or not, he couldn't stop himself.

Bridget made a dismissive sound. "My best friend is *Kalisha* Harris of the Sports Network. I'm sure she'd be willing to make a few calls, see who's in town."

Lucy bounced in her chair. "This is amazing. Thank you so much. We've been so stressed about the possible shortfall in our budget. But this makes me feel so much better."

"You know what else would be amazing?" Camila said, her grin growing wide. "If you played in the tournament, Bridget. That would be so cool."

Bridget's smile fell. "As an organizer, I think I should be available to help rather than play."

Camila waved her off. "It would be all set by then. I'm sure our staff and Blake could field any issues. Should I mark you down as our first player?"

"No." The sharpness in Bridget's voice caused everyone to

still and Charlotte to stand up with a whine, dropping her head back on Bridget's leg. "I just meant that I think we'll find plenty of people to play."

"Okay," Lucy said quietly. "So, how about this? I'll start working on a logo for the event and Camila can send out an email blast asking for volunteers. And the two of you," she pointed at Bridget and him with her pen, "can work out the schedule and recruit players for the tourney. Oh, and maybe some silent auction items? Could you do that too? Staff is swamped with the influx of new dogs and locating fosters."

"I'm pretty open until Storyhill leaves on tour," Blake said. "I can take on the schedule and budget if Bridget's willing to brainstorm with me and call in a few favors."

"I can do that," she answered, not looking at him.

"This room is open for the rest of the day," Camila said. "It's yours to use."

"Well, um, I . . ." Bridget stuttered.

"Do you have meetings this afternoon, Bridget?" he asked. Discussing things over the phone or email would be the smarter choice, but for reasons he refused to examine, he wanted her to stay.

She sighed, her shoulders dropping. "No."

"Great!" Lucy clapped her hands. "We're right down the hall if you need anything. I'm so excited to have such fabulous co-chairs."

"So excited," Bridget mumbled under her breath, but he heard it.

Lucy and Camila exited the room with Charlotte and Archie in tow, leaving the two of them on opposite ends of the small conference table.

"Where do you want to start?" he asked, opening the notebook in front of him, attempting to move beyond the last awkward thirty minutes. "With the schedule of events or brainstorming people to contact?"

She clicked the end of her pen several times in rapid succession. "How is this whole tour thing working? With Andrew on his honeymoon? Don't you need to practice?"

He shifted in his chair, his mind wrestling with her abrupt change of subject. "Oh. Um. Tour. Right. We, ah, added a few extra practices in Minneapolis the week before the wedding and we have three days in Nashville to iron out any wrinkles—Andrew and Grace will be back by then. Since we've performed all the sets before and it's a short tour, we all agreed that was enough prep time."

"And you'll be back in time for this event?"

"Worried or hoping?" he asked.

She adjusted her glasses and met his eyes for a single beat. "I'm sorry?"

"Worried I'll be back, or hoping I won't?"

"Both?" she said, pressing a finger between her brows and rubbing. "Admit it, this is weird. Uncomfortable. Awkward."

"There you go with all that sexy honesty."

"Blake."

He looked out the window over her shoulder, anything not to look directly at her. He pushed his fingers into his hair and gave what he hoped was an undetectable tug. "You said it earlier. We agreed to be friends."

"We did," she said. "But . . ."

"But?" he asked against his better judgement.

Something that sounded like a cocktail of a sigh, a groan, and a laugh fell from her lips. "I thought it'd be a while before we saw each other again."

He nodded. He'd banked on the same thing. That he'd be over it—whatever *it* was—by the time their paths crossed again. But since they didn't get that time . . . "Like the Flames for you, this organization is important to me. How about, until this thing wraps up, we set aside what happened last weekend and focus on that?"

"Do it for the dogs?" she said, a tiny smile flirting with the edge of her lips.

"For the dogs," he said. They should shake on it or something, but he knew better than to touch her—in any capacity. Her eyes traveled from his face to his hands and back again, silently acknowledging that she knew it too.

An hour later, with a notebook full of ideas and duties divvied up, Blake pushed back from the table. "I think that's a solid plan for now. Do you agree?"

Bridget stood and smoothed her jacket. "I do. You've got my phone number" —she pointed at his notebook— "text me if anything comes up before our next meeting." When he nodded she left the room with a tentative wave.

The minute he could no longer hear her shoes click against the terrazzo floor, he slumped forward, releasing the breath he'd been holding for . . . well, since she'd walked into the room.

Volunteering with Woof Watchers was his escape. With the staff, with the dogs, he let all his masks fall. *Kind of like your night with Bridget,* a little voice whispered. His shoulder muscles tightened. He needed to stop thinking about that night. And about her. In that way.

She was his friend. The event co-chair. And Andrew's sister. The last one did it. Cooled his swirling thoughts immediately. He ran his finger down his to-do list, thankful they could complete most of the items individually. And the best way to distract himself was to get started immediately.

Item number one was to call Ford Marini at Storyhill's record label and ask for silent auction items. Easy enough. He picked up his phone and opened his contacts. As his finger hovered over the call button, a cacophony of barks, snorts, and growls bounced off the walls.

He stepped out into the hallway and made his way to the lobby. Sometimes when a new dog came in for evaluation, things could get a little crazy.

In front of the reception desk, Charlotte woofed, Archie yipped, and the dog in Camila's arms snorted.

"Can I help?" Blake asked over the barking.

Spinning, Camila locked eyes with him. "Yes. Blake. Yes, you can."

The glint in her gaze had him contemplating a quick escape. He knew that spark—it happened every time a woman wanted something. Usually something big. Like Comic Sans training.

"This is Destiny," Camila said, lifting the black and white French Bulldog in her arms.

Blake stepped forward, stretching out his arms. "Do want me to take her in the other room while you get Charlotte and Archie settled?"

"Yes. And no."

"Okay," Blake said, laughing. "That's incredibly clear."

"Yes, I want you to take her." She handed the roly-poly fur ball to him. "But not to the other room. I want you—*need you*—to take her home with you."

Blake raised a hand, palm out. "You know I love fostering dogs, but I'm leaving on tour in three weeks."

"Destiny's foster broke her leg, and no one else is available. You'd only have to take her until I can locate another foster." Camila softly patted the dog's plump jowls. "Look at this face. How can you say no?"

He sighed and pressed his lips together to stem a smile. "Saying no to beautiful women has always been my weakness."

"Yay!" Camila bounced on the balls of her feet. "I know you

have some supplies at home, but I'll go get you a fostering kit."
She raced past Blake on her way to the conference room.

Destiny turned in his arms and licked his chin.

"Just so you know, the last woman who kissed me and asked
me 'to take her home' couldn't get away from me fast enough.
Knowing that, you up for this?"

Destiny sighed a shuttering breath. And let out a giant fart.

Perfect. Absolutely perfect. "I'm going to take that as a yes.
But just so we're clear" —he scratched the heart-shaped patch of
white on her chest— "next time a bark or simple head nod will
suffice."

Blake slipped inside the entryway of the brownstone he called
home and surveyed the three flights of stairs. This was the only
part of fostering that he didn't love—up and down the three
flights of stairs every time the dog needed to go outside. He
stepped onto the first stair and the leash went taut in his fingers.
Destiny had dropped her butt to the floor, a "no way, mister"
expression on her face.

He gave the leash a gentle tug. "Come on, Destiny." He
shook the bag in his hand. "There will be treats at the top."

Destiny's ears perked up and she waddled up the first stair.
She placed her paws on the next stair and hopped three times
before clamoring on to the second stair. Blake smirked and
scooped her up. "Don't get used to this, little girl. I won't carry
you every time, but at this rate we won't make to the third floor
until tomorrow morning."

"That's where Gramps lives," he said, pointing at the door
to the left. "And Bette—aka Mom—lives on the second floor.
You should definitely call her 'Grandma.'" He chuckled at the
idea of anyone daring to call Elizabeth Kelly "Grandma." He

might try it just to see what happened. The word apoplectic sprang to mind.

"You'll be bunking with me on the top floor." The dog grunted. "Yeah, I know. What does it say about us that we all live in the same building? Most people assume it's because we're close, but they'd be wrong. Except me and Gramps, we're solid." He unlocked his apartment door and set Destiny down. Her nails scrabbled against the hardwood floors as she zipped—well, Destiny's version of zipping—around the furniture. Reaching his vintage Eames chair, she hopped up on the chair with ease, spun three times, and flopped down.

"So that whole stair thing was an act? Well played." He emptied the foster kit on the kitchen counter. The dog's eyes followed his movements as he filled the water and food bowls, but she didn't move. He grabbed a beer from the fridge, uncapped it, and downed a long pull. "It's a good chair, right?" He strode to the chair and sat beside her, pulling her into his lap.

She wiggled her butt between his arm and waist and sighed. "Since you're going to be here a while, maybe you can help me with something. What do we do about Bridget Hayes?"

Destiny turned and licked his face.

"Normally, I'd say that was a good idea, but I already kissed her. And it's probably not a great idea to do it again." He tipped the beer back, taking another long drink. "Why is that you ask? Excellent question, Destiny. I knew you were a smart dog. Does it have to do with what I said when we walked up the stairs about me not being close to my mother? Again, so astute. She was always busy when I was a kid—still is. I was really lonely. Until we formed the band. They became the family I never had and the thought of losing that scares me."

Destiny woofed and placed a paw on his chest.

"What does all that have to do with Bridget? Well, it means her brother is my brother."

Blake laughed and scratched the dog's head. Wow, that sounded bad. That phrasing alongside having a full conversation with a dog confirmed dangerous levels of sleep deprivation. He emptied the beer and stood, hoisting the dog into his arms. "It's bedtime, doggie." Hopefully, the beer mixed with the fatigue would guarantee an eight-hour reprieve from all Bridget-related thoughts. Either way, he had a week before he saw her again. A week to pack the memories of their night together into a tiny box in the recesses of his mind. Deep enough to quiet the warring thoughts of "I want more" and "You got too close."

CHAPTER TEN

Bridget walked into Sid's a few minutes after five and scanned the room. Close to the arena, basketball memorabilia covered every inch of the bar's wall space and tables barely fit in between every known (and a few unknown) basketball arcade games.

Kalisha sat at a table tucked between a life-size cutout of Maya Moore and a Michael Jordan pinball machine. The NBA playoffs were in full swing, commanding nearly all of Kal's time, so they were squeezing in a quick happy hour instead of their weekly lunch.

Quick, because Blake was meeting her here in an hour.

"Come here often?" she said, walking up to the table.

"As often as I can. I love the understated decor," Kal deadpanned.

"And the cheap beer," Bridget added, sliding onto the stool opposite Kal.

"Everyone knows that themed bars next to sports arenas never overcharge for their beer."

Bridget snorted. "In my defense, it's convenient."

A good-looking server ambled up to the table, sliding bar

napkins in front of them. "Well, if it isn't UConn's version of Stockton and Malone."

"Great location *and* charming staff," Kal added, rolling her eyes. "We haven't played for UConn in over a decade, Billy."

"At Sid's, once a star, always a star." Billy winked at Kalisha and flashed his I-live-on-tips smile. "What would you like tonight, Kal? Something tall, brown, and spicy?" He ran a hand down his chest.

"Tempting, but I think I'll start with a gin and tonic."

"Your loss." He scratched a couple of things on his pad and turned to go.

"Billy," Bridget called after him, "I didn't tell you what I wanted."

"You always order the same thing, chica," Billy said over his shoulder.

Bridget cracked a peanut, tossing the two halves into her mouth. "Am I so predictable?"

"Best friend code prevents me from having to answer that question."

She crushed the peanut shells in her fingers and dropped them into an empty bowl. "Fine. Here's something unpredictable. You'll never guess who is co-chairing the charity event with me."

Kal leaned back as Billy dropped off their drinks. "Please tell me it's Idris Elba."

"So close." Bridget unwrapped her straw, dropping it in her glass. "Blake Kelly."

Kal choked on her drink, coughing, and wiping her nose. "I'm sorry, what?"

"Yep. Blake Kelly. Storyhill tenor. Friend to all who know him. Skilled lover of women." She paused for effect. "Co-chair."

"And I'm just hearing about this now?" She threw a peanut at Bridget, bouncing it off her forehead.

Bridget shrugged, ignoring her question. "Unpredictable enough for you?"

Kal hummed. "Maybe not so unpredictable. It seems the universe is conspiring to bring you together."

Bridget rolled her eyes.

"What?" Kal asked, at Bridget's disbelieving expression. "How would you explain it?"

"Coincidence seems like the obvious answer."

Kal wiped the condensation from the outside of her glass with a long, manicured finger. "How completely unromantic of you. And unsurprising."

"Unsurprising?"

"Remember when I say this, that I love you."

Bridget pushed back in her chair and grabbed another handful of peanuts. "Says no one who's delivering good news."

Kal put a hand in front of her face. "Do not throw those at me."

"Um, you were the one throwing the nuts. I'd never waste stale peanuts by throwing them at my best friend."

"Because you're above that type of behavior?"

Bridget sniffed. "Clearly." She rolled her hand, signaling Kal to get on with it. "Now you were about to school me on my unsurprising-ness."

"Okay, well . . . you have a tendency to push away anything that doesn't fit into your itemized long-range plan."

"What's wrong with having a plan?" Things in her life were comfortably predictable. Just the way she liked them. Just the way she needed them to be. And more importantly, sticking to a plan kept her from being buried under the "what-ifs" that hummed just under the surface.

"Nothing, *if* you allow for deviations and spontaneity."

Bridget tilted her chin up. "I was spontaneous at the wedding and look what happened."

"You had the best sex of your life?" Kal asked, looking at her over the top of her drink.

Bridget snorted. "Chaos ensues."

Kal laughed. "Your post wedding activities are hardly the definition of chaos, Bri."

Bridget shrugged, waving a hand in the air. "Po-tay-to, Po-tah-to."

"Can anyone get in on this conversation about farm produce?" a familiar voice said from behind Bridget, lighting up her nerve endings like a summer thunderstorm. A *chaotic* thunderstorm.

She attempted to catch Kal's gaze, warn her to behave herself, but Kal stared at the man hovering behind Bridget. A smile pulled at the corner of Kal's lips, and she turned to Bridget and mouthed, "Conspiring."

Bridget flicked a peanut shell across the table, hitting Kal in the abdomen. If the universe was sending a message, it was a warning to rein things in, not whatever romantic nonsense Kal was peddling.

"You're early," Bridget said, swiveling toward Blake.

He lifted a shoulder. "I planned to get a drink and look through my notes before you arrived. I know how you like a well-thought-out plan."

Kal did her second spit take of the evening.

"Blake Kelly," he said, sticking out his hand. "You must be Calvin."

Kal brushed a napkin across her chin and shook his hand. "That's me. Best friend. Supplier of condoms and lingerie."

Bridget groaned. "You're both menaces."

"Nice to meet you finally, *Kalisha*," Blake said, charm set to dazzle.

"Likewise," Kal said, a smile curling her lips.

Bridget fidgeted in her chair, annoyed by how much she

hated it when he turned his stun gun on other women. "Didn't you say something about wanting a drink?" She tried for a light tone, but her irritation seeped through, and she sounded testy and . . . *ugh* . . . jealous.

Blake gestured to the table. "Right. Can I get anyone a refill?"

"I'm headed to an interview in a few minutes, so no more for me," Kalisha said.

And I'm headed into a meeting with Blake Kelly and need all my senses. "I'm good too," Bridget said.

Blake nodded and turned toward the bar, weaving around an At The Buzzer arcade game and a tower of signed basketballs.

Kalisha pulled her gaze from his retreating form and skewered Bridget with a look. "Appears there's a lot you're not telling me."

Bridget sucked down half of her drink. "We needed to meet about the charity gig. Figured it saved time for him to meet me here. No biggie."

"And you didn't tell me because you thought I'd be gone before he arrived." It wasn't a question. Kal let out a low whistle. "Bri, the pictures do not do him justice."

She wasn't wrong. He was good looking by anyone's standards, but what made him utterly attractive was the charm that oozed from him, something a camera couldn't capture.

"I get why you can't shake the crush."

"I got him out of my system at the wedding, remember?" Bridget brushed her palms together in an "all finished" gesture. She'd keep saying it until they *both* believed it.

"Yep." Kal nodded, not hiding her grin. "That's why you turned every shade of pink when he walked up behind you."

Bridget shrugged a single shoulder. "Pfft. That happens every time someone mentions produce."

"Maybe if it's eggplant or a cucumber, but I don't think potatoes count." Kal rolled her lips in, holding back a smile, clearly thinking she was all kinds of clever.

"Wow, Calvin, you're really scraping the bottom of the humor bucket."

"I'm up for bad humor. Can I join you?" Blake asked, returning from the bar, holding a beer. "Or should I grab a different table until our designated meeting time?"

"Thoughtful," Kal said, "but unnecessary. Pull up a chair."

Blake grabbed a stool from a neighboring table as Bridget frowned at Kal. She shrugged and turned her attention to Blake.

"Bridget mentioned the two of you are co-chairing an event, but didn't mention any details. Tell me about the organization."

Bridget touched his arm, immediately regretting the decision. Fire singed her fingertips. "Fair warning. Kal is a skilled interviewer and really doesn't know how to shut it down in her personal time."

"Pot meet kettle," Kal mumbled.

Blake laughed. "So, you're both former players *and* current workaholics?"

Bridget wrinkled her nose. She hated that word. "If what you mean by 'workaholic' is that we're committed to our jobs and have to work harder in an industry dominated by men, then yes, we're both workaholics."

Ugh. Blake Kelly brought all the emotions. Lust. Longing. Confusion. Irritation. *Et cetera.*

She and Kal both watched as he covered Bridget's hand with his own. "I'm sorry. Poor choice of words. My mother and I aren't close, but I've watched her struggle with misogyny her entire career. It makes things unnecessarily difficult. Let me try again. I can see why the two of you are close friends. Both equally skilled, driven, and dedicated to your chosen careers."

Kal chuckled. "Nice reframe, Mr. Kelly. Now, about the charity organization?"

He removed his hand from hers and wrapped his fingers around the base of his beer. "Woof Watchers," he said, tapping the side of the glass. "They rescue dogs from a variety of situations and place them in foster homes until they find a permanent home." A smile tugged on his lips. "They recently celebrated their ten-year anniversary and have placed almost fourteen thousand dogs. I started volunteering and fostering about eight years ago."

"You foster?" Bridget asked, surprised.

"I do. When I'm in town. With all the Storyhill-related travel, it's not fair to have a dog full time, so fostering is a good solution. In fact," he said, pulling his phone from his back pocket, "after you left the meeting the other day, they had an emergency foster situation and I ended up taking this pretty lady home with me." He opened his photos app and showed them a picture of a black and white French Bulldog.

"Look at that adorable squishy face," Bridget said, scissoring her fingers to enlarge the photo. "What's her name?"

"Destiny."

Bridget chuckled. "So Blake Kelly is finally having his date with destiny, huh?"

He laughed at her pun. "Seems that way."

"So why dogs?" Kalisha asked, still in full-on interview mode.

Blake trailed a finger around the rim of his pint glass. "They're easier than people. Unconditional love, and all that."

Bridget's eyes flashed to his face. She suddenly realized that this was the first time she'd heard sadness in his voice. His expression made her want to reach out and wrap him in a hug.

"And you know, they don't talk back or drink all your beer

like other friends," he said, the pensive expression replaced with a wink and his far more familiar, toothy grin.

Her heart squeezed. Was the cavalier attitude a mask? She understood burying pain and disappointment behind another persona. She was something of an expert at it. Had she misjudged him? And, if so, did that make her feelings for him more, or less, dangerous?

"How about Storyhill? How long have you been with them?" Kal was a master of body language and nonverbal clues, so Bridget knew that the abrupt change of subject was intentional. She'd heard the melancholy in his response, too.

"Founding member," he said, this time with a smile that met his eyes.

"Yeah," Bridget chimed in. "Blake and Nick picked up Andrew in a seedy bar in Nashville. By Andrew's account, they *begged* him to join the group."

Blake laughed. "That's not exactly how I remember it."

"With Andrew's wedding and this event" —Kal motioned between Bridget and Blake— "am I right in thinking you have some time off between gigs?"

This was how Kal built a reputation for being one of the best in the business—she hardly let a person breathe between questions. She swore it was the only way to get honest answers.

To his credit, Blake rolled with it. "We have—or had—about a month between the wedding and a short tour of the western US. Colorado, New Mexico, Arizona, California, Vegas." Blake counted off the locations on his fingers. "Andrew and Grace squeezed their wedding and honeymoon in during the break." He shrugged. "I guess that's the life of a traveling musician."

A string of notes pealed from Kal's wrist, and she tapped her Apple Watch to life. "Sorry. That's my fifteen-minute warning. Time for me to go. I'll leave you to your *meeting*." She winked and stood from her stool. "Nice to meet you, Blake." Kal stepped between him and Bridget and leaned in, whispering something to him.

Kal waved and yelled, "Goodbye Billy," to their server on her way out the door.

"My heart breaks a little more every time you leave, Kalisha," he yelled back.

"What's with that?" Blake asked, pointing to the man watching Kal leave.

"A little harmless flirting," Bridget said with a shrug.

"You sure? Because when I went to the bar, he asked me if I was here for Stockton or Malone. It took me a minute to get the reference, but when I answered Stockton, he looked visibly relieved."

Bridget's gaze traveled back to the bar. "Maybe a little unrequited love?"

He held her gaze, unblinking, as something enigmatic passed behind his eyes. The noisy bar went instantly quiet, and her lungs stopped filling.

"Can I ask you something?"

A tremor ran through her body. She prided herself on her tough negotiation skills, her ability to stare down defenders, to hold her own with the toughest people in the business, but a single question from him had her contemplating the quickest route to the door.

"I suppose," she whispered.

"Why did you refuse when Camila asked you to play in the three-on-three tournament?"

She shook her head. That wasn't even in the family of questions she'd expected. She shrugged. "Events like this rely on name recognition to be successful. I wouldn't want to take a spot away from someone else. Nobody knows who I am anymore."

He tipped his head toward the bar. "The server does."

"This is a very insular, basketball-crazed bar. That's not a good litmus test."

"You set a shit-ton of records at UConn—many of which still stand today."

She tried to laugh it off. "I don't think 'shit-ton' is an official basketball analytic."

He reached across the table and tapped his fingers against her knuckles. "If it wouldn't cause you pain, it'd be really cool if you played."

She sighed. "Playing ball is my history, not my present or future. I need to stay focused on the business side of the game. I'm sure you understand."

He narrowed his eyes, neither agreeing nor disagreeing. Didn't matter. She would not be playing. Dealing with Blake Kelly was disruptive enough. She wouldn't voluntarily complicate her life further.

She reached for the remainder of her watered-down her drink and nearly dropped it as her phone . . . vibrated *and* rang? No, her phone vibrated with an incoming text at the exact time Blake's phone trilled the opening notes to Storyhill's latest release. They both grabbed their phones as if they were the final lifeboats on the Titanic. And groaned simultaneously.

"Did you just get a dinner invitation?" Blake asked with a sigh. "Yep."

"I totally forgot they were coming to New York."

Bridget circled her thumb around her temple. "I remembered, but assumed they'd be" —she raised her fingers in air quotes— "otherwise occupied."

"Should we go?" Blake asked, indecision registering on his normally confident face.

"Grace knows I'd move heaven and earth to eat at Curtis' restaurant. I can't say no."

"Other than short notice, there's no reason pre-Minneapolis Bridget and Blake would say no to this invitation, right?" Blake reasoned.

Bridget knocked her fist against the table. "Right."

"I'm responding yes," he said, grabbing his phone, thumbing in a response.

"Wait." Bridget grabbed his forearm and his gaze dropped to her fingers. "There's something you should know first."

"That there will be, like, five forks on the table?" he said with a laugh. "You don't need to worry. Etiquette lessons preceded the dance lessons."

"No." Bridget pulled in a breath. "Grace knows."

He set his phone on the table. "Grace knows what?"

Bridget grimaced and waved a finger between them.

"What the hell, Bridget? We promised to keep what happened off the record."

She squared her shoulders. "I didn't tell her," she said through clenched teeth. "She guessed."

He wrapped a hand around the back of his neck and squeezed. "And?"

"And I panicked and instead of denying it, I pleaded with her to not tell Andrew."

He pounded his fist on the table, the vibration setting off the lights and music of the closet pinball machine. "Shit."

"Give it a kick, Stockton," Billy yelled from behind the bar. "Right side, by the flipper button. It says Michael Jordan on it, but for as often as it goes off for no reason, it's clearly channeling Dennis Rodman."

Bridget quieted the game and set her hand on Blake's shoulder. "I don't think she'll tell him."

"Why not?"

"Because she knows how irrational he is about me. And you.

You with me. Plus, I have a really hard time believing that they're going to spend their honeymoon talking about *us*."

"Fair point," he said, his shoulders coming down from where they'd nearly attached to his ears. "So, we should go?"

"I think it would look more suspicious if we didn't. But Blake" —she squeezed his arm again— "no more lying, okay?"

His mouth dropped open. "You want to tell him? Are you crazy?"

"I meant about working together on the Woof Watchers thing."

Blake tipped back the dregs of his beer. "He won't like that either."

"He doesn't run either of our lives. He's just going to have to chill the *Walt Frazier* out."

Blake chuckled, the tension breaking. "Walt Frazier, huh? Going pretty far back in the archives for that one."

She bit her bottom lip. "I couldn't think of another name that started with F."

He laughed. "Sylvia Fowles?"

She snapped her fingers. "Yes, that would be more on brand for me." She tipped her head, searching his face. "And . . ."

"And?"

Don't say it, Bridget. It's only going to make it weird. Weirder. "And it's actually pretty sexy that you know the names of WNBA players." She'd done it. She'd blurted it out.

"Yeah?"

"Yeah," she breathed out.

They stared at each other for, like, six beats longer than necessary. He blinked first and looked down at his phone. "So, we're doing this?"

Doing what? Oh right, the dinner thing. She nodded slowly. "It seems so. But what about all this?" Bridget pointed to the papers in front of them. "We really need to talk about the event."

"How about we join Grace and Andrew for dinner and meet tomorrow morning at my place?"

"Y-your place?" A shiver raced down Bridget's spine, settling low. Based on what happened the last time they were alone together, his place was not a good idea. *Or at least unproductive for planning,* a little voice taunted. "We could meet at a coffee shop or a restaurant or a—"

"Relax, TNR. I'm not luring you into my den of iniquity. I can't leave Destiny alone again. Not twice in twenty-four hours when she's just getting settled in."

"How about FaceTime?" she asked, disgusted at the desperation coating the question.

"Everything goes faster when you're in the same room." He tapped his finger against his chin. "How about this? I'd planned on checking in on my grandfather tomorrow morning. Why don't you meet me there? Gramps would love the company and could act as a chaperone." He smirked—and winked.

Candace Nicole Parker. Turning her into a melted chocolate bar with a single wink was completely unacceptable.

He smiled, indicating he knew exactly the effect he had on her. Because she'd told him about her crush *and* then admitted his knowledge of the WNBA was sexy. Rookie mistakes. Coach had always harped on them not to telegraph plays. And she'd gone and done it. Twice.

"I'll stop dropping the names of WNBA players, if that would help," he said, once again reading her mind.

"Fine," she said, fishing out her phone. "What's the address?"

"Same as mine."

Bridget frowned. "You live with your grandfather?"

"Not exactly. He lives on the bottom floor of the brownstone. I live on the top."

"And the middle floor?"

A pinched, tension-filled expression covered his normally handsome face. "Elizabeth Kelly."

"Your mother?"

"Yep, one big, *happy*," he said, sarcasm lacing his voice, "family."

Had she ever heard Blake talk about his family? She didn't think so. She knew, through the Storyhill grapevine, that he grew up in New York City with a single mother. Elizabeth Kelly. Why was that name familiar? "Wait. Is your mother *Bette* Kelly?"

Blake drummed his fingers on the table and nodded. "The one and only. Clearly her reputation precedes her."

Indeed, it did. Legend had it she'd started one of the country's most powerful marketing and branding companies with a few hundred dollars and a single client. "I haven't worked with her directly, but her company represents several of our bigger advertisers."

He didn't lift his head, his fingers now tracing the grain of the wood. "I don't really deal with her directly, either."

"Blake . . ."

He held a hand up, stopping her question. "I don't want to talk about my mother."

"Okay. What time should I plan on meeting you tomorrow morning?"

"I get to choose? You don't need to check your calendar?" he teased, though with half his usual energy—and no signature wink.

She smiled and tapped a finger on her temple. "It's all right here, Kelly."

"How about nine?"

Bridget nodded her agreement. "Now, about tonight, since we're going with an honest approach—"

"*Mostly* honest."

She studied his face. Something kept nagging at her. "Can I ask you something?"

"I guess it is your turn."

She drummed her fingernails rhythmically against the table, pondering if she truly wanted the answer to her question. Yep, if she didn't ask, it would just keep eating at her. "I know why I'd prefer Andrew didn't know about our indiscretion. But why is it you don't want him to know?"

"First" —he pointed a finger at her— "please stop calling it an indiscretion. I don't like what that implies. And second" —a second finger rose to match the first— "that was your stipulation, TNR, not mine."

"Okay, evade if you must, but did you, or did you not, just have a teeny, little freak out when I told you Grace knew the truth?"

He flashed his practiced get-out-of-jail-free smile. "There you go, using the word 'teeny' again."

"Blake." She used her best "stop playing around" negotiation voice while peering ever so slightly over the top of her glasses. She'd spent nearly a decade honing it, and it had a 97 percent success rate. Though, in fairness, everything that worked in the rest of her life failed around Blake Kelly.

His gaze fluttered over her face, his expression unreadable. But if she had to guess, he was deciding whether to tell her the truth, to trust her.

Bridget grabbed her handbag, pulling the strap over her shoulder. She slipped to the edge of the barstool, tentatively placing weight on her leg. "It's fine. You don't have to tell me."

He grabbed her hand, pulling her back. "I can't risk doing anything that will upset the dynamic in the band," he said so low she barely caught it. "They're my family. I can't lose them. Outside of my grandfather and a distant relationship with my mother, they're all I have."

She stepped closer to him, laying her hand on his arm. "So, the *mostly* honest answer is that we're both scared."

"You're scared too?" he asked, tucking a piece of her hair behind her ear.

Always.

But admitting that wasn't *mostly* honest, it was entirely honest, and she wasn't ready for that. Maybe never would be. So she placed her hand over his and nodded.

His eyes drifted to her lips, and his head dipped toward her. If he was thinking about kissing her, she wouldn't stop him. Couldn't stop him. Scared or not, the decision-making part of her brain, the part that understood consequences short-circuited when near this man.

"Somebody order a Lyft?" Billy yelled from behind the bar, causing them to flinch away from each other.

"We better go before they drive away," she said, waving at Billy and turning toward the door. Her fingers and knees trembled. Whether from relief or disappointment, she'd never know because with Blake Kelly, simple, straightforward answers didn't exist.

CHAPTER ELEVEN

THE FIFTY INCHES BETWEEN THEM WAS A GULF AND A sliver. They'd climbed into the backseat of the Lyft, each hugging a door with the silent understanding that proximity was both dangerous and tenuous and now was an especially bad time to test their resolve.

"You keep looking at me," she said, staring out the car window.

Yep, his ass might be on the other side of the vehicle, but he hadn't been able to keep his eyes there. "Just looking out the window. You have the better view."

She snorted. "I expect more of you, Blake Kelly. You're usually far more creative with your dodges and redirects." She turned and pierced his heart with a soft smile. "Am I no longer worthy of your best?"

The car window should be wide open for how much caution he was about to throw to the wind. "You're worthy of my best and then some, but when you're this close to me, the heat of you, the birthday cake smell of you, muddles my brain and makes finding words difficult."

She stared at him, mouth hanging open.

He shrugged. "You said tonight was about honesty."

The car came to a stop in front of a nondescript brick building, and Bridget scurried from the car. Blake paused before following her, drawing in a breath.

"Hey man," the Lyft driver said, grabbing the headrest of the passenger seat and turning to Blake. "That was one hell of a line." He chuckled. "Probably gonna steal that one."

"Have at it," he replied, stunned, and a little mortified, that he'd said it out loud. He slipped out of the car and walked to where Bridget stood staring at the heavy silver front door. Deciding it was best to ignore his declaration, he reached around her and grasped the door handle. "You ready?"

"Not sure," she whispered.

His thoughts exactly. "Let's focus on the food rather than the company," he said, projecting far more confidence than he felt.

She nodded and he opened the door. As luck would have it, Andrew and Grace stood at the host stand, turning in tandem as the spring wind swirled in the door.

Grace offered a soft, teasing smile. "What a coincidence, you two arriving at the same time."

Honesty. Bridget wanted honesty. He swallowed past the lump in his throat. "Not a coincidence. We came together," he admitted while his heart hammered against his ribs.

Grace's eyebrows shimmied up her forehead.

"Ms. O'Connor," the host said, "your table is ready."

"You came together?" Andrew said, ignoring the host.

Bridget smiled and wove her arm through Andrew's. "It's a funny story, big brother," she said, all signs of discomfort gone. Or buried, more likely. "One I'll tell you over dinner." She tugged his arm and signaled for Grace to lead on.

Seated, Bridget glanced at him, pointed at the middle fork, and mouthed, "Salad fork."

He laughed, and the ropes of tension crisscrossing his chest loosened a little. He tapped her napkin and whispered, "That goes on your lap, not under your chin."

"Got it," she said, before turning to Grace and asking, "Are Curtis and Megan joining us?"

Grace shook her head. "Curtis tries to pop out of the kitchen when I'm here, but Megan is at Delia's—their restaurant in Cali—so it'll be just the four of us tonight."

"Thanks for including us," Bridget waggled her eyebrows, "on your honeymoon. Your invitation surprised us."

"Us?" Andrew nearly growled. Or that was his normal voice and Blake's nerves were getting the better of him?

Grace laid her hand on Andrew's arm, and he visibly relaxed. "You mentioned a funny story?"

Bridget slid her foot next to Blake's and he forced himself not to react to the contact. "Well, it's not funny ha-ha, more like funny-surprising. Right, Blake?"

"Surprising for sure." He smoothed the napkin on his lap and forced himself to look at Andrew. "You know that foster organization I work with, Woof Watchers? Well, they emailed me right after the wedding, asking if I could assist with an emergency fundraiser."

"Because they had a large influx of dogs needing homes," Bridget added.

Blake nodded. "I agreed and they told me they'd asked someone from the Flames to co-chair the event with me. Long story short, that person from the Flames turned out to be Bridget."

"My marketing manager, the original co-chair, needed to hand off the project. Bed rest. Her first baby is due in about four weeks."

They were babbling, trying too hard to sell the story. Time

to wrap it up. "We were meeting about the event when your text came in."

"Seemed impractical not to share a ride here," Bridget added, suddenly very interested in her water glass. "Funny, right? What are the chances?"

"Yes," Grace said, light dancing in her icy eyes, "what are the chances that just a few days after *seeing* each other at the wedding, you'd bump into each other again so soon? In a city of nine million people, no less."

"Bridgie, you sure it's wise to take on more?" Andrew asked, thankfully missing Grace's intimation.

Something in Blake bristled. "She can handle it." In all the years he'd known her, there'd never been a single sign that she couldn't handle anything thrown at her. Sure, her accident had terrified Andrew, and Blake understood wanting to protect her, but it happened ten years ago. Andrew needed to ease up.

"Because you know so much about her?" Andrew asked, his words slightly clipped.

"Much as every woman loves two men trying to decide what's best for her, how about I decide what I can and cannot handle?" Bridget said, placing her palms on the table and giving them both an icy stare.

Her look should scare him, not turn him on, right? Then again, nothing about his reactions to her made any sense. When it came to Bridget Hayes, up was down and down was up.

"It's just that—" Andrew started.

"New rule," Bridget said, cutting him off. "You are no longer allowed to start a sentence with 'it's just that.'"

"Or what?" Andrew challenged, their brother-sister dynamic coming to the forefront.

Bridget straightened the dessert fork above her dinner plate and drew in a breath. "Or I tell Mom what really happened to the rug in the den."

Andrew's eyes went wide. "You wouldn't."

She leaned toward him. "Try me."

"What happened to the rug in the den?" Grace asked, leaning her elbows on the table, and dropping her chin into her hands.

Bridget opened her mouth, and Andrew slapped his hand over it while they glowered at each other.

"So, Grace," Blake said, interrupting the standoff—and trying to ignore how much Bridget playing the badass turned him on. "You've started your honeymoon here in the Big Apple. Where to next?" He knew the answer, but they needed a subject change. Fast.

"London and then Dublin—just like my first tour with Storyhill. Then Andrew will fly back to Nashville for practice and tour, and I'll go to Minneapolis for a couple of weeks. I've got a project to finish up with Chris Cooper, and it'll give me a chance to spend some time with Annie, Will, and the girls while you guys are gone."

"And a chance to get away from Andrew for a while," Bridget grumbled.

Blake tipped his head back and laughed.

Bridget narrowed her eyes and did a close impression of Andrew's earlier scowl. "What's so funny?"

"My impression of you is as polished, award-winning, take no prisoners business executive, not sullen, little sister."

Bridget wrinkled her nose and shrugged. "He brings out the best in me."

A server halted additional comments by placing four small plates in the center of the table. "Compliments of the chef." He pointed to each dish.. "You have poached lobster in popcorn foam, a miniature eggplant timbale, dates stuffed with chorizo and wrapped in bacon, and crab over an apple and citrus salad. Enjoy."

"Think you can share with your sister, Cowboy?" Grace asked Andrew with a wink.

"Hilarious," he said with a low growl, but a smile curved his lips as he looked at his new bride.

A pang of jealousy spiraled through Blake. He brushed it aside. It wasn't productive. He wasn't long-term relationship material. But sometimes he still wondered what it might be like. No, that wasn't quite right. He wondered what it might be like with *her*.

"You're fostering a dog?" Grace's voice sliced through his thoughts.

He blinked, looking around the table. "I'm sorry?"

"I told Grace and Andrew about Destiny," Bridget supplied.

Yes. Destiny. Dogs. A subject he was comfortable talking about. He pulled his phone from his pocket, opened the photos app, and shared a picture like a proud papa. And it did what dogs always do—it siphoned the tension away from the table.

"Who's up for an after-dinner drink?" Grace asked an hour, and three courses, later.

Bridget sighed and folded her napkin, placing it on the table. "Not me. It's been a long day and if I had another drink, I'd be asleep on the table. Someone would have to carry me out of here."

Blake resisted the temptation to volunteer for that job.

"Are you sure?" Grace said. "Curtis makes a mean bittersweet chocolate-mint martini."

"Tempting, but I'll take a raincheck. Next time you're in the city?" Bridget asked.

Grace and Andrew nodded in unison. "Blake" —Grace turned to him— "how about you?"

"I have a dog to get to," he answered, pushing back in his

chair. "And Bridget and I should leave you to enjoy your honeymoon. I'm no expert, but from what I understand of these things, three is a crowd."

They stood and exchanged hugs. Andrew clapped him on the back and asked, "You'll wait with her until her ride arrives?" Good to know that, in Andrew's mind, he at least ranked higher than the dark streets of Brooklyn.

"Of course," he answered.

"Thanks, brother."

Brother. A powerful reminder of Blake's priorities. But was it enough to shut down the eddy of emotions that churned through him anytime he was near Bridget Hayes? It had to be. His family—and his job—depended on it.

Blake opened the door to his apartment and nearly tripped over Destiny. He crouched down and scratched behind her ears. "I'm sorry, little lady. I didn't expect to be gone for so long. You ready to go outside?"

She spun in three circles and grabbed her leash from the bench flanking the door.

"Such a smart girl." He clipped the lead to her collar, and she jumped toward him. He scooped her up with a laugh. Excellent actress or not, three flights of stairs were difficult for her squat legs.

Weaving through parked cars, Blake sprinted across the street, Destiny in his arms, football style. He set her down once they got to the Riftstone Arch. "Alright, little lady, right or left tonight?"

A gentle breeze swirled around them, lifting a cluster of recently fallen tulip petals. Destiny yipped, and with a tug on her leash, chased them down the paved trail. "Left it is," Blake said with a chuckle.

Destiny stopped and sniffed, or more accurately, *snuffled* nearly every plant and fence post lining the pavement, and Blake's mind replayed the day's events. Well, not so much events as images—the way Bridget's smile made the corners of her eyes crinkle, the softness of her skin when she touched him, how she clearly loved hard *and* fought hard when it came to Andrew.

He stopped at the next bench and sat down. "Destiny," he said. "I think I'm in trouble. I need some advice." She waddled to the bench, dropped onto her hind end, and stared up at him.

He looked left and right. Was he ready for people to see him conversing with a dog? What the hell, it was New York City. Last week, he'd walked past a guy screaming about the dangers of eating tuna. *Eating tuna fish is a death wish*, the guy had chanted, never breaking stride on his path through the park. Talking to a dog was tame in comparison.

Destiny set her front paw on his foot.

"Okay, okay, I get it, get on with it." He leaned forward, arms on his thighs. He scratched under her chin. "There's this woman. And I like her. A lot. Shouldn't be a problem, right?" He fisted his hands in his hair. "And it's not *a* problem, it's *so many* problems. For years, I've denied my attraction to her. Made up reasons like, she works all the time and I'm constantly traveling. Or it was a one-sided attraction. And then there's the very real rationale that if we tried something and it went sideways, I could lose a job I love and the family I've made. And the excuses worked. Until I slept with her."

Destiny let out two sharp barks.

"Hey, hey, now. I thought this was a no judgement zone."

She barked again and pulled on her leash.

"You're right. Time to go to bed. Everything will feel better in the morning. Good advice."

Stepping inside the brownstone, he let Destiny wobble up

the first flight of stairs. At the landing, he pulled a treat from his pocket and opened his hand, letting her take it.

He looped an arm around her middle, hoisting her up, as the door next to him flew open. He reared back, just barely hanging on to the dog. "Mom! You scared the crap out of me." He set Destiny back on the floor as he caught his breath. "What are you doing?"

"Checking out the strange sound I heard." She peered down at the pooch currently sniffing the air, but not getting too close to his mother. Smart dog. "I didn't realize you had a new dog."

You might know that if we talked more than once every two weeks over overpriced Cobb salads. Per usual, he kept the thought to himself. "I'm surprised you're still up."

Bette Kelly shrugged. "I had some emails to get through and a proposal to proof. Work never ends, you know."

A chill ran down his spine. His mother's words could have just as easily come from Bridget's mouth. How had he not seen it? His mother consistently put work ahead of everything else in her life, including him. If he explored his growing feelings for Bridget, would the same thing happen with her?

He shook his head. Cart before horse. There was no relationship with Bridget. There would be no relationship with Bridget.

"Work ends the minute you decide to end it," he snapped back. Both of their eyes flew wide. He never said things like that to his mother. He learned a long time ago that calling out her behavior didn't change a thing.

"Never mind," he grunted, stooping to pick up Destiny.

Bette tentatively reached out, allowing Destiny to sniff her fingers before giving the pup's chin a scratch. "I've been meaning to email you."

He rolled his eyes. "Mom, I live eleven steps away" —he

pointed to the stairs behind him— "you could knock on my door."

"I never know when you're home."

Again, something easily remedied. *Pick your battles, Blake.* "I'm here now. What did you need?"

She twirled the pen she was holding between her fingers. "About dinner next week. How about we change things up? Instead of dinner at Cuisson, we go to Chix?"

"Really?" His heart squeezed the way it used to when she made a rare appearance at a concert or piano recital. Huh. He thought he'd shut down that feeling—that sense of hope—a long time ago. Didn't matter, he was shutting it down now. "You know that place serves fried Korean-Nashville Hot Chicken, right? It's fusion and spicy—neither of which you love. And you're not likely to rub elbows with the wealthy and powerful at that place."

"Fried chicken is one of your favorites, isn't it?" she asked, running her fingers through her perfectly styled silver bob.

"When I was sixteen." Still, the fact she remembered made that pesky hope flicker in his chest again.

"A client is considering expanding his restaurant holdings to include soul food. We can have dinner, chat, and I can do a little research. It's win-win."

Blake's shoulders dropped and his hope deflated like a mylar balloon in freezing temperatures. "Sure, Mom. Sounds good." He sighed. Thirty-five was too old to keep believing that she'd change "someday."

"Monday night, then?" she asked, already retreating into her apartment.

"Yep," he said, turning and taking the stairs two at a time, careful not to jiggle Destiny. Stepping inside his apartment, he set Destiny in her crate and turned toward the hall. After a meeting with Bridget and a dinner with Andrew, Bette Kelly had sucked out the last of his energy. He'd be lucky if he didn't fall asleep brushing his teeth.

When he returned from the bathroom, Destiny was curled up on the pillow next to his. "You're supposed to be in your crate."

She opened one eye, snuffled, and burrowed in deeper.

"Fine," he said, pulling back the comforter. "Consider this my apology for leaving you alone for so long. But this is a one-night thing."

Blake sighed. Promises of a single night were really becoming his thing.

"We're going to visit Gramps tomorrow," he told his new companion. "Check in. See how he's doing and what he needs. Bridget will be there too, so you can meet her and see what I'm talking about. Sound good?"

This time, the dog opened both eyes and stretched. He'd take that as a yes.

He climbed into bed, and she nuzzled under his chin. He itched her belly, tracing the heart-shaped patch of white on her chest and, despite everything, he couldn't help wishing it was a different dark-haired woman curled up next to him.

Tomorrow, he thought mid-yawn, a solution to this Bridget-business would present itself. Now he just needed some sleep.

CHAPTER TWELVE

BLAKE ROLLED OVER AND A DROP OF WATER SLID DOWN HIS cheek. And then another. What the . . . He opened his eyes and saw nothing but black jowls. Wet black jowls. He swiped at his cheek with a prayer that his new foster dog had not been drinking out of the toilet.

He pushed himself up on his elbows. "Good morning, Destiny. What can I help you with at this early hour?"

She nudged her square head against his chin.

"Let me guess, you want food?"

She yipped and tapped her front paws on the bed.

Blake blinked a few times, pushing fingers through his hair. "Why do I get the impression your previous owner taught you a fair number of tricks?"

Destiny's owner had surrendered her when his new assisted living apartment didn't allow pets. An aging dog parent separated from their beloved pet always broke Blake's heart. His therapist would likely say it had something to do with his fear of abandonment. It was a rare session when she didn't bring it up. Maybe he should see if the guy left a forwarding address with

Woof Watchers? Or would it be too painful to see Destiny when he knew he couldn't keep her?

He threw back the covers and ambled out of bed. Questions like those would have to wait. He had a dog to feed, a grandfather to check on, and a meeting with a woman he couldn't get out of his mind.

An hour later, he carried Destiny down the three flights of stairs and knocked on Gramps' door.

"Come in if you have a key or are a beautiful woman," the older man hollered from behind the door.

Blake smiled and slipped his key in the lock. "I have a key and a beautiful woman," he said, releasing Destiny. The dog scrabbled over the herringbone patterned wood floor and jumped into Gramps' lap.

Clyde Kelly laughed and patted her head. "Well, now, not exactly what I'd imagined, but she is handsome. Who do we have here?"

"This is Destiny. She's a new foster."

"Welcome to the building, Destiny," Gramps said, feeding her a scrap of bacon from the TV tray on his left.

Blake smirked. "I think you just assured her undying love and affection."

"Always have had my way with women." He ran his thumbs under his bright pink suspenders and winked at Blake. "We've got that in common."

Blake rolled his eyes and unpacked a bowl and toys from Destiny's bag, setting them near the wall, assuring Gramps wouldn't trip on them. "When was the last time you went on a date, Gramps?"

Gramps snorted. "I might be a little past my prime, but I still got game. I've been chatting up a lady at the senior center. Might take her to bingo tonight."

Blake bit back a smile. "Got game and chatting up, Gramps? Where are you learning sayings like that?"

Gramps shrugged. "I got 125 channels and the Netflix" — he pointed at the 54-inch TV Bette had purchased for him— "and not much else to do."

Blake narrowed his gaze. "What's this lady's name?"

"Sounds like you might not believe me, son. Her name is Sharon Adair. Not a good Irish name like your grandmother, God rest her soul, but she's spunky for an octogenarian."

"That means she uses a cane instead of a walker?"

Clyde huffed. "The insolence."

Blake laughed. "I learned from the best, Gramps."

"Speaking of commonalities, there's bacon left if you want some." Gramps tilted his head toward the kitchen in the back of the apartment. "You look like you could use a little sustenance this morning."

Blake nodded. "If you're okay with Destiny" —who was now snoring lightly in his lap— "I'll grab a piece and do the dishes while I'm in there."

Clyde rolled his eyes. "I've told you a thousand times, I can do that stuff myself."

"And I've told you, a million times, I'm going to do 'that stuff' anyway."

"Stubborn," Gramps grumbled.

"Again, wonder where I got that from?" Blake teased as he walked into the kitchen.

"From your mother," Clyde said, not missing a beat.

"And she got it from . . .?"

"Point taken."

Blake filled the sink with water, squeezing a few drops of dish detergent, and collecting the dishes from breakfast and last night's supper. He needed a moment to clear his head before Bridget arrived.

As Blake shut off the water and placed the last plate in the dish drainer, Gramps yelled, "Come in if you have a key or are a beautiful woman," followed by scrabbling nails and a series of barks.

Gramps' vintage wall clock chimed nine times. She was right on time. He wondered if she was naturally punctual or if it was another way for her to control a situation. Blake hadn't locked the door behind him and it creaked open slowly.

"I don't have a key," a familiar female voice said. "But I come bearing gifts."

Blake held back, waiting to hear Gramps' response. "Your beauty is all this apartment needs."

Yep. Clyde's game *was* better than Blake's.

Bridget laughed softly. "No need to wonder if I'm in the right place," she said. "It's clear you're as big a flirt as your grandson." She leaned down and petted the dog prancing at her feet. "You must be Destiny," she said.

Blake stepped through the small dining room in time to hear Gramps say, "Taught Blakey all my best lines."

"Says the man who was married to his wife for over fifty years." Blake placed a fresh glass of water on the TV tray.

"Fifty-*three* years. I wish we would have lived closer so you could have spent more time with her."

"Me too, Gramps, me too." Blake squeezed his grandfather's shoulder. Maybe if he'd spent more time with Clyde and Norah, he'd have a better sense of healthy relationships. Instead, the woman who raised him expressed her love through a hefty allowance and networking opportunities.

Years in therapy helped him see Bette craved security and to her that meant making and accumulating money. But knowing that now hadn't stopped him from making impulsive decisions. He'd been so hungry for attention that he handed his heart over too easily to people who didn't handle it with care. After several painful heartbreaks, he opted for casual, short-term relation-ships—companionship without the drama.

"I'm Bridget Hayes," she said, holding her hand out to Gramps. "I brought you a small gift for hosting us today." She handed him a small stack of chocolate bars tied with a large red bow. "They're Cadbury Dairy Milk bars—the ones made in Ireland, with real Irish milk."

Clyde reached for the chocolate, looking between it and Bridget. "How did you find these? Outside of Ireland?"

Bridget smirked and smiled. "I have my ways."

"Hmm," the older gentleman said, pulling the ribbon and investigating the flavors. "And how is it that my grandson came to know such a thoughtful woman?"

"I'm Andrew Hayes' sister. From Storyhill?" Bridget answered.

"And what exactly am I hosting?" Clyde asked, continuing to pepper her with questions. "Blakey, did you bring her here to tell me something?" He wrapped his fingers around Blake's wrist. "Like you're marrying this woman? I know you're not stupid enough to let a woman with Irish chocolate *and* an Irish last name get away."

Bridget blushed a deep red, and Blake coughed. "She's here to help me plan that event I told you about, Gramps. The one with Woof Watchers? You're actually hosting Destiny" —he pointed at the snoozing pooch— "so we can work. That okay?"

"You going back to your apartment?" Clyde waggled his eyebrows.

"No," Bridget and Blake said in unison.

"We're going to work right there," Blake said, pointing to Clyde's dining room table.

Clyde harrumphed. "Maybe you're not as much like me as I thought. At your age, I'd never have courted a beautiful woman in the apartment of an old man."

"Gramps," Blake said, "I'm not courting her and—"

"Why not?" Clyde said, peeling back the deep purple Cadbury wrapper.

Blake blinked. "You're especially persistent this morning, Gramps."

"Neither one of us is getting any younger, and this is the first woman you've brought to meet me in a decade. It seems like now or never. I'd like to see you settle down *before I die*."

"Persistent *and* melodramatic," Blake said.

"You'll have to excuse an old man, Bridget. It's just that my grandson has developed a severe case of constipation when it comes to love. Someone needs to give him a push, so to speak."

A bark of a laugh fell from Bridget's lips. "It's okay, Clyde. I am *very* familiar with family members wanting to help. But I really am here just to work."

"For now," Clyde said, pinning Blake with a look over his wire-rimmed glasses.

"Behave," Blake said, pointing a finger at his grandfather. Not that it would help. He turned to Bridget, gesturing to the oak table in the adjoining room.

Bridget nodded and walked to the table, pulling three colorful file folders from her bag.

"Sorry about all that. Maybe this wasn't such a good idea," Blake whispered, pulling out a chair for himself and one for Bridget.

"I'm old, not deaf, son," Clyde hollered from the adjoining living room.

Blake lifted his eyes to the ceiling. "He hears perfectly when it suits him. Other times, not so much."

"I heard that too."

Bridget sank into the chair Blake had pulled out. "It's okay," she said with a soft chuckle. "You ready to get started?" She opened the top folder and pulled out several spreadsheets.

Blake peered into the living room. Destiny had clamored back into Gramps' lap and Clyde had turned on the Food Network. Man didn't cook much, but he loved his food TV. And the volume was much lower than normal, meaning he had every intention of eavesdropping.

"Let's do it," Blake said, already anticipating the slew of questions he'd get the minute Bridget left.

Within a couple of hours, they'd reviewed their initial plan, brainstormed a few more people to contact, and emailed a tentative schedule to Woof Watchers for final approval. He'd concentrate his efforts in the next ten days before Storyhill left on tour, and Bridget would follow up with people while he was gone. They'd check in via text or email from here forward, leaving him feeling equal parts relieved and disappointed.

"Think we can get it all done?" Bridget asked, placing her hands on her lower back and stretching.

"With my charm and your unparalleled organizational skills?" He smiled. "We're the perfect team."

"Team," she hummed so low that he doubted she realized she'd said it aloud. Her eyes met his and it was as if two live wires crossed. The sparks were undeniable. She cleared her throat and dropped his gaze, shuffling the papers spread across the table into her file folders. "Are we done for today? I should probably get up and move around so my leg doesn't get stiff."

The need to touch her, to bring her attention back to his, was so strong he slipped his hands under his thighs to stop himself. "Do you have anywhere you need to be?"

"There's always work to be done, but no, nothing specific."

See, a little voice whispered, *she's willing to do something other than work. Totally different from your mother.*

"Want to take a walk with me and Destiny? She hasn't been outside since we arrived."

They both turned, looking into the living room. Clyde was asleep, his head lolled to the side, Ina Garten making some chicken dish in the background. Destiny's eyes had popped open at the word "walk." Her expression read cautious anticipation—excited but unwilling to move until Blake confirmed that yes, he'd really meant it was outside time.

"Want to take a walk with Bridget?" he asked the dog.

Destiny rose, stretched, and slid down Clyde's legs, waking him. She ran to the door, did her now recognizable three spins, and pulled at the leash hanging from a hall tree hook.

"You're leaving already?" Clyde said.

"Just for a little while," Blake said, smiling at his grandfather. "Going to take Destiny for a walk, but I'll be back to take you to the senior center."

Clyde leaned forward in his recliner. "Then I'd better get myself ready."

"For Sharon?"

"Yep," he said with a wink. "There's only one constipated Kelly in this room. When it comes to love, anyway," he added with a shoulder shrug.

"Maybe that's enough talk about constipation for one day, Gramps," Blake said, clipping the leash to Destiny's collar.

Clyde's lips twisted, his gaze going to the ceiling.

"Gramps?" Blake asked, backtracking toward Clyde's recliner. "You okay?"

"Fine, Blakey. Just couldn't decide what made the better joke: something about being the Love Doctor specializing in getting things 'moving' or the Metamucil for love." Clyde hardly got the last word out before he started laughing.

"Ugh, Gramps" —Blake rubbed his forehead— "they're both terrible. And laughing at your own jokes? Not good."

Bridget walked up beside him. "Don't worry, Clyde. I laugh at my own jokes all the time. Someone has to, right?"

"See, Blakey," Clyde said, rising from his chair and poking Blake in the chest, "she *is* the perfect woman."

"Enough." Blake walked to the door, gesturing for Bridget to go first. "See you in a little while, Gramps."

"Take your time," Clyde said with an exaggerated wink.

Blake shook his head and let the door drop shut behind them.

"I'm sorry about all that. Gramps was like a dog with a bone today," he said as they waited for the traffic signal to change. Destiny barked and spun toward him. "Figure of speech, little girl," he said, reaching down to pat her head, "not a real bone."

"No worries," Bridget said. "I meant it when I said I understood families" —she raised her fingers in air quotes— "helping."

The walk sign lit up, and they followed the throng of people across the street to the park entrance. Blake cinched Destiny's leash as a bicycle messenger sped by. "It's not just Andrew? They're all up in your business?"

"Not so much up in my business as constantly treating me like I'm fragile. It drives me crazy. The accident happened ten years ago. And, yes, I almost died, but I didn't. Yes, they told me I likely wouldn't walk again. But look at me" —she waved her hands in front of her body— "completely ambulatory. Every time they ask me how I am or tell me I shouldn't do something, it reminds me of . . ." she trailed off.

"Of?" he said, suddenly desperate to know everything about her.

"Nothing," she said. "Right or left?" she asked, pointing at the fork in the path.

"Hey," he said, reaching for her hand, but pulling back, "it's okay if you don't want to talk about it, but for what it's worth, I think they're just scared."

Her eyes whipped to his face. "Scared of what?"

"They faced the possibility of losing you. It would make anyone cautious. After the accident happened, Andrew was out of his mind with worry. When he left the tour, Joe offered to travel with him because we weren't sure he could make it back here safely."

She visibly stiffened. "I never wanted Andrew to leave the tour."

"I know you would have done the same for him." He hooked a left on the path leading to Strawberry Fields.

She nodded. "Enough of that," she said, waving her hand in the air, as if pushing away the memories. "Tell me, who is Sharon?"

The quick change of subject had his mind spinning. "Sharon?"

"The woman Clyde is getting all spiffy for?"

Blake laughed. "Right. Sharon. Apparently, she's the woman Gramps is flirting with at the senior center. According to him, she's spunky and one hell of a bingo player."

As they continued down the path, skirting rushing locals and oblivious tourists, the light spring breeze picked up the ends of her hair and twisted them around her face like a chestnut brown halo. She tucked the strands behind her ears and smirked. "You and Clyde seem close."

They slowed so Destiny could fully inspect a particularly interesting puddle. "We are now."

"But not previously?"

Blake pointed to a bench facing the lake, dappled in sunlight. "Let's sit."

Bridget tapped her thigh. "I'm good," Bridget said.

"You might be, but I think Destiny needs a rest." He pointed down to the dog, her tongue hanging out. "Her previous owner was elderly, and I don't think she got a lot of exercise."

"Right," Bridget said, dropping to the bench. "So, you and Clyde?" she asked again.

Blake nodded, absently scratching down Destiny's spine. "Until my grandmother passed, they lived in a small town in Pennsylvania. They didn't like to drive into the city and my mother was always too busy with work to go out there. She sent me to stay with them for a week every summer, and we talked often on the phone, but other than that, time together was rare."

"How did your mother end up in New York?"

He pulled out a small water bottle from the pocket of his hoodie and opened it, encouraging Destiny to drink from the stream he poured. "She attended NYU and never looked back."

"And Clyde moved to New York after your grandmother passed?"

He screwed the cap back on the bottle and wiped some drops from Destiny's nose with the back of his hand. "I thought Kal was the interview expert."

Bridget shrugged. "We've been friends a long time. I've learned a few things. You don't have to answer if you don't want to."

Did he want to? Normally, talking about his family was one of his least favorite pastimes, but there was something about sitting here, in the sun, his attention focused on the dog that made him want to tell Bridget about his mother, Gramps, about how lonely he was growing up.

"When Grams died, my mother renovated the brownstone and moved Gramps into the bottom floor."

"So, they're close? Your mother and Clyde?"

"No," he answered. "My mother's not close to anything except her business. For family, it's all about money. She pays for the best of whatever is needed but doesn't get involved otherwise."

Bridget wrapped her hand around his forearm, and he tried

to ignore the tingles climbing his arm. "I'm glad you and Clyde have each other now."

He nodded, slumping a little further down on the bench. They sat in silence watching runners skirt the tourists posing for selfies in front of the *Imagine* mosaic in the distance.

"Did you know that was donated by Naples, Italy?" she asked, pointing at the circular tiled memorial.

He nodded. "And done in a Portuguese pavement style."

She turned to him. "How do you know that?"

"I came here a lot as a kid." He pointed at the benches further down the path. "I liked that it's a designated quiet zone in a city full of noise. I researched the area and the mosaic for a seventh-grade report."

"Were the Beatles an inspiration? Is that how you got started singing?"

"No," he said, smiling at the memory. "In elementary school, I stayed with a woman in the building after school. Imagine every stereotype of an Italian grandmother and you had Mrs. Romano. She had a beat-up upright and played it every day with me sitting beside her, explaining everything she was doing. I guess I took to the piano right away. Mrs. R must have mentioned it to my mother because it wasn't long before a secondhand keyboard showed up in the apartment with a few music books from the 70s. Piano and voice lessons came after her business took off."

"70s music, huh?" —she tapped a finger to her chin— "Let me guess, the first song you learned was 'A Horse with No Name' by America."

He laughed. "Close. 'Sailing' by Christopher Cross. And I can still play it from memory."

"You'll have to prove it to me sometime."

"Are you asking to see my piano, Bridget Hayes?"

"The *keys* to your heart, you mean?" she smiled, but it faded quickly. She cleared her throat and dropped her gaze. "Sounds like she loves you in her own way. Your mother, I mean."

"So says my therapist," he said with a hollow laugh. Sun dappled Bridget or not, this conversation had gone far enough. Time to head it off.

"How about you? How did you start playing ball?"

She shrugged in a way that only another avoider recognized. "Andrew did the music thing. Colin is the bookworm. I wanted to be different, so I did the sports thing."

"I'm guessing, based on your success, you were a natural."

Bridget scratched Destiny absently. "I'm competitive and driven. Always have been. If I had a free moment, I was running drills, practicing my shot."

"So same work ethic as now?"

She turned to him, an unidentifiable emotion passing over her eyes. "I guess," she said. "But playing basketball came easier than the business of basketball does. Probably came too easy." She rubbed her fingers over the wood bench slats, flicking off the seed pods floating down from the trees overhead.

"Too easy?"

She stared across the path, quiet. He was about to suggest continuing their walk when she turned her head and said, "I took it for granted. Pushed limits. Took too many chances. I was cocky. Believed my talent would open any door."

"Hey," he leaned toward her, placing a finger under her chin, tipping her face up. "That's not uncommon. It's the hubris of youth."

She searched his face. "Maybe not. But the way I acted, that hubris, cost me my dreams."

His heart ached seeing the unmasked pain and regret in her expression. In this moment, he'd give anything to ease it. "Certainly not *all* of your dreams."

She held his gaze until he lurched forward. Destiny had stretched her leash taut, pulling toward the paved trail.

"Looks like Destiny is ready to go," Bridget said, standing.

"Bridget," he reached for her hand.

She stood, flipping her hair over her shoulder, not looking at him. "You should get back to Clyde. I certainly don't want to be the reason he's late for his date."

"I said the wrong thing. I'm sorry," he said, rising to stand next to her.

"Not at all," she said with a wave, slipping easily back into all-business-Bridget.

He hated it. And recognized it. She wasn't the only one with practiced masks.

"You have grandfather duty, and I should get a few things done this afternoon. And we both have Woof Watchers-related things to do. You're still okay if we handle everything from now on through email or an occasional phone call?"

"Yes." Meeting virtually was the smart thing to do. Then why did it feel like something he really wanted was slipping through his fingers?

"Great. Then I'm going to head back through the park to my apartment." She pointed in the opposite direction from his brownstone. "Please tell Clyde that it was a pleasure meeting him."

"I will."

And with a quick scratch on Destiny's head, she was gone. And, despite all his efforts to keep his feelings in check, she took a piece of his heart with her.

CHAPTER THIRTEEN

BRIDGET PUSHED HER GLASSES INTO HER HAIR AND massaged the back of her neck. It felt like the more she gave this job, the more it demanded. Logistics for the second half of the season needed final approval. The DEI consultant needed to reschedule, meaning Bridget had to identify a new date where staff, coaches, and the consultant all had availability. It wasn't ideal but pushing it back to the All-Star break seemed to be the only workable solution. On the heel of that news, the accounting department had emailed, claiming that corporate sponsorships had a budget shortfall of about ten grand. Not an unsurmountable figure but putting something *back* on her to-do list was her least favorite thing to do. It disrupted her system, her plans.

And none of that included her Woof Watchers responsibilities. Since their meeting at Clyde's, Blake had emailed twice, asking for an update. Each time, she'd promised to get back to him—and hadn't.

She opened her calendar app to verify the date Storyhill planned to gather in Nashville. Tomorrow. Wait. What? *Tomor-*

row? Son of a *Shaq* burger. She set a reminder to email—scratch that—call Blake tonight.

"How about a super-sized iced latte?" Kristina asked from her office doorway.

"With a shot of hazelnut?" Bridget asked, setting her phone aside.

"Of course," the woman said, placing the magical elixir on the corner of Bridget's desk.

Bridget ripped the paper from the straw, stabbed the lid, and inhaled a glorious dose of caffeine. "Are you the world's best assistant, or are you buttering me up?"

Kristina laughed shakily. "Both?"

Bridget sucked down another six ounces and circled her hand in the air. "Hit me."

"Every time I walked by today, you were sighing. Call it assistant intuition, but I figured the best way to combat that kind of day is with a vat of espresso."

Bridget smiled. "So that's the excellent assistant bit. What's the other part?"

"Tricia is unreachable—"

Bridget set down her coffee, bracing her hands on her desktop. "Oh no. Is everything okay?"

Kristina lifted her hands, palms out. "She's at a regularly scheduled doctor's appointment and, when there, she turns her phone off."

Bridget dropped her mouth open in mock shock. "Hold up. Phones have an off button?"

Kristina laughed. "I can show you where it is."

Bridget matched her assistant's smile. "No way. That's too much power. If I turned it off, I'd probably never turn it back on."

"I doubt that," Kristina said, dropping into the chair in front of Bridget's desk. "You are the most dedicated person I know. I don't know how you do it all."

Fatigue seeped into Bridget's bones, suddenly making her feel very heavy. She forced a smile. "Well, I certainly don't do it by turning off my phone. Now, what's in the folder?"

"Lisa is wrapping up the collateral materials for the Flames Academy summer camps and needs final approval on the copy and photos."

Bridget motioned for the folder. "There is certainly no need to bother Tricia with that. It would eventually end up on my desk, anyway. When does she need it by?"

Kristina cringed. "Three."

Bridget's eyebrows shot up. "Three, today? That's in twenty minutes."

"With Tricia out, projects are backing up a bit."

Bridget sighed. "It's okay. I'll look at it right now. And, thanks for the coffee," she said, tipping the plastic cup in Kristina's direction.

Kristina stood, nodded, but didn't move.

"Something else?"

"I'm always here to help, you know," Kristina said, taking a step toward Bridget's desk.

"Thank you for that, but I'm good."

"Okay. Let me know when you're finished reviewing that" —she gestured to the folder— "and I'll run it back to Marketing."

Bridget nodded, already flipping through the mock-ups. She circled a typo, rearranged the order of the first two sentences, easy fixes. The next page featured a collage of photos, determined kids, smiling Flames players.

Her rookie season, every player committed to attending a day camp, their game schedule preventing more involvement. Bridget could still see the little girl standing in the back, hair pulled into fat braids, colorful barrettes dangling from the end of each. She stood a couple feet away from the rest of the kids, doing her best to fade into the bleachers. Bridget had set up a drill on ball handling skills and surreptitiously partnered with the little girl. The wider the girl's smile grew, the more often she met Bridget's gaze, the warmer Bridget felt. When the little girl was finally brave enough to join the other kids, Bridget thought her heart might burst.

That memory, these photos, were an unwelcome reminder of the life Bridget assumed she'd be living. She threw her pen across the room, ironically bouncing it off the team photo of the sole championship she'd won as a pro. Why couldn't she leave the past in the past and settle into this life?

She was the youngest woman to be named WNBA Executive of the Year. Any outsider would say she'd turned lemons into lemonade. But she didn't see it as a redemption story. Redemption stories didn't open with the constant refrain of *what if, what if, what if?* Redemption stories didn't include blocking out memories by working constantly. Or always making the safe choice. Or refusing to dream new dreams.

Maybe she could work a little less? Maybe she'd done enough to prove herself? Maybe she could trust that accepting help was not the same as admitting failure?

"Kristina!" she called, a little more forcefully than planned.

"Yeah, boss?" Kristina said, popping into Bridget's door frame.

"Do you really have time for another project?"

The younger woman's eyes widened, and she nodded. "I'd love to take on more responsibility."

Bridget unearthed the Woof Watchers folder from the towering stack on her desk. "The Woof Watchers event, the one Tricia agreed to sponsor, I could really use some help." Bridget ignored the trickle of guilt running down her spine, reminding herself that this event *was* work-related. A detail she often forgot, as the event had become, in her mind, all about interacting with Blake. "Inside the folder is a spreadsheet listing the individuals and organizations approached for either a silent auction item or event sponsorship. If there's not a blue check next to their name, I need you to send a follow-up email, or better yet, call them."

"Easy enough. I'll get started right away." Kristina tapped the folder and smiled widely. "Thanks for trusting me with this."

"And the proofs are ready to go back to Marketing." Bridget passed off the pages, realization hitting her with the subtlety of a 2x4 strike. By trying to prove she was indispensable to the organization, had she unwittingly made her staff feel like she didn't trust them? Is this why they called her at home on the rare days she took off? Why Kristina called her at the wedding? She bumped her fist on her desk. *Dirk Nowitzki.* She never wanted her hang-ups, her limitations, to cause issues. Not for her family. Not for her staff.

Her phone buzzed with an incoming text. She shook her head. She'd been staring at her door since Kristina left. She grabbed her phone, but not before it buzzed a second time. And a third.

Bridget flipped her phone over and held it up to her face to unlock it. Three texts from Blake.

Blake: I need a favor.

Blake: A big favor.

Blake: Call me when u r free. Pls.

She scrolled to his name in her contacts and jumped an inch off her chair when her phone buzzed again.

Blake: Better yet, can I meet you at your office?

Meet her *here?* She hit the message icon instead of the call button. *Everything ok?*

Blake: Yes. No. Maybe. I hope so.

Bridget: I find your decisiveness very calming.
Blake: No one's bleeding. Just a schedule issue.
Bridget: With Woof Watchers?
Blake: Sort of. Can I come there? What time are you finished?

She wanted to say "never," but she didn't want to inspire another lecture about her long work hours. Plus, hadn't she just decided to ease up a little? Isn't that what asking Kristina for help was all about?

Bridget: The building locks at five. So 4:30?
Blake: Thx. C u then.

She looked at the time on her phone. Three pm. Great. An hour and a half to think about him and what he wanted. She sucked down the last third of her iced latte, turned back to her computer, and read the same email four times without retaining a word of it.

At 4:25, Bridget closed all the windows on her laptop. She needed to collect the Woof Watchers folder before Blake arrived.

She rose with a glance back to her desk. "Kristina?"

"Blake," said a voice just inside her door. "Disappointed?"

Wasn't that a loaded question? And one that had no good answer. She smiled and pointed at the chairs facing her desk. "Have a seat. I need to grab the Woof Watchers folder from Kristina."

Returning, Blake stood in front of the credenza, looking at her photos. "You have a picture of Storyhill?"

Her heart skipped a beat. This was one of those scenarios where a little white lie was not only excusable but completely necessary. "It's a picture of my brother."

He turned to her, a smile curling his lips. "And the rest of us?"

She shrugged and eased back into her chair. "Photo-bombers." She motioned to the chair in front of her. "Sorry that I've been remiss in getting back to you. Your departure date snuck up on me. I planned to call you tonight about the event. I'm assuming that your issue pertains to that."

"Sort of," he said, folding his six-foot three frame into the chair. "These are comfy," he said, running his hands over the arms. "Not used to that."

"That's because, in this office, you're entirely average."

He cocked an eyebrow and smirked.

She waved a hand, motioning to his body. "Size-wise, I mean."

His smirk stretched into a smile, dimples on full display.

Heat gathered in her cheeks. "I mean," she said, steadying her voice, "we selected all the furnishings in the building to accommodate tall people. At six-three, you fall in the middle of the height chart. *Average.*"

He leaned forward, bracing his weight on his elbows. "You know how tall I am?"

"What is the issue you wish to discuss, Mr. Kelly?" she said, opening the Woof Watchers folder.

"Right." He leaned back, draping his arm across the chair next to him and holy forearms, Batman.

Nope. This was a place of business. *Her* place of business. Drooling and ogling were for personal time. Or never. Never would be better.

"The foster that was supposed to pick up Destiny tonight had to cancel—for the entire tour run," he said.

"And?"

"And Woof Watchers can't find anyone on such short notice." His features scrunched. "I'm hoping you'll take her."

"Me? I'm hardly home. Seems unfair to her."

"Gramps can help with her during the day if you can drop her off and pick her up at night."

She shook her head. "I don't know, Blake."

"Please," he said, pulling the best puppy dog eyes she'd ever seen from a human. "I'd ask Gramps to take the whole time, but I don't want him taking her out at night. If he fell, I'd never forgive myself."

She'd always struggled with saying no and thinking of Clyde made it almost impossible. "Fine."

He slapped a hand on her desk. "Seriously? That's great!"

"But," she said, raising a finger. "I'll need very detailed instructions. Food time. Potty time. Emergency vet phone number." She looked up to find him smirking at her. "And absolutely no TNR comments."

He mimed zipping his lips and throwing away the key.

"I'll bring her to your place tonight."

"T-t-tonight?" She twisted her hands together under her desk. Alone. In her apartment. With Blake Kelly. And no charming eighty-year-old chaperone.

"My flight is at 5:00 am. Meaning I have to be at LaGuardia by, like, 3:30."

She blew out a breath. "Fine, but let's plan on discussing Dribble and Dunk at the same time." If she made it about work, maybe she'd think less about . . . the other stuff.

"Seven or eight?" he asked, pushing himself out of the chair.

"Eight." That would give her an extra hour NOT to be alone with him.

At 8:10, Bridget's phone rang, lighting up with a call from "Front Door." She mumbled a prayer for strength and fortitude, quickly wondering if an incantation for an instant case of pimples and flatulence—*for him*—might better ward off her flourishing crush.

When she finally answered, the male voice that made her belly flip and her heart squeeze said, "It's your turn for a date with Destiny." For added effect, a bark punctuated the sentence.

She buzzed them in, sucked in a calming breath, and opened the front door. Blake unclipped Destiny, and the pooch shot inside, scurrying through Bridget's apartment, her nose pressed to the floor.

"Come in," Bridget said with a laugh. "Sniff around. Make yourself at home."

"No need," he said, stepping over the threshold. "I already know it'll smell like cake."

"I opened wine," she said, gesturing to a bottle on the counter and doing her best to ignore his comment. "Would you like a glass?"

"You just opened it?" he asked, walking into the kitchen and holding up the half empty bottle.

"Long day," she said with a sigh. "And that was before one of my brother's friends asked me to watch his dog. For three weeks."

"Bastard. You'd think he'd have asked your brother to do it."

The mention of Andrew twisted something in her belly, but she played along with a roll of her eyes. "As luck would have it, my brother is also traveling."

He took a step closer to her, his eyes washing over her. "Well, let me be the first to say, your brother is very lucky to have such a kind, accommodating sister."

A nervous laugh fell from her lips. "Oh, you're not the first. Everyone says I'm the nice one in the family."

He held her gaze, not moving. The dimpled smile she couldn't resist firmly in place.

"Wine?" she said, shoving the bottle between them.

"Sure," he said, taking the bottle, setting it back on the counter, and following her into the kitchen. "These from Curtis' restaurant?" he asked, picking up a cookie from the counter and popping it in his mouth.

Her lips curled in, biting back a smile. "Do you like them?"

He cleared his throat and swallowed, his Adam's apple dipping down the length of his throat. "Little meatier than I expected," he rasped.

"That's because they're dog treats. I bought them for Destiny on my way home from work."

He swiped a finger under his bottom lip—and her eyes didn't have a choice but to follow. "So not from Curtis, then?"

"Nope" —she laughed— "but they are organic, and all the ingredients have less than two syllables."

He pounded a fist against his chest. "Protein is important."

"Especially before nightly shows."

"Correct," he said, moving away from her, walking into the living room.

She watched him from the corner of her eye as she poured him a glass—and refilled her own. He was studying the contents of her floor-to-ceiling bookshelves.

"You have some pretty unique bookends, TNR." He ran his fingers over the engravings on her trophies. "Louisiana Player of the Year. WBCA All-American. A Naismith award. How come they're shoved into the corners?"

Her gaze paused on the dusty bronze and silver statues. "Because they're from a lifetime ago." No, that wasn't right. They were from an entirely different life. Her two lives—before the accident and after. From a girl who acted impulsively to a woman who planned everything. A life that, in a blink, went from unlimited potential to unrealized dreams.

She took a sip of her wine, fighting to regain her focus, to stay present in the moment. "You ready to talk about the event?" she asked, sinking down into one end of her plush velvet sofa, gesturing for him to sit on the other.

He nodded, pulling two bowls and a single sheet, double-sided, from the large duffel he'd dropped by the door. "Water and food bowls and the care information you requested." He circled the kitchen island, filled the water bowl, and placed it on the floor. "Speaking of which, when's the last time you saw her?"

Bridget scanned the room. No Destiny.

"She's mostly well-behaved, but she does like to get into—" Blake's face broke into a smile and laughed.

Bridget followed his gaze and caught sight of a little black blur running toward him—with something hanging from her mouth. She dropped whatever it was at Blake's feet, looking up at him, clearly waiting for praise.

Blake bent to the floor and picked up . . . oh my god . . . a pair of her underwear. He held them up and a devilish glint danced in his eyes. "As I was saying, she likes to get into laundry baskets. Unless you left these lying around for me?"

Bridget stomped from the couch to Blake, ripping the panties from his hand. "How does this keep happening?" she asked between clenched teeth. She grunted and walked down the hall, throwing the underwear in her small laundry room, and slamming the door.

"You really need to stop throwing your lingerie at me, Bridget," he teased when she returned to the living room. "A guy could get the wrong idea."

"I had nothing to do with either incident," she said sharply.

"But you have to admit, lacy underwear is quickly becoming your calling card, at least where I'm concerned."

She didn't have to admit anything of the sort. She picked up the dog care instructions from the coffee table. "So, she eats breakfast at seven every morning?" She kept her eyes glued to the paper.

"Impressive deflection skills, TNR." He sat on the couch and patted the space next to him. "Come, Destiny."

But instead of following Blake's command, the little underwear thief jumped up next to Bridget and stared at her. Bridget chanced a quick glance at Blake. "What does she want?"

"Dogs can be very sensitive to tone of voice. She probably thinks you're mad at her."

"I am mad at her," she said, trying to sound stern, but the corners of her mouth turned up.

"Go on," Blake urged. "Give her a pet. Let her know that it's not her fault that I'm a panty magnet."

Bridget rolled her eyes. Hard. She leaned down, meeting the dog's gaze. "We girls have to stick together, Desi, and that means staying out of the laundry basket and not padding men's already large egos." She scratched between the dog's ears. Destiny sighed and flopped down, curling up next to Bridget's thigh.

"Girl power," Blake said, curling his fingers into a fist.

Bridget snorted. "I think it's time to get to work."

"Want a refill?" Bridget asked, gesturing to Blake's wine glass. "You earned it. We got a lot accomplished tonight."

"I could have another," he said, sliding to the edge of the couch. "You pour, and I'll move Destiny's crate. She'll do best with the transition if the crate is in your bedroom. That okay?"

"I can do that," she said, unsure she wanted Blake Kelly anywhere near her bedroom.

"I know you can, but you're helping me by taking Destiny. Let me help you."

Bridget looked at the floor. "I'm not very good at that."

"I've noticed." He placed a finger under her chin, tipping her face up. "Is that just about me, or is it everybody?"

"Everybody," she whispered.

"Why is that?"

She levered out of the couch and walked to the kitchen. "How long you got?" she said with a forced laugh.

"My flight leaves at five am."

Bridget slowly exhaled and wondered about her sudden urge to tell Blake everything. Fears she'd never shared with anyone. Things she hadn't even told Kal. How she longed to go back and end her career on her own terms, instead of giving that power over to a moment of shattering glass and bending steel. How on a good day, her scar was a badge of honor and on the bad days, it was a flaming red slice of shame.

Whoa. How much wine had she consumed?

She blinked several times and uncorked a second bottle of wine. "Bedroom's the second door on the left," she said, needing a moment for her thoughts—and heart rate—to settle.

"Should I be mindful of more panty traps?"

She laughed, and a few of the bubbles of tension in her chest popped. "You're safe. I only had time to set one and Destiny already found it."

"Second door on the left?" Blake confirmed, pointing down the hall.

Bridget nodded and filled both of their glasses, carrying them back to the living room. Destiny had rolled to the side and stretched out all four legs, easily taking up a third of the sofa. "Make yourself at home, little girl," Bridget said with a laugh, settling beside her.

"She takes up a lot of space for such a small dog," Blake said, returning to the room. He eyed the space next to Bridget on the sofa before sitting in the chair to her right.

He plucked his glass from the coffee table, leaned back, and lifted an ankle over the opposite knee. "So, you were about to tell me why you don't like to accept help."

"Was I?"

He laughed. "How about this? You answer one of my questions and I'll answer one of yours."

Her nerves flared again. Over the years, she'd bottled up her feelings because it felt like if she let one thing out, the rest would burst through the dam, and she had no idea if she had the power to stop the tsunami.

"Why?" she said, stalling.

He tapped the stem of his wineglass, silent for a few moments. "I could make some joke about both of us needing some 'master deflector therapy,' but the truth is" —he pinned her with his gaze— "I'd like to get to know you better, Bridget."

"Why?" she repeated, this time barely over a whisper.

"Because I'm curious. Because I like you, Bridget. I'd like to be friends. Real friends."

She turned her attention to the dog, now snoring, and mindlessly ran her fingers down Destiny's back. "I thought we were already friends."

"As a product of our proximity to Storyhill," he said, reaching out and squeezing her hand before rubbing Destiny's belly. "And I'd like to get to know Bridget, not Andrew's sister."

The specter of what getting closer meant hung in the air. Were they ready to confront all that came along with that? She shivered under his gaze. When his eyes dipped to her lips, she blurted out, "Go ahead. Ask your question." Who knew she'd find it easier to answer a personal question than to have him keep staring at her?

He blinked several times and his fingers flexed over the chair cushion like he was trying to hold himself in place. "I'll give you a choice. Either tell me why you think of those trophies" —he motioned to the bookcase— "as part of a different life, or tell me why you don't like accepting help?"

"You don't want to know my favorite color or my middle name? You know, ease in a little?" she said with a nervous laugh.

He watched her, waiting her out.

Which was the less dangerous question? Which one made her sound less crazy? "The trophies represent an unrealized dream," she said, echoing her earlier thoughts. "I struggle with how my career ended." She stood and walked to the bookcase, turning the Naismith award forward. "I've tried to pack them away, but I can't bring myself to do it. Maybe because they're a good reminder of what I owe the Flames." And look at that. In a roundabout way, she'd answered both of his questions.

"What do you owe to the Flames?" he asked, his forehead crinkling.

She wiped the dust from the top of the gold basketball atop the trophy. "Nope. You said one question. You asked, I answered. Now it's my turn."

He smiled. "Ah yes, I momentarily forgot that you're a stickler for the rules."

He dropped back against the chair, unbuttoned the cuffs on his shirt and rolled up the sleeves. And the forearms were back. Distracting little buggers.

"Bridget." Her name cut through the forearm lust fog.

"Huh?"

"Your turn?"

"Right." She pushed her spine against the bookshelves. What was she the most curious about? His music goals? His mother? No . . . "Tell me about your longest relationship."

He grinned. "That's not a question."

She sighed, walking back to the sofa. "Fine. What's been your longest *romantic* relationship?"

He dropped his foot to the floor and leaned forward, elbows

propped on his knees. "I don't do long-term *romantic* relationships."

"If it pleases the court, I'd like to amend my question."

He smirked. "I'll allow it, but only because I feel like I should model flexibility."

She rolled her eyes. "How to word this?" she said, tapping her chin. "Are you not interested in long-term relationships because settling down with one woman means you can no longer sample all the world has to offer?"

His smile fell. "No. It's not about sampling. It's because I'm not good at them. I've tried. I've failed." He looked at her like he wanted to say more, but instead rose from the chair. "I should go."

"I'm sorry if I overstepped, but you're the one that said you wanted to get to know each other better," she said, the words coming out harsher than planned.

"I did. I do. But you've got work tomorrow and I want to be respectful of that."

He extended his hand, and she took it, allowing him to pull her up from the couch. But he pulled a little hard and her leg was a little stiff from sitting and she ended up pressed against his chest.

His hand fell to her waist, his fingers slipping just under her t-shirt. "Bridget," he whispered. "I very much want to be your friend, but I'm not feeling very friendly right now. Tell me it's a bad idea to kiss you."

"B-b-bad idea."

He traced a finger over her jaw. "You're going to have to say it like you mean it."

She sucked in a breath and let her eyes drop shut. "It's a bad idea, Blake. Last time I checked, friends don't kiss." *Even if they are friends that have slept together.* She opened her eyes to find him still staring at her.

"You're absolutely sure about that rule?"

"Not even a little bit," she whispered, the truth slipping from her lips. "But until I research it fully, it's probably better to assume it's true."

"Ignorance of the law is no excuse and all that?"

She couldn't do anything but nod.

He caught her fingers, twining them through his own. "Thanks for watching Destiny. Gramps is expecting her tomorrow morning. I gave him an extra set of bowls, food, and a few toys, so you don't need to take anything but her leash."

"Okay," she said, still unable to put more than a few intelligible words together.

"And I'll check in from the road."

"Mmhmm." She pulled her hands from his and tucked them behind her back before she changed her mind and reeled him back in. "Good night, Blake."

He pulled the door open. "Good night, Bridget."

She locked the door behind him and flopped down on the couch, causing the cushion to bounce and Destiny to let out a sharp bark. "I agree, Desi. Spending more time with your foster dad is not a good idea." She scratched the top of the dog's head. "Why? Because a guy telling you he's no good at relationships is never a good sign. You should remember that if you're ever in the market for a canine companion." The Frenchie cocked her head. "Still not convinced? Well, there's the fact that he's distracting, and my work needs to come first. And let's not even get started about Andrew and Storyhill." Bridget looked at the empty wine glasses on the table. "Plus, there's that mysterious thing about him that makes me want to answer his highly inappropriate personal questions. That is a slippery slope, my friend."

And iron willpower or not, she doubted she could be "just friends" with someone she shared such undeniable physical chemistry. Look what happened in Minneapolis. Sleeping with him was supposed to get him out of her system, and that had been a complete miscalculation.

The dog climbed into her lap and licked Bridget on the chin.

Bridget laughed. "Who needs Blake with kisses like that?"

Destiny sighed and plopped into Bridget's lap. Clearly, the dog knew denial when she heard it.

CHAPTER FOURTEEN

A LOW RUMBLE VIBRATED NEXT TO BRIDGET'S EAR. SHE cracked open an eye. The only thing that sounded remotely similar was the weekly garbage truck and she was pretty sure it wasn't Friday.

Maybe her phone was vibrating?

She slapped a hand over the top of her bedside table, feeling for her phone. Her fingers brushed the top of it. No buzzing. She rolled back over, bumping up against a large lump. A warm lump.

Bridget propped herself up on her elbows, grabbing her glasses from the table, the room coming into focus. The door on Destiny's crate stood open, and the little escape artist was not only on the bed, but she'd burrowed under the covers and laid her head squarely in the middle of a pillow.

"Your friend Blake didn't mention your Houdini act," Bridget said to the snoring lump.

She grabbed her phone and snapped a photo of the sleeping dog. Blake was likely still in the air, but she texted the pic to him with the caption: *Dateline, NEW YORK. In a Goldilocks Imita-*

tion, French Escape Artist, Le Destin, Picks Lock and Makes Herself à L'aise.

The three dots jumped immediately. Must have landed early.

Blake: You speak French?

Bridget: That's all you have to say?

Blake: Would you prefer the truth?

Bridget: That you left out some very important details about this dog? Yes.

Blake: No. That I'm jealous.

A shiver raced down her spine. Refusing to think too deeply about his meaning—and unable to conjure up any of last night's excuses of why flirting, even via text, was a bad idea—she shot off a response.

Bridget: Yes, jealous of the fact that she is still asleep and we're both up.

She waited for the jumping dots and when they didn't appear, she shimmied out of bed, not reaching her en suite before her phone pinged. She turned it in her hand. A single word response: *Deflector.*

She dropped her phone on the bathroom vanity. The truth needed no response. And she didn't want to risk saying something that would come back to bite her. Instead, she'd focus on this morning's priorities: showering, taking Destiny to Clyde's, and getting to work. Texting Blake Kelly didn't make the list.

Bridget knocked on the large oak door while Destiny pawed at it. "Are you knocking too, little girl?"

The door swung wide, and Clyde stood on the other side wearing a mint button-up, pink suspenders, and a lilac bowtie. It shouldn't work, but it did. It brought out the twinkle in his eyes.

"Good morning, Clyde. You look dapper."

He playacted straightening his tie. "I wanted to look good for my two favorite ladies."

"Why, Clyde" —she placed a hand on her heart and fluttered her lashes— "we've only just met and I'm already one of your favorites? I'm flattered."

"I'm an excellent judge of character." He stepped back with a wink. "Good morning, Destiny." He pulled a doggie treat from his pocket and held his hand down to her. The dog lapped up the treat as if it was a secret handshake she and Clyde had practiced.

Bridget closed the door behind her and unclipped Destiny's leash. "You're sure you're okay with this?"

"Yep. Got the whole day planned. We'll do the Times Crossword, watch a couple of episodes of Cupcake Wars, take a walk in the park, and then Destiny will probably need a nap."

Bridget bit back a smile. "Destiny helps with the crossword, huh?"

Clyde's ever-present smile widened. "You'd be surprised."

Bridget found Destiny's bowls and filled one with water and one with food. "She did figure out how to unlatch her crate last night," she called from the kitchen.

Clyde appeared beside her. "Smart dog."

"Apparently." Bridget scanned the room. "Do you need me to do anything else before I go?"

Clyde stepped back across the faded hand braided rug and sunk into his well-loved recliner. Destiny hopped into his lap and licked his chin. "Maybe we should take one of those selfie things to send Blake. So he doesn't worry."

Bridget's eyebrows shot up. "Blake worries?" Outside of the thing with Andrew, it seemed like everything rolled off his back.

Clyde studied her. "He keeps a lot to himself. Thinks other people don't notice. I've always thought if he could just find someone to share his life with, like my Norah, things would be easier for him. Maybe you could be that person."

"Friends are important too," she replied lamely. People either pushed them together or apart. What was wrong with a little middle ground? *You mean the same middle ground you couldn't seem to find last night?* She shut down the image of being pressed against his chest, feeling his heart beat against hers and turned her to attention back to Clyde. "Ready for that selfie?"

Clyde pulled the latest model of iPhone out of his pocket and motioned for her to stand behind him.

"That's a pretty fancy phone you got there, Clyde."

"Lizzie likes to buy me things," he said with a shrug.

She'd recently heard something similar from another Kelly man.

He turned the phone around, so the camera lens faced them.

"May I?" Bridget asked, reaching for the phone.

Clyde nodded, dropping the phone into her hand.

"There's an easier way to do this." She turned the phone and showed him how to flip the camera to front-facing.

He chuckled. "Would you look at that? I always wondered how people didn't constantly cut their heads off in these selfies."

Bridget snapped the photo and handed the phone back to Clyde. "Do you know how to send it?"

He blew out a breath. "Of course."

Bridget smiled and rubbed her knuckles over Destiny's head. "Okay. I'll be back at five to pick her up."

"And you'll stay for dinner."

"Oh no, I couldn't—"

"Wasn't a question, Hayes."

Bridget smirked at his use of her last name. "Gotcha, *Kelly*. See you at five, then."

"For dinner," he repeated, picking up a pencil and unfolding the newspaper over Destiny's head.

"For dinner," she confirmed, unable to hold back a smile.

Bridget hung her laptop bag on the hook just inside her front door, kicked off her shoes, and massaged her fingers into the tight muscles in her leg.

Destiny ran to her bowl, picked it up, pinned Bridget with her puppy eyes, and dropped the bowl emphatically.

"Um, I was there when Clyde fed you, remember?"

If dogs could roll their eyes, Destiny had just done it.

"When he fed both of us," she whispered. Bridget had arrived a little after five and Clyde had set the table and was slicing grilled cheese on the diagonal, placing them next to bowls of tomato soup. She couldn't remember the last time she'd had a home cooked meal in a home that wasn't her mother's.

They'd had a lively conversation. Turns out he'd taught economics at a small liberal arts college for forty years. An institution with a well-known Division I women's basketball program. He'd surprised her with his knowledge of the sport, claiming Norah was an ardent supporter of women's athletics and whatever Norah loved, he loved—or learned to. "A woman ahead of her time," he'd claimed. "Lizzie and Blake might have gotten their stubbornness from me, but they got their drive from my wife," he added, his expression a mixture of pride and melancholy. "She made sure Lizzie understood she could accomplish anything. Maybe too well."

Earlier in the day, Bridget thought she'd be keeping a lonely man company, but had quickly realized it was the other way around. He talked about his friends at the senior center. His streak of bingo and pinochle wins. About how he'd once met the Barefoot Contessa at a local deli—and if he ever got the chance again, he'd ask for her Perfect Roast Chicken recipe instead of bumbling around like a star-struck fan. And, of course, Clyde had quizzed her about the Flames and her opinion on whether they'd make the playoffs this year.

His life was active and colorful. Much more than hers, she thought ruefully as she changed into a hoodie and yoga pants. Normally, she'd go from work clothes to pajamas, but Destiny needed another trip outside before bed.

Returning to the living room, she dropped onto the couch and flipped open her laptop. Before her fingers met the keys, a ball rolled over the keyboard. Destiny stood in front of her, tapping her paws against the floor.

"Are you *and* Clyde trying to teach me work-life balance?"

Her tongue lolled out and she tapped, tapped, tapped the floor.

Bridget threw the ball across the room and Destiny lumbered after it, her booty wiggling back and forth. This went on until Bridget's phone pinged.

Kal: Dinner tomorrow night?

Dinner with Kal. Right. This thing with Destiny had popped up so fast she'd forgotten to tell Kal.

Bridget: I'd love to. But could you come here? I'm dog sitting.

Kal: What???????

Bridget: Long story. Will tell you tomorrow night.

Kal: Will you also be cooking?

Bridget snorted. *And deny you the opportunity to flirt with the delivery guy. What kind of friend does that?*

Kal: You're right. What was I thinking?

Bridget: Obvs not. How about 6pm?

Kal: Perfect. See you then.

Bridget picked up the damp ball. "You ready to meet Auntie Kal, Desi?"

The dog spun in three quick circles and ran to the door.

Bridget laughed. "She's not coming until tomorrow."

Her phone chirped again. "What do you think she forgot?" Bridget asked the dog.

But it wasn't Kal.

Blake: What did you do?

What was he talking about? She ripped the Woof Watchers folder from her bag, flipping to the daily schedule. She ran her finger down the list. Nothing for today. Had she forgotten to write something down? *"Lindsay Whalen,"* she muttered under breath. How had she missed something?

A second text.

Blake: Clyde's in love.

She reread the two texts. "I think your foster dad has been drinking, Desi." The dog plopped down with a heavy sigh. "I agree. Alcohol is not a good idea the night before a long day of singing practice."

Are those two things related? she thumbed in and hit send.

Blake: Clyde is in love with YOU. He's sent me three texts since your dinner "date." Apparently, you are smart, funny, pretty, and a tech genius . . . something about his iPhone camera???

Bridget typed and backspaced, deleting the message. She nibbled on her thumbnail and then retyped the same message. *Are you saying he's wrong?*

Blake: Is that your one question for tonight?

Bridget: I wasn't aware we were still playing that game.

Blake: We are. And no, he's not wrong. And I'll allow one additional question, if you give me one.

"What do you think, Desi? Should I give him another question?" Bridget blew out a breath. Was she seriously asking a dog for advice? On the other hand, her puppy power had gotten her out of her crate without the use of opposable thumbs.

"Here goes nothing," she said to her phone screen.

Bridget: Since my date with Clyde was the best I've had in a long time, I'll allow one question.

She closed her laptop and waited for a response. Why was her heart trying to break out of her chest? It was one question.

As if sensing her discomfort, Destiny jumped on the couch and laid a paw on Bridget's thigh.

Blake: What's your middle name?

A laugh ripped from her chest. She'd braced for impact, and he lobbed a softball. She pulled her legs underneath her and Destiny scrabbled onto her lap, looking from Bridget's face to the phone and back again. Sign number one that she needed to get out more? The fact she was certain Destiny's expression said, "Go on, get on with it, text him back." Must stop anthropomorphizing the dog and start talking to more humans. About things other than work.

Destiny nudged her hand. "Fine, little girl, I get it." She typed back, *Asher. My mother's maiden name. And here's a freebie: my favorite color is blueish green—like the ocean or a Tiffany's box. What's yours?*

Blake: Color or middle name?

Bridget: Both

Blake: If I say anything other than emerald green, I'll get kicked out of the Irish Heritage Club.

Bridget: The Irish Heritage Club? Is that an after-school program for you artsy types?

Blake: I refuse to be shamed by you jock types. And my middle name is Thomas.

Bridget: After your dad?

Blake: No idea.

"For the love of Udonis Haslem." She punched the pillow next to her. She'd hit send before thinking. He'd never mentioned a father. I guess that was one way to bring flirty texting to an end.

I'm sorry, she typed. She stared at the phone for what felt like forever, waiting for a response, or at least the three dots indicating he was replying. She grabbed the blanket from the back of the couch and wrapped it around her and Destiny.

"C'mon, c'mon, c'mon," she whispered at the phone, willing it to light up.

Her phone finally pinged, and she let out a breath she hadn't realized she was holding.

Blake: No worries.

Clyde's words replayed in her mind. *He keeps a lot to himself. Thinks other people don't notice.* Before she formulated a response, he texted again.

Blake: Before I wish you a good night, promise me I'll be the first person you call if you become my step-grandmother.

Who was deflecting now?

Bridget: Good night, Blake.

Blake: Goodnight TNR. I'll check in tomorrow. Try not to miss me too much until then.

Bridget reread the message. What were they playing at? She wasn't entirely sure, but it felt a long way from friendship.

"Why is the door locked?" Kalisha's muffled voice called through the door.

Bridget scooped up Destiny, scurried to the door, flipped the deadbolt, and pulled it open. "Because dog." She lifted Destiny for emphasis. Destiny let out a soft "woof" and started wiggling, trying to get out of Bridget's grasp. "She's a lover and I didn't want her to attack lick you."

On cue, Destiny turned and licked up the entire side of Bridget's face. "See? Can't hold her licker."

"Funny," Kal said, stepping through the door. She scratched

Destiny under the chin and said, "My rule is that you buy me dinner before I allow any attack licking."

"Good rule," Bridget said, releasing Destiny to the floor.

Kal shrugged. "It's served me well so far."

Bridget poked at her phone, opening the food delivery app. "Thai or pizza?"

"Thai," Kal said, helping a scrabbling Destiny onto the sofa.

"The usual?" Bridget asked, thumbing in the order.

Kal twisted her lips and nodded. "Plus an order of mango sticky rice."

Bridget finished the order and pulled out another bottle of wine. She'd drained more bottles in the last couple of weeks than she'd consumed in the last year. She turned to find Kal curled up with Destiny. "Are you a dog person? That could be one of the few things I don't know about you."

"I don't really know. Never had one. Never dated anyone with one, now that I think about it. But this little roll of lard is damn cute."

Destiny turned and licked Kal on the chin.

"Not sure I like that part, though," Kal said, wiping at her chin.

Bridget laughed. "Like I said, she can't hold her licker."

"Now, tell me, how did one of New York's busiest basketball executives agree to dog sit?"

Bridget wiped at some crumbs on the counter. "Favor to Blake." Seconds passed and Kal said nothing. Bridget dared a glance at her best friend. "Don't look at me like that."

Kal dipped her head to Destiny. "How are we supposed to look at her, Destiny? Like after effectively ignoring her crush for years, she finally sleeps with your dad, claiming it's a one-time thing, and now you're here? That kind of look?"

"*Foster* dad and" —Bridget leaned over the counter and

183

covered Destiny's ears— "Destiny does not need to know about our . . . exploits."

"Is the dog going to tell Andrew?" Kal asked with an arched brow.

Bridget rolled her eyes. "I was trying to be funny."

"I think you better start at the beginning."

Bridget flopped down on the couch next to Kal and threw her arm over her eyes. "It's simple, really. A tale as old as time. Overworked executive loses her mind at her brother's wedding, throws all caution to wind, sleeps with one of her brother's best friends, qualifies for a free bottle of wine by completing her first Frequent Drinker card in three years, and is now 'friends' with long-time crush, and likely in love with said crush's grandfather and dog."

"You're right," Kal said. "If you take the sex part out, it's practically a Disney classic. Animal sidekick included."

Bridget grabbed a pillow from the couch and slapped Kal with it. "It's not funny."

Kal giggled. "It is, Bri. It really is."

Bridget groaned. "You know why Disney never shows what happens after they get together? It's because it looks like this." Bridget waved her hand from her chin to her waist.

"It looks like pining?"

"No." Bridget shimmied into a sitting position. "Dark circles" —she gestured to her eyes— "fatigue, heartburn, new wine habit."

"So pining."

Bridget's phone lit up with a call from the lobby. "That's our food and your chance to flirt with the delivery guy. Go get it. Please."

"Aye, aye, captain," Kal said, rising from the couch. "Think I can get us a handful of coupons again with just a smile and hair toss?"

Bridget smirked. "Hashtag life goals."

A laugh ripped from Kal. "I think you're too old to be saying things like that."

"Thanks for the reminder." She pointed at the door and circled her hand. "Think before I get and older I could eat some hot food?"

"Pining makes you cranky," Kal said, slipping out the door, just missing getting hit with the pillow Bridget threw at the door.

After a metric ton of Thai food, Bridget had walked Kal to the door and taken Destiny out for her final potty run. Now, she was in bed with team travel itineraries strewn across her lap.

The furthest paper rose and fell with Destiny's inhales and exhales. Yep, Destiny was on the bed. Her Houdini act continued last night, so Bridget gave in.

Bridget massaged her forehead, attempting to release the building tension. Between Woof Watchers event planning and having to leave work at five every night to collect Destiny, she was falling behind. Okay, not behind, exactly, but not in the position she preferred. Which, let's face it, was ahead.

Somewhere under all the paper, her phone buzzed. Didn't matter that it had never happened, Bridget always assumed a text after 11:30 at night meant someone was hurt or dead. Nervously digging for her phone, she read the screen, and her frown morphed into a smile. She forced her expression flat. She shouldn't be this excited to hear from Blake. Not pining, indeed.

The preview screen showed the entire text: *Too late for a question?*

Bridget: Is this an emergency? That's the only reason people text this late.

Blake: The only emergency is me checking to make sure my dog is still alive.

Bridget snapped a picture of Destiny, her body under the papers, her head on the pillow. *Your trust in me is shockingly low*, she typed below the photo and hit send.

Blake: She's on the bed again?

Bridget: She wore me down.

Blake: In two days? Where's the infamous Bridget Hayes' spine of steel?

Bridget: In my defense, this is the third *night. And you know what they say about the third date.*

Elena Delle Donne! Why had she said that?

I save my spine of steel for the boardroom. When it comes to something cute in my bed, my willpower goes out the window, she quickly typed.

The three dots appeared, disappeared, and appeared again. Bridget reread the message and gave herself a mental slap. She was in fine form tonight. When had she become someone who—even unintentionally—threw around innuendo?

Blake: So you think I'm cute?

How the Horace Grant was she supposed to reply to that?

She tapped her fingers against her lips. What would she do in a tense meeting?

Redirect.

Is that your one question? she thumbed in, buying herself some time.

Blake: Hmmmmmmmmmmm? No.

Bridget: Then I'm not answering it.

Blake: Chicken

Bridget: I am a middle child, stuck between two obnoxious brothers. Baiting me will not work.

Blake: Another question then?

She should say no. But somehow, cuddled in her bed with

only the light of her laptop and a small bedside lamp, it felt safe to answer his question. *Okay,* she typed, *but I want a Comic Sans credit for breaking the rules.*

Blake: Done. Did you ever attempt a comeback after the accident?

Bridget collected the papers spread over the bed. This guy didn't pull any punches. She could delay answering by acting like she didn't understand his question, but he'd already caught on to her deflection game. And there was no better time to answer that question than now, when she couldn't see his face or watch his body language change or see his expression filled with pity or worse, something that read "just get over it already."

Bridget: No. My mobility and speed likely would never have cut it and . . . She stopped typing, her fingers shaking. "You can do it, Bridget. Tell someone. Tell *him,*" she mumbled under her breath.

The phone pinged with an incoming message: *You still there?*

She curled her fingers, trying to stop the tremble. With another cleansing breath, she finished her response, deleting the "and" and replacing it with "but."

Bridget: but the issue isn't so much physical as mental.

Would he leave it at that? Not likely. He was like Destiny with a stuffed toy, chewing it until she pulled all the stuffing out, exposing the squeaker.

Blake: Maybe I should call you? Suddenly this doesn't feel like a text conversation.

Yep. He didn't leave it.

Bridget: Don't call. Please. I don't think I can talk about it. Outside of therapy, I never have.

Bridget nibbled her thumbnail. She didn't need to talk to him, but she could still tell him. Or she could shove it all back into the box in her mind that held everything painful and embarrassing. Before she could change her mind, she typed, *I'll share, if I can do it this way.*

His response came immediately. One word. *Listening.*

Bridget: I woke up in the hospital angry. I rehabbed angry. Angry at myself. Basketball was my only dream, my entire identity, and I'd destroyed it. Without the game, I didn't know who I was. You'd think that would have made me try playing again. But every time I thought about getting back on the court, I couldn't do it. Couldn't risk being devastated again.

She touched her finger to the small arrow beside her confession, sending it, and felt both raw and strangely soothed.

She waited for his response. Something that would likely chide her about dreams changing or remind her of being thankful for the career she'd had now. When his reply came, she toyed with not looking at it, but curiosity won out.

Blake: I understand wanting something so badly and not getting it. It messes with a person.

Tears burned behind her eyes. He hadn't shamed or belittled her. And somehow, in his two short sentences, she felt completely seen. She reread his words, this time feeling *his* pain.

Your mother? she typed back, pulling at the threads of the only sorrow she'd ever heard in his voice.

Blake: Yes, but more the idea of being part of a family. Gramps is fantastic, but for so much of my life, he felt just out of reach. It's why Storyhill is so important to me.

Bridget sighed. He'd told her that several times, but this was the first time she was really hearing it. For him, Storyhill wasn't just a group of friends that had grown close enough to feel like brothers. It was the place he received the love and attention he missed growing up.

Her fingers hovered over the keypad, words escaping her. She typed *Family is important.* Anything else felt like too much and not enough.

Blake: Give Destiny a goodnight kiss for me?

Seemed they'd both had enough vulnerability for one night.

Bridget: Of course. Put $20 on red for me when you get to Vegas—or whatever people who understand gambling say.

Blake. Will do. Thanks TNR. For all of it. Sleep well.

Bridget: You too.

She closed the text app and gingerly set the phone on her bedside table—as if she laid it down with too much force, everything that had just transpired between them would spill out. She rolled toward Destiny, pulled the dog to her side, and forced her mind blank, needing the respite that only a deep, dreamless sleep provided.

CHAPTER FIFTEEN

BLAKE SCRUBBED HIS HAND DOWN HIS FACE AND OPENED the curtains. More mountains. Last week it was the verdant green and soaring heights of the Rockies. Today the sun rose over shorter red rock and stubby desert scrub, punctuated by towering cacti.

They'd traveled yesterday, giving them a full day off before their first performance here in Tempe. This morning's schedule included an excursion to the Desert Botanical Garden. Blake chuckled, knowing that minutes after boarding the bus, Nick would school them on desert topography and plant life. On the two-hour trip from Boulder to Colorado Springs, Blake learned enough about Tavá Kaa-vi to make a geologist jealous.

Nick loved performing but hated leaving his son. Before leaving on tour, long or short, he and Henry learned all about Storyhill's destinations and Nick would bring back artifacts from each stop. It made the time apart easier. Then, while on the tour bus, he'd "teach" the guys all the things he'd learned. It occupied his mind, kept him from worrying about Henry and the unique rigors of being a single parent *and* a traveling musician.

While the other guys left wives and kids at home, Blake traveled untethered. Until this trip. Destiny wasn't his permanently, but right now she was his responsibility, and he felt the weight of it. For the first time, home tugged on his mind and his heart.

You sure it's Destiny tugging on your heart, a little voice asked.

He jumped when a fist pounded on his hotel room door. A deep voice hollered, "Breakfast." *Andrew.* "You in there alone, Kelly?"

"Just me and my thoughts," he said, pulling the door open.

"So entirely alone then," the bass teased, stepping inside the room.

"Ha, ha," Blake said, trying to shake the unease he felt around Andrew lately. He kept reminding himself Andrew couldn't read minds—that seemed to be his wife's talent. Blake's eyes flashed to his phone, sitting on the bedside table. Thankfully, it was face down. The last thing he needed was for Andrew to see the string of texts he and Bridget were exchanging.

Yep. He was still texting her. Every day. Sometimes several times a day. Under the guise of checking on Destiny or discussing a detail about the Woof Watchers event. Maybe the key to Blake Kelly maintaining any kind of relationship was keeping it text only.

"You ready for some bacon and carbs covered in syrup?" Andrew asked, breaking into Blake's thoughts. "And iced coffee. Nick said it's going to be about a hundred degrees today."

"I saw that." Nick had sent a group text early this morning. And had Blake pounced on his phone, hoping it was Bridget? Yes, he had. And he wasn't proud of it.

"But it's a dry heat, whatever the hell that means," Andrew said with a laugh.

Blake tucked his room key into his wallet and slipped it into his back pocket. "Yeah, I don't think that's a thing."

"We'll know after a couple of hours out in it this morning. You ready to go?"

Blake grabbed a ball cap and a tube of sunscreen approved for cave dwellers and pasty redheads. He pocketed his phone as it chirped with an incoming text. His fingers twitched to open it.

"Let's go," Andrew said. "It's probably just Nick with some fun fact about how tall saguaros grow."

"Probably," Blake said with a tremulous laugh. "But I should check. It might be Bridget with something about the dog." As soon as the words fell from his mouth, Blake went stock still.

Andrew turned to him, hand gripping the hotel room door handle. "Bridget? As in my sister?"

Shit. Shit. Shit. He'd meant to tell the guys about Destiny and the foster situation. But it never seemed to come up. *Or* he'd conveniently forgotten to mention it. "Yeah, funny story."

"Where have I heard that before?" Andrew said, his eyes narrowing.

Blake motioned for Andrew to exit the room, but he didn't move, blocking the door. "It's all tied together, actually."

"Go on."

"Remember the dog I mentioned at the restaurant?" When Andrew nodded, Blake continued. "The foster scheduled to take her when we left on tour backed out, and Woof Watchers didn't have anyone else available, so I asked Bridget to watch her."

"You asked my sister, who already has too much going on, to watch your dog?"

Blake held up his hands, palms out. "Technically, not my dog. And Bridget is only watching her at night. The dog is with Gramps during the day."

"And you've been texting about it?"

Blake shifted from one foot to the other. "That, and the Woof Watchers event."

"So, this texting is happening often?"

More often than I'll be telling you. Blake shrugged. "You know, every so often." Blake reached for the door handle again, and this time, Andrew let him pass. "You ready for that bacon?"

"I thought you needed to check that," Andrew said, pointing at Blake's pocket.

"I'll check it at breakfast," he said, opening the door and ushering Andrew out.

Andrew grunted, but followed him into the hallway. "I'm not sure I like this."

Blake didn't want to do anything to disrupt the band, but he was growing weary of Andrew's suspicion. "It's business and one friend helping another, that's all." Not the entire truth, but not a total lie either.

"It tracks. Bridget gives one hundred and ten percent to anything involving the Flames and she has a hard time saying no when someone needs her help." They walked to the elevator and Andrew punched the down button. "But maybe I should see those texts."

Irritation soared up Blake's spine. "You want to share what Grace texts you?"

Andrew had the decency to go a little pink in the cheeks. "No," he said, his deep voice falling further. "But that's different."

"The only thing that's different is that I have a healthy respect for other people's privacy," Blake said, stepping out of the elevator and scanning the lobby for directions to the café.

Andrew clapped Blake on the shoulder. "You're right, man. I'm sorry. I worry about her and I get crazy."

"You do." Blake wanted to add something about how Andrew should trust him, but that would be hypocritical after what had happened in that Minneapolis hotel room. "Sometime I'd love to know why you do that, but right now I need a stack of pancakes, a few eggs, and a gallon of coffee."

"Not sleeping well?" Andrew asked, pointing at the other members of Storyhill already occupying a corner booth.

"Not particularly," Blake said. "But it's not unusual on tour —sleeping in a different bed almost every night." Also, not a lie, but hardly the entire truth. He wasn't about to tell Andrew that he woke nightly, hard as stone, after a recurring dream about a certain brunette basketball executive.

"Did you know saguaro cacti regularly grow to forty feet tall, but the tallest one measured over seventy-eight feet?" Nick said as Blake and Andrew arrived at the table.

They turned and smirked at each other; the previous tension gone.

"Be pretty hard to get one of those in a suitcase for Henry," Matt said, pouring cream into his coffee until it could no longer be called brown.

"I'm sure the Desert Botanical Garden gift shop will have a replica," Nick said. He passed the plate of pancakes to Blake and the plate of bacon to Andrew.

Emotion welled in Blake's throat. Growing up, with his mother working late hours and weekends, this is what he craved. A place to belong. People in his life who understood how much he loved pancakes—and handed them over without needing to ask.

Storyhill had given him that place to belong. And the idea of losing it made the fluffy buttermilk pancakes turn to sawdust in his mouth.

But lately he'd started craving something else, too.

Something that could take this from him. If only he hadn't slept with her. Felt the softness of her skin. Heard her sigh into his shoulder as he wrapped his arms around her. He surveyed each of his "brothers." Would he ever know acceptance like this again? He didn't know how to do relationships, but he understood how to do this.

Or did until *she* turned his life upside down.

How could a guy who'd never had a healthy relationship modeled for him, never succeeded at one, risk all this for the slight chance that maybe something special was happening between him and Bridget?

He couldn't.

But the idea of walking away from Bridget seemed impossible, too.

He pressed his thumb into a temple, his fingers massaging along his hairline.

"Will another piece of bacon help?" Nick asked softly, holding the plate aloft.

Blake grabbed three pieces off the platter, biting the first one in half.

Nick's eyebrows shot up. "Wow. A three-piece problem. Must be a woman."

"No problem," Blake said around a full mouth. "Just like bacon."

Nick scratched his beard, cocked his head, and stared at him. "Sure. Okay. Just know that I'm here when you're ready to talk about it."

"Talk about what?" Joe said, pulling his chair closer to the table.

"Saguaro cactus," Blake said, dropping his gaze to his half-eaten pancakes.

"Yep," Nick said without missing a beat, "Blake, here, is challenging my assertion that a typical saguaro lives 100 to 200 years."

"Shit, really?" Joe said.

"Truth," Nick said. "And they can weigh more than a ton."

Blake slumped against the back of the booth and stuffed a full fork into his mouth. He knew what he needed to do. There were millions of women who weren't related to his brothers, but there was only one Storyhill. This is the place he belonged. With the family that had his back.

Any texting that wasn't about Destiny or Woof Watchers had to stop.

Blake flopped on the bed, over-baked and exhausted. The trip to the botanical garden had been awesome—especially when their guide threw up his hands and let Nick take over the tour—but he wasn't used to this kind of heat. He needed a shower and a nap before dinner.

Thirty minutes should do it. He pulled his phone from his back pocket to set an alarm, and a text from Bridget showed on his home screen. He checked the time. She'd sent it while they were walking around the botanical garden. He'd turned the ringer off, but strange that he didn't feel it vibrate.

The text was a single sentence update. *Knicks ponied up a suite—with all the food and drink—to auction off for WW!* His thumbs immediately went to the keyboard to reply, but he stopped himself. This wasn't something that needed comment. He pressed down on the message and selected the thumbs up icon.

There. He'd kept it professional. Just like he'd promised himself.

He set the timer and chucked his phone into the chair across the room, assuring he'd get up to turn it off. And, honestly, to ensure he wouldn't text her. Because not texting her was the right thing to do, even if it felt like the complete opposite.

He startled when his phone pinged. Had thirty minutes gone by already? He cracked an eye and looked at the digital clock on the bedside table. Nope. It'd been seven minutes. He scrabbled over to his phone. Maybe the guys needed something? Or Gramps?

Blake let out a groan and stared at the ceiling. Bridget. Seriously?

It was a photo of Destiny—sitting on a stool at Bridget's counter with her food bowl in front of her with the caption, *Think I'm spoiling her?*

He should just send another icon or emoji, but he couldn't do it. And, really, what was a few more texts? They were on opposite sides of the country. No harm, no foul. After the Woof Watchers event, he wouldn't need to see her. Plus, she absolutely could not let the dog eat from the counter.

He dropped into the chair. *Please tell me you are not letting her eat at the counter*, he typed. *And isn't it a little early for dinner?*

Three dots jumped immediately, and a mixture of dread and excitement corkscrewed through his chest like one of those twist cones.

Bridget: Totally staged it. Employed desperate measures since you didn't respond to my last text. And, not too early, it's 6:20 here—3 hours ahead of you.

Right. Touring always did this to him, threw off his clock and his sense of the day of the week—one day bled into another day on the road.

Blake: Didn't answer earlier b/c was busy learning all about Sonoran Desert plants.

Bridget: ???

Blake: Day off. One of those group field trips Brad loves to schedule. Thought it'd be a good idea to take my fair-ass self out into the sun in the name of team building. He attached a photo of all five guys standing in front of a giant cactus.

Bridget: Nice pic. Tho, you are a little more tomato-like than the other guys.

Blake laughed, but quickly sobered. He owed her a heads up. *FYI, I mentioned to Andrew that you're watching Destiny.*

Bridget: Did he realize it's just an extension of the WW thing or did he flip his shizzle? (Per usual)

Blake: Flipped. But small win, he seemed to calm down quicker than usual.

Bridget: Baby steps, I guess.

"Congratulate her on the Knicks thing and say goodbye," he mumbled to himself. Instead, he asked about her day. Something he'd ask any other friend.

Bridget: No cactus or sun worshipping here. Put out a fire in ticket sales and had a league-wide business meeting on Zoom. Efforts are underway to modify the league's business model. I, among others, would like to see the WNBA a little less reliant on the NBA for financing.

Blake smiled. He had no doubt she'd managed both with ease. *So, the usual then? Kicking ass and taking names,* he thumbed back.

Bridget: Living the dream.

He didn't know how to respond to that statement. Star ball player moving into the front office was usually a success story. But from their recent conversations, he wondered if it was true for her?

Blake: One question?

The three dots jumped, disappeared, and jumped again. Finally, a single word popped up. *Okay.*

Blake: I know your career didn't end the way you wanted, but are you living your dream now?

The screen remained blank. He stood from the chair and paced the length of the bed. Had he finally pushed her too far?

For someone who'd sworn off non-work-related texts, he was desperate for her to respond.

The phone pinged, and his shoulders dropped an inch.

Bridget: Yes and no.

He stared at the phone. That answer was an invitation to ask for clarification, wasn't it?

Blake: Who's being decisive now?

There. That sort of asked for more without pushing.

The phone lit up with an incoming call. Bridget. He stared at it, the refrains of a Storyhill song playing, and froze. Texting was safe. Casual. But a call? The ringtone stopped. Not cool. You asked her a very personal question and then refused to answer a call. He scrolled his recent calls and hit her number.

"Hi," she said when she answered, "That question seemed a little complicated for text, but maybe I crossed a line by calling?" she said quietly, echoing his thoughts.

"Had stepped into the bathroom," he answered, the lie tasting bitter on his tongue.

"Do you have time to talk?" she asked, sounding more tentative than usual.

"I do if you do. Got nothing until I meet the guys for dinner." A reminder of the band should keep him in check. He heard snuffles in the background. "Is that Destiny that I hear?"

Bridget laughed, and the tension hanging on the line eased a little. "I can hardly sit down before she's clamoring into my lap. Currently, there are tiny bits of kibble falling from her jowls onto my pants."

Blake chuckled. "You can forward me your dry-cleaning bills."

"No worries. I changed into yoga pants when I got home. She's got me trained."

Blake's mind immediately flashed to the soft fabric pulled

tight over Bridget's curves. He shook the "not friendly" thought from his head.

"Bet you'll be happy to give her back to me in ten days."

A sigh echoed through the phone. "I don't know. It's been nice having her. She's made me realize . . ." Her voice faded off.

"Realize what?"

"Having her here, going to Clyde's every day, it's made me see how lonely I've been. I hate to admit it, but maybe Andrew's right. Maybe I have been working too hard." She laughed. "Do not tell Andrew that I admitted he was right. He'll be insufferable."

"No way. Your secret is safe with me." He wouldn't tell Andrew anything about this conversation—for so many reasons. "And I get being lonely."

"You mentioned you were lonely as a kid. Are you still? It's hard to believe what with all the Comic Sans living and dating."

Blake fisted his fingers in his hair. How honest should he be? She'd given him an out with her Comic Sans joke. He cleared his throat and dove into the deep end. "Sometimes I'm the loneliest when I'm around friends or on a date."

If he didn't hear Destiny softly snoring, he would think the call had dropped.

"Aren't we a pair?" she finally said.

"Looks like we have more in common than we originally thought," he said, feeling equal parts nauseous and liberated by his admission.

"You mean, I haven't always been a buttoned up nine-point Times New Roman and, maybe, once in a while, you hide behind a Comic Sans mask?"

Direct hit. Her words sent a tremor through the length of his body. He wasn't sure exactly when it happened, but somewhere along the way, he'd adopted a confident, casual, nothing bothers me attitude. And people liked it. So he kept playing the role. With it, he didn't have to face more rejection. But hiding things, hiding big parts of himself deepened the loneliness.

"Maybe," he said, "but I'm far more interested in the fact that you weren't always a TNR. Is that true?"

She sighed, and he could hear her moving the mountain of pillows on her sofa. "Before the accident—Kal can confirm—I was the very definition of Comic Sans."

"You've mentioned that before. That you pushed limits. Took things for granted. What did you do?"

"Mostly stupid kid stuff. Took risks I'd never take now. When you're eighteen, nineteen, twenty years old, you think you're immortal. Until something happens that proves you're not."

"What happened, Bridget? What caused the accident?"

Silence hung like the cloying humidity right before the skies erupt into a major thunderstorm.

"If it's too hard, you don't have to talk about it."

"No, it's okay. It's just been a long time since I've talked about the details. Most of the people close to me know the story."

"I'd like to know, if you'd like to tell me."

He heard what sounded like the refrigerator door and then the unmistakable sound of a soda can being opened. He kept quiet, giving her the space to talk when she was ready.

"I'd had a terrible day. Coach had pulled me aside in practice and told me I wasn't putting in enough effort. That I might have been the best player on my college team, but here, in the WNBA, everyone was a superstar. Pieces of that day are totally lost to me, but I remember every single word she said to me." She sighed. "Probably because she was right.

"I know now that she was trying to help me elevate my game, help me transition from rookie to veteran player. But I was young, and as I've said, I took my talent for granted."

She sucked in a rattling breath, and he knew without a doubt she was struggling to hold her emotions at bay. Just when he thought she might not continue, words poured out of her.

"I was hurt and upset—so I drove out to the guy's house that I was seeing at the time. He was surprised to see me. He shouldn't have been. I did a lot of spontaneous things back then. He said he was glad I was there, but it turned out he wasn't happy to see me. My unplanned visit made it convenient for him to break up with me. He said—wait for it—" she laughed a mirthless laugh— "I was too unpredictable. He never knew when he'd see me. That I took him for granted. His words echoed Coach's.

"I needed to get out of there. I didn't want to cry in front of him. Long story short" —she exhaled, the sound was thick, like she'd started crying— "ten minutes later a minivan crossed the center line. We were the only two cars on the road. Teenage kid fumbling with his phone, they told me later. He hit me head on. Apparently, the car spun and when it hit the gravel shoulder, it flipped and rolled into the ditch, flipping several times. I totaled the car . . . and my leg."

Holy shit. He wiped away the tears tracking down his cheeks. "I thought you said the accident was your fault?"

"It was my fault. I got into a car when I was upset. I was crying, my vision was blurry."

"Bridget, honey," —the term of endearment slipping from his lips— "even if that much was true, the kid came across the center line. What could you have done?"

"I could have swerved. The ditch was deep, but likely the damage would have been less. Coach was right. My boyfriend was right. I took too much for granted. I thought I was invincible. And I lived my life that way. And it was all taken away in a moment. All those months in rehab, I promised the universe that if I walked again, I'd never be cavalier again."

He pushed out of the chair and walked to the bathroom, yanking two tissues from the standard hotel-issue box, and wiped his face. "And that's why you work so much?"

She laughed, again completely without humor. "I give all I've got to repay the Flames."

"Repay them?"

"They gave me a job when I had no idea what to do next. I didn't die in that crash, but I did kill their star point guard and greatly wounded an entire team's chance to get to the playoffs that year because of my carelessness. And they still gave me a job. They didn't need to do that."

"Shit, Bridget, that's a lot of weight to carry around. Is that why, when I asked if you're living the dream, you answered yes and no?"

She hummed. "I love my job, Blake, and I'm good at it, but playing basketball was my dream. And I didn't get to finish that dream. Plus, I've never really known if I earned the job or they just gave it to me."

"Maybe that's true about your first position, but how many promotions have you earned since then?"

"Three," she said quietly.

"Bridget," he said, his heart cracking down the center.

Destiny barked, the sound reverberating through the phone.

"She needs to go out, Blake. And, as you know, her bladder waits for no one."

"Bridget, wait," he said, knowing Destiny was a convenient excuse.

"I know you have back-to-back concerts until Vegas. I'll text if I need help on a Woof Watchers thing, otherwise you can consider no news as good news."

He could almost hear her pushing everything back inside. And he could hear it because he'd done it himself more times than he could count. He wouldn't push, but . . .

"Bridget, thanks for telling me all that."

"Yep, okay," she said, as the sound of her deadbolt unlocking echoed in the background.

"I'm here if you need to talk," he said, repeating Nick's words from earlier in the day. They'd physically crossed the line of more than friends in Minneapolis, but tonight they'd obliterated the line emotionally.

"Thanks, but I'm good," she said, her voice changing as she entered the hallway outside her apartment. "Good luck at the concerts."

"Thanks," he said, but she'd already ended the call.

CHAPTER SIXTEEN

BLAKE TOSSED HIS CARRY-ON INTO THE OVERHEAD BIN AND re-checked his boarding pass. Maybe it had magically changed in the last five minutes, and he wouldn't be sharing an armrest with Andrew. He glanced at the thin slip of paper in his hand. Nope. Still the same.

They'd left the tour bus in Los Angeles, opting for the inexpensive flight to Las Vegas. Two more concerts, then they'd all fly home for a few days of R&R. *Home.* It used to be a quick pit stop between tour dates. A time to squeeze in as many dinners as possible with Gramps, maybe tag along to a couple of bingo nights. Volunteer a few hours with Woof Watchers. Meet his mother for dinner and a drink. And then pack his bags again and get back to his real life on the road.

Now, however, thoughts of home included a portly pooch and a woman with a soft smile. Before they appeared in his life, he thought he had it all worked out—casual dating, foster dogs, on the road as much as he was home. Nothing too permanent. The perfect life. But now he wondered if his transient lifestyle was truly his dream or just the path of least resistance?

"You look like hell," Andrew said as Blake dropped into the seat beside him.

"Yeah. Still not sleeping much."

"Because you went out last night?" Joe called from behind Andrew.

Matt peeked his head in between the seats. "And a woman kept you up?"

Yes. But not in the way you're thinking. He couldn't admit that dreams replaying their night in Minneapolis had been replaced with Bridget achingly retelling the story of her accident. The sound of her voice. Her misguided belief that somehow, she was entirely responsible for the end of her playing career. For the accident. And when that conversation wasn't playing on repeat, he chided himself for getting this deeply involved with her. This deeply *connected.*

Plus, there was the fact that in the last week, he'd only heard from her once. To get his approval on an event vendor. He'd picked up his phone to text her so many times. But he'd always set it back down, wanting to respect that she might need some space after their intense conversation.

Blake pinched the bridge of his nose. "I did not go out and I wasn't with a woman, you band of idiots. Can't a guy just have a restless night?"

"*Band* of idiots," Nick chortled from across the aisle. "That's a good pun."

"Not meant to be," Blake said, letting his head fall to the headrest.

Nick shrugged. "Just saying."

"Nick would know. He is the undisputed king of dad jokes," Matt said, poking a finger into Nick's shoulder.

"If you think that's an insult, Mattie, try again," Nick said, never looking up from his book.

"It's not even nine am. Why are you guys so chatty?" Blake said.

Their manager, Brad Rodgers, came down the aisle, handing each of them a single sheet of paper. "You look like hell," he said to Blake.

"That seems to be the consensus," Blake mumbled.

"You've got about an hour and fifteen from here to Vegas. Try to get some rest. We've got a full couple of days." Brad tapped on the paper in Blake's hand—an updated itinerary—that now included a video shoot. This afternoon. In the desert. Super.

Andrew leaned over. "You sure you're okay? Tired is one thing, but I've never seen you in a wrinkled shirt. This situation" —Andrew tugged at the tail of Blake's untucked oxford— "causes me serious concern."

And your sister is causing me some. But no way he was admitting that aloud. Though, if he did, the plane could probably make it to Vegas on Andrew's righteous indignation alone.

"No worries," Blake said, slipping in his AirPods. "Quick nap and I'll be good as new."

"Dude," Nick said when Blake walked into him, nearly knocking him into the revolving door.

Blake gave his head a little shake. "Sorry." Turns out a bumpy flight from the City of Angels to Sin City does not make one good as new.

They exited the door and Nick wrapped his hand around Blake's forearm, stilling him. "You're acting like Andrew when he met Grace or Matt after he'd learned Avery was his new co-host. Is there something you'd like to share with me?"

Should he tell Nick? Get someone else's opinion? He scanned the lobby. The other three members of Storyhill were a rooms-length away at the hotel check-in desk. Nick *was* the most discreet among them. But admitting his growing feelings for Bridget still felt too risky.

Nick's brows dropped, and his eyes narrowed. He also had the most sensitive bullshit meter in the group. Thankfully, he was saved from whatever Nick was about to say when Joe handed them each a room key and Brad yelled, "Huddle up, we need to talk itinerary."

"I noticed a video shoot on today's schedule," Blake said, happily turning away from Nick's perceptive gaze. "What's that all about?"

"A few minutes outside of town is the perfect location to shoot a video for 'Under a Desert Moon.' We'll meet back here" — Brad gestured to the lobby of their newest, and last, hotel stop on the tour— "in two hours. Lunch will be on location and Julia has coordinated wardrobe. She'll bring items to your individual rooms in a few minutes. The rest of the schedule is standard. You'll find call times on the sheet I gave you on the plane. Questions?"

"No," they all said in unison.

They crowded into a single elevator and dispersed when the doors opened on the eleventh floor. Reaching his room, Blake tossed his bag on the hotel luggage rack and went about hanging up his clothes in the small closet. After twelve years on the road, he did it without thinking.

He glimpsed himself in the mirror and groaned. The guys were right, he did look like hell. He yanked the iron and ironing board from the closet. He might not be able to do anything about the circles under his eyes, but he could do something about the wrinkles in his shirt. He didn't get it. People always said love was supposed to give you energy, make you feel good.

He stopped in the middle of the room, iron dangling from his fingers. *Love?* Where the hell had that come from? He wasn't in love with Bridget. Couldn't be in love with her. No, no, no, just no.

A knock rapped against his door, and he nearly jumped out of his skin. "Shake it off, man, you're just tired," he mumbled.

"Blake, it's Jules."

He stumbled to the door and pulled it open, thankful for something, anything else, to think about. "Hey Jules." He pointed at the dry-cleaning bags slung over her shoulder. "What delight do you have for me this time?"

She extracted the bag marked "B" and held it out to him.

He reached for it, and she pulled it back. "Wait. No flirty comment about the B standing for beautiful or bewitching?"

He sighed. "Not today."

"Bewildering," she said, smirking.

A soft laugh fell from his lips and some of the tension in his chest eased. "I see what you did there, Jules. Very clever. Now what's under the plastic?"

She winced and handed him the hanger.

"Seriously? Embroidered chambray with pearl snaps?" He was tired, but he'd have to be dead not to be slightly scandalized about wearing a denim country shirt from—he tore the plastic to reveal the tag—he couldn't even say the name.

"I just follow the brief. And aren't you always telling me it's your confidence that makes you sexy?" She rolled her lips in, clearly biting back a smile.

That is what he'd normally say, but today he was lucky to manage a shrug and a weak wink.

She pulled back, lifted to her toes, and placed her hand on his forehead. "Are you sick? You are seriously freaking me out."

"Just tired," he said for what felt like the millionth time.

"Okay," she said, still searching his face. "If you're sure?"

"I'm sure. Thanks for the, um, shirt, Jules."

"Would it help if I sewed in a Tom Ford label or put a polo player on the pocket?"

He laughed, a real one, and her shoulders eased. "And take attention away from this beautiful embroidery?"

"Okay, I can leave now that I've seen a glimpse of the real Blake Kelly." She headed down the hall, hollering back, "Pair it with the darkest jeans you have along."

He nodded and let the door fall shut, wondering how much of the real Blake Kelly they could handle. Before he decided, his phone vibrated. He pulled it from his back pocket and nearly dropped it.

It was a text from Bridget. After nearly four days of silence. "Calm down, it's probably just a message about the event," he chided. But when he opened it, it was a short video of Destiny's head trotting down the sidewalk, a toy he didn't recognize in her mouth. The caption read, *On our way home from Clyde's. Via the pet store.*

He wanted so desperately to ask how she was, to apologize for pushing her to tell the accident story, but he settled for, *Did you buy her a new toy?*

Her response was immediate. *I gave her the choice of a basketball or a stuffed microphone. She chose correctly.*

Blake laughed, making a mental note to buy the microphone toy as soon as he got home. He'd do his own test to see which toy their dog truly preferred. His smile slipped. *Their* dog. Destiny wasn't *their* dog. She wasn't even his dog. Someone could adopt her at any point. The reminder hit him like a punch to the gut. How could he be in love with Bridget when he couldn't even manage a long-term relationship with a *dog*?

He pressed down on the photo of Destiny to enlarge it. Maybe there was a way to keep her.

Which her? the little voice that was becoming more and more of a nuisance prodded.

That troubling thought was interrupted by a second text flashing across his screen.

Bridget: You're in Vegas now, right? Have you won any money for me yet?

Ignoring the pounding in his chest that ratcheted up with every new interaction with Bridget, he quickly typed back, *Got here about an hour ago. No time to gamble. Brad scheduled a video shoot this afternoon/evening.*

Bridget: I forget what you're doing is "work."

Blake: Wasn't it Snoop Dogg that said, "If you love what you do, you'll never work a day in your life."

Bridget: Pretty sure that was Mark Twain.

Blake: Right. Right. I mix up the great writers.

Bridget: Ha! Enjoy the shoot, Blakey.

Blake: Blakey? Now I know you're spending too much time with Gramps.

He waited for a response and when none came, he ignored the disappointment gathering in his chest and headed for the shower.

"I think that's a wrap," the video production manager called out.

Blake exhaled, pulling the snaps of his shirt open in one go, exposing the t-shirt beneath. Even with the sun dipping in the sky, the desert temperatures had only slipped from blistering inferno to pot ready to boil over.

"Wait," Matt yelled, "let's get a selfie for social media."

"It's too damn hot, Mattie," Blake grumbled. "Can we at least do it under the tent?" Blake pointed at the small canopy erected over top of the camera equipment and food.

The guys tromped to the edge of the shade, turning their backs on the desert scene. Matt held up his phone, angled it several ways before handing it to Andrew, standing on the end, to take the shot.

"Mattie," Andrew said with a sigh. "Your phone died."

"Use mine," Blake said, passing his phone to Andrew, "so we can get this done and get out of this heat."

Andrew grabbed it and flashed it in front of Blake's face to unlock it. He held it up and lowered it, staring at the screen.

"What the hell, Blake? You've been texting my sister?"

Blake blew out a breath. He was exhausted, sweaty, and in a shirt clearly made from synthetic materials. He was done. With this shoot. And with Andrew's bullshit. But he was the peacekeeper, the guy who didn't rock the boat, so he pulled in a breath and grabbed for his phone. "We've already discussed this, Andrew. We are working on that event together and she has my foster dog," he said, his voice as steady as he could make it.

Andrew held the phone out of reach. "You said you were texting occasionally" —he swiped a finger over the screen— "this looks like you've been texting several times a day, *every* day."

Something snapped in Blake. Calm, cool, and collected Blake Kelly had just located his breaking point—something he wasn't even aware he had. He stepped up to Andrew and ripped the phone from his hand. "Enough," he growled.

"You lied to—"

"Stop," Blake roared, causing everyone to turn to him. Blake never raised his voice. Ever. "Of course I lied to you. It's not like you gave me another choice. You don't even see her. She's a kick-ass businesswoman who beat incredible odds and you treat her like she's fragile and can't handle her own life. And you think I'm" — he shoved a finger into his own chest— "some sort of giant asshole who would take advantage of her. News flash, Andrew, NO ONE takes advantage of Bridget Hayes."

"So you *do* want to be with my sister?" Andrew said.

Blake shoved his hands into his hair and pulled. "Maybe,"

he yelled, letting some truth drip out. "But that's not what this is about!"

"Then what is it?" Andrew's voice raised to match Blake's.

"That you're out of touch with reality. That somehow you get to decide what's best for her. That you don't trust her. *Or me.* That you'll call me 'brother,' but won't trust me with other members of your family." He dropped his voice, his chest heaving. "It's really shitty that the people I love most in this world" —he gestured to the group— "think I'm an inconsiderate jerk. That I'm not good enough." Blake turned, grinding his heel in the sand.

Andrew's head snapped back, his expression full of surprise. "Blake, wait, it's just that—"

Blake stepped up to Andrew, inches from his face. "If you're thinking of telling me I don't understand because I don't have siblings, because I don't have a family, I'd think twice," he growled through clenched teeth.

Blake stormed toward the van, registering Joe's low words to Andrew. "Let him go."

He hopped into the passenger seat, unwilling, and unable, to face his bandmates. He sat silently as everyone got into the van and the driver pulled out. Outside the windows, the twisting roads and bleak landscape were the perfect metaphor for his feelings. The desert giving way to the assault of colors fighting for attention on the Strip mirrored his thoughts—loud, congested, and all over the map.

Back at the hotel, Nick had straightened an arm, barring his bandmates from entering the elevator, allowing Blake to ride solo.

The elevator beeped rapidly, not stopping between the lobby and the eleventh floor. Odd for a Vegas hotel. Seemed the entire city knew he needed time to collect himself. Time to be alone.

But apparently, time alone was a euphemism for frantically pacing.

He desperately needed a shower, but his feet and his thoughts wouldn't stop moving. One minute, he angrily decided he didn't need any of his bandmates. The next, his stomach squeezed at the possibility that he'd blown up the only family he'd ever known. And somewhere in between, he paused with the thought that maybe Bridget could be his family.

But how realistic was that? Sure, it was obvious she was attracted to him, but attraction wasn't love. And he'd shown her all his broken parts. Who wanted a guy who admittedly didn't know the first thing about being in a committed relationship?

He paced from the door to the window, contemplating the other thing his outburst might have cost him—his job. Yes, Story-hill was his family, but they were also how he paid his bills. He could go solo. He had the talent and, he thought with a humorless laugh, his mother had the connections. Wouldn't that be rich, after years of complaining about her insistence on the importance of networking, that he'd have to ask her for help?

But he really didn't want to be a solo act. He'd spent his childhood alone and had no desire to start down that path again.

It felt like his skull—and his heart—were cracking open. He stuffed his phone and key card in his pocket, his only destination being "out."

He wandered the casino, weaving through the labyrinth of slot machines before finally sitting down in front of video poker. He played long enough to consume three and a third, free, fuchsia-colored cocktails, win $458, and avoid dinner with the guys.

Figuring it was late enough to get back upstairs without being seen, he gave a large tip to his server, and walked a mostly straight line to his room, praying the upside to strangely flavored pink drinks was a full night of dreamless sleep.

The next morning, instead of joining the group for breakfast, he slept in, showered, and wandered the Strip in search of the biggest, cheapest breakfast buffet he could find. Not his best decision. The all-day breakfast of steak and eggs for $6.99 with country potatoes and toast on the side mixed with remnants of pink drinks and a stomach full of panic turned out to be a volatile combination.

Lumbering back to the hotel, his phone pinged, and his heart leaped. Maybe it was a text from Bridget? He covered the screen with his hand, trying to block out the blinding Vegas sun. It wasn't Bridget, it was a calendar reminder of his call time. He picked up the pace, because while he didn't know exactly what would greet him in the green room, he wasn't about to make things worse by missing run-through.

When he pushed open the door, all eyes turned to him and the silence in the room hung heavy. The perfect reminder of why he'd hidden his attraction to Bridget for so long, why he buried his anger deep, and why he never set his expectations too high.

Calm-and-casual Blake got to keep his friends. Hot-headed Blake risked everything.

He opened his mouth to speak, but Nick beat him to it. "The guys and I have been talking and we'd—"

"How about we get through this concert and then we can talk about my role in the band?" Blake said, unable to meet anyone's eyes.

"What?" four voices said in unison.

Blake pushed his spine against the nearest wall, needing the extra support. "I never want to be the reason for issues in the group and if one of us needs to go, it should be me."

"Andy," Joe said, pushing Andrew forward.

Andrew cleared his throat. "It's been brought to my attention, by them" —Andrew gestured to the group— "and my wife, that I've been acting like a horse's ass. And I'm sorry. Truly."

"Grace weighed in?" Blake asked, unable to process that *Andrew* was apologizing instead of him.

Andrew nodded. "She said, and I quote, 'You're acting like some toff in a regency romance who's trying to take away a woman's agency,' whatever the hell that means."

"And not being a very good friend," Matt added.

"Mattie," Nick said, shaking his head.

"What?" Matt said with a shrug. "That's what she said."

"She did," Joe said, clasping Matt's shoulder and pulling him back. "But this is between Andy and Blake. Let them work it out."

"Matt's right and so is Grace. I've been a shit friend. I let the lingering fear of losing Bridget color everything." Andrew paced, pulled his long hair behind his head, and let it drop. "Blake, I need you to hear this. No one would ever ask you to leave the band," he said, closing the distance between them. "Do you know why? Because we're family and families fight, but they still love each other. I know you don't have experience with that—"

Blake met his gaze, his brows pulling together.

"Right. Not supposed to bring up the family thing. And I'm not saying I can change the Bridget thing overnight—"

"Or ever," Matt said.

"Mattie!" Joe and Nick chorused.

Andrew placed his hands on Blake's shoulders. "But," he continued, "I will try, and more than anything, I'd like your forgiveness."

Blake dropped into the nearest chair. Of all the scenarios he'd imagined, this was not one of them. The panic that coursed through his system for the last twenty-four hours rushed out. His body felt like it'd been through the wringer and spit out the other side. He couldn't believe it. They didn't want him to leave?

"And?" This time it was Joe chiming in.

"And," Andrew gritted out between clenched teeth. "If you and Bridget want to be together, it's none of my business."

At that declaration, Blake's head popped up. He didn't know what, if anything, Bridget wanted from him, but he was relieved knowing the possibility of having the band and Bridget existed.

"It's none of my business, *mostly*," Andrew added.

"Mostly?" Blake asked, his voice low and raspy.

Andrew chuckled. "She's still my baby sister. And what's that saying? A tiger can't change its spots overnight?"

Blake smiled—for the first time in what felt like a very long time. "A tiger has stripes, not spots, but I get your meaning." He stood and extended his hand to Andrew. "I accept your apology, *brother*," he added with emphasis. "And I owe all of you an apology as well" —his eyes fell to each band member— "I'm sorry I lost it out there."

"It's cool," Matt said. "We all agreed at dinner last night that we're relieved."

Blake's eyes widened. "Relieved?"

"Yeah," Joe said. "We've always thought it was a little weird how you never get mad. After yesterday, we know you're human, just like the rest of us."

Blake smirked. "Well, maybe a *little* more like the rest of you. Let's not get crazy. I'm still the most exceptional guy in the group."

After the laughter died down, Matt asked, "Can we finally take that selfie now?"

"I thought the purpose of that pic was to capture the desert," Nick said.

"This green room is pretty bleak," Matt said, gesturing to the sparse décor. "Especially for Vegas."

They stepped together just as Blake's phone rang. Not a

text, but an actual phone call. It was likely not important—the people closest to him were in this room or knew it was almost concert time.

He went to flip the ringer to silent, but the name on the screen caught his attention. "It's Bridget," he said. Out loud.

"Can I talk to her?" Andrew said.

"Why?" Blake asked, voice laced with suspicion.

"Since I'm already in groveling mode, might as well apologize to her too."

Blake swiped the screen to answer. "Hi Bridget, Andrew's here and wants to say a few words really quick." He handed his phone to Andrew.

"Hi Bridgie, I want to . . . yes, okay, but if I could just . . . I know, but it'll only take . . ."

"ANDY, SHUT THE HELL UP AND PUT BLAKE ON THE FUCKING PHONE!" Bridget's voice rung through the space.

"She cursed," Matt and Joe whispered in unison.

Andrew's eyes were enormous as he handed the phone back to Blake.

"Hey Bridget, that was some lang . . . what?" Blake felt the color drain from his face, and he reached for the chair behind him, dropping into it. "Oh my god, is he . . ." He nodded, barely able to process her words. "Where . . ." His hand shook so hard, he could barely hold the phone. "Is my mother . . . Right. Okay, I'll be there as soon as I can." He ended the call and sat staring into space, unable to move.

"Is it the dog?" Andrew asked.

"Do you need a flight home?" Nick asked, already scrolling on his phone.

"Not the dog." He turned to look at Nick. "Yes, I need a flight."

"What happened?" Matt asked, crouching next to Blake.

Tears burned behind his eyes. "Gramps had a heart attack."

"Nick, book the next the flight to NYC," Joe said. "I'll find Brad and have him order a car from here and from Kennedy."

The tears spilled over. "But what about the concert?"

"Matt and Nick can cover any of your leads, or I could shock the crowd and prove I can sing up there, too." Andrew smiled. "You go, we've got it covered."

"Because that's what family does," Nick said without looking up from his phone.

"Because that's what family does," Andrew repeated.

CHAPTER SEVENTEEN

BRIDGET ALTERNATED BETWEEN SITTING, MINDLESSLY flipping through months old magazines, and pacing the small waiting room. She kept seeing Clyde slumped in his chair, his face growing paler, the pain evident in his expression.

The ambulance arrived in minutes, but it felt like hours. When the EMTs asked if she was family, Clyde had nodded, fear in his eyes, and she'd gone along with the lie, telling them she was his granddaughter-in-law.

A heart attack and a marriage all in one day. Big day.

She'd climbed into the ambulance, holding his hand, whispering things she hoped were true. She'd waited to call Blake until the ER doc came out and gave her an update. They were taking Clyde for an angioplasty or surgery if the results warranted it.

Bridget pressed a hand to her belly. The sounds and smells of the hospital were making her stomach churn and bringing back memories she'd rather not revisit. She hadn't set foot in a hospital since being discharged after the accident.

But every time the nausea rose, she reminded herself that

until Blake arrived, she was all Clyde had and she could power through the memories.

Blake texted a brief message from the Las Vegas airport saying he'd be there in five hours and that he'd been unable to get through to Bette, who was currently in Paris on business.

It was her and Destiny until then.

She stopped pacing. *Destiny.* She'd left the dog alone in Clyde's apartment. And she didn't know how long she'd need to stay here. She rummaged through her bag for her phone and the apartment key Clyde had given her this morning, claiming she didn't need to knock every time she brought Destiny.

Best friend SOS, she thumbed in, and prayed Kal had wrapped tonight's broadcast.

The response was immediate. *What do you need?*

Bridget: Are you free right now?

Kal: I can be.

Bridget: It's a long story, but can you meet me at Mount Sinai ASAP?

Bridget: I'm okay, she quickly added.

Kal: Thanks for the second text—I can breathe again. I'm in Midtown. I'll be there in under 20.

Bridget: Thanks. Text me when you're 5 minutes away. I'll meet you in the lobby.

She explained her situation to the team at the nurses' station and they handed her a pager, promising to buzz her when they had news about Clyde. She slipped inside the elevator doors as they closed and punched the button for the lobby. For a brief few moments, the sounds and smells of the hospital faded away. Though maybe that was because the guy standing in the opposite corner of the elevator reeked of weed. Bridget didn't know whether to laugh or inhale deeply.

She didn't have time to decide as the doors popped open, and the guy sprinted for the entrance. She wandered into the middle of the hallway, knowing she couldn't leave, but unable to sit down either. People flowed around her as she tried to get her feet to do something. Anything.

Kal flew through the sliding glass door and let out a visible sigh when she caught sight of Bridget. She put her hands on Bridget's cheeks, staring into her eyes. "You're really okay?"

"Physically I'm great."

Kal led her around a tropical fish tank to a nearby sofa and guided her down. "Mentally?"

Bridget wheezed out a breath. "Not as much."

"Why are you here?"

Bridget glanced at the pager in her hand. No lights flashing. "Clyde—Blake's grandfather—had a heart attack."

Kal's brow furrowed. "And *you're* here because?"

"Blake's in Vegas with Storyhill, well, he's on his way back from Vegas, and his mother is in Paris," she rattled off, adrenaline still pumping through her. "I picked up Destiny after work and Clyde didn't look good. Said he'd been feeling off all day. I made him dinner and when he still didn't look good, I stayed. He stood to walk me and Destiny out and grabbed his left arm and nearly crumpled to the floor. Somehow, I got him to his recliner, but . . ."

Kal strung an arm around Bridget's shoulder. "Take a breath."

Bridget bobbed her head, sucking in and blowing out the biggest breath she could manage. "I hate hospitals," she whispered.

"I know. I know," Kal said, wrapping her arms around Bridget and rocking slightly side-to-side.

"He told the EMTs I was family and he looked so scared, I couldn't leave him. So I said I was married to Blake and they let me ride in the ambulance." Tears welled in her eyes, threatening to spill over.

Kal pulled a package of tissues from her bag, handing them to Bridget. "I bet that was terrible."

She balled her fists, trying to stem the trembling. "I was so focused on keeping Clyde calm, I didn't even think about my last ride in an ambulance."

"That's good, I guess. Though I'm pretty angry about not being invited to the wedding."

An unsteady laugh gurgled from Bridget. "If it makes you feel better, I don't really remember it, either."

Kal nodded sagely. "Because of all the Jägermeister you drank that night?"

Another laugh fell from her mouth, this one a little stronger. "You're the world's greatest friend. You know that, right?"

"I do." Kal swiped a thumb over Bridget's cheeks, wiping away the tears. "Now, what do you need?"

Bridget looked at Kal's TV-ready outfit. "Are you free right now?"

"I am. I finished five minutes before your text."

Bridget pulled a key from her pocket and pressed it into Kal's palm. "Destiny is at Clyde's apartment. Any chance you could go get her? As soon as Blake gets here, I'll come and collect her."

"I have no idea what to do with a dog, but of course I will."

The pager in Bridget's fist lit up and vibrated. "That's the nurses' station. I have to go." She quickly texted Clyde's address to Kal. "Destiny's bag is right next to the door. It's black and white with dog bones all over it. And grab her food and water bowl from the kitchen."

"Go," Kal said. "I'll figure it out."

"Thank you." And with a squeeze of Kal's hand, Bridget ran down the hallway and into an open elevator.

The doors opened and she sprinted to the nurses' station.

"Someone paged me," Bridget said, trying to release her death grip on the buzzing device. "About Clyde Kelly."

The nurse smiled softly. "Mr. Kelly is back in his room and the doctor is with him. She can fill you in on your grandfather."

"In-law. My grandfather in-law." Bridget didn't know why she felt the need to explain that, but she was sure the nurses heard all kinds of weird stuff.

Bridget turned, looking up and down the long white tile corridors. A pair of soft hands turned her toward the left. "Room 425."

"Thank you."

"I can take the pager now," the nurse said, holding out her hand.

Bridget handed it to her, stretching out her fingers.

She slowed as she came to the room. Clyde was hooked up to all kinds of tubes and monitors. Bridget's stomach threatened to empty itself all over the floor for about the hundredth time since arriving. *You can do this, Bridget. For Clyde.*

She fixed her attention on the doctor standing behind a rolling cart holding a laptop. "Hi," she said, pushing out the sound. "The nurse told me you could give me an update on Clyde. I'm Bridget Hayes," she added.

"Ah, yes," the doctor said, smiling softly, "the basketball player. I'm Dr. Singh—and a Flames season ticket holder." She pulled the surgical cap from her dark hair. "It appears Mr. Kelly had a few heart attacks—"

"*A few?*"

"Yes, I'm guessing from what you told the EMTs, he'd been having them throughout the day. We did the angioplasty, hoping we could solve the issue with stents, but his blockage was too severe. We performed a triple bypass, and he handled the surgery well."

"Thank you," Bridget whispered, not sure what else to say. "What now?"

"We'll try to rouse him over the next hour and then, because of his age, we'll keep him here for a few days."

Bridget smirked. "If you can."

Dr. Singh smiled knowingly. "Bit feisty, is he?"

Bridget nodded. "Feisty might be an understatement. That's why this doesn't make sense to me. Outside of a bacon habit, he eats well and walks daily."

"Coronary artery disease has a large genetic component so that, along with his age, may be the root cause."

"Can I stay with him?" She understood how frightening it was to wake up in a hospital, not immediately remembering how you got there.

"Of course," Dr. Singh said, pointing to a large recliner in the room's corner.

"Thank you," Bridget said again.

"Thank *you*, Ms. Hayes. If you hadn't been there and acted so quickly, we'd likely be having a very different conversation."

The tears welled again and a lump clogged Bridget's throat. She could only nod.

"The nurses will be in shortly to take vitals and start waking him."

Bridget dropped into the chair, sent Kal an update, and texted Blake that Clyde was in the cardiac unit, 4th floor. He'd see it when he landed.

The nurse came in, pushing yet another cart with a laptop positioned on top. After checking several monitors, she squeezed Clyde's hand. "Mr. Kelly, you're at Mount Sinai and we'd like to see your sparkling eyes." She tapped a little harder.

"Bridget," he mumbled, eyes still closed.

"She's here, Clyde. If you want to see her, you'll have to open your eyes." The nurse motioned for Bridget to come to the bedside. Her emotions ping ponged between feeling like a fraud to just so happy someone was here for him—even if it was a fake relative.

"Talk to him," the nurse mouthed.

"Hi, Clyde, it's Bridget. I know the Kellys are not fond of rules, but the nurses would really like you to wake up."

"Where's Destiny?"

The nurse raised an eyebrow and Bridget nodded, trying to communicate he was making sense.

"My friend Kal picked her up. She's safe. Kal texted me a picture. I can show you if you open your eyes."

He squirmed, the bed sheets rustling around him, but his eyes remained firmly closed.

"You are connected to a lot of things right now, Mr. Kelly. It's best you don't move too much," the nurse said, placing a hand on his shoulder.

He drifted back to sleep until Bridget got an idea. "Clyde, you don't want to miss the pretty nurse, do you?"

His eyes popped wide, and Bridget stifled a laugh. His eyes shifted to where the nurse stood. "Can I have my glasses?"

The nurse nodded and pulled a large blue and white plastic bag marked "Personal Belongings" from underneath the bed. She extracted the glasses, placing them on his face, careful to slide them under the tubes coming from his oxygen cannula. "Better?" she asked.

His eyes swiveled back to Bridget. "I feel like I've been hit by a car."

And just like that, Bridget's nausea returned, and she fought the urge to run. Again. She pushed the images out of her mind and focused on Clyde. "No cars involved," she said, her voice trembling. "But you have had an exciting last few hours."

The nurse moved into his vision. "Do you remember what happened, Mr. Kelly?"

His fingers hovered over his chest. "Chest pain. And this beautiful lady" —he looked at Bridget— "was my angel. My grandson has exquisite taste."

"Very good," the nurse said, typing something into his chart. "You had a heart attack and one of our talented cardiac surgeons fixed you up. We want you to stay awake for a little while and then you can rest again. Okay?"

"Aye, aye, captain," Clyde wheezed out, attempting a small salute.

She smiled and repositioned the pulse oximeter on his finger. "I'll be back in a few minutes."

Bridget leaned in and whispered, "You know that Blake and I are not together, right?"

His eyes came together, three lines forming between his white bushy brows. "I have no memory of any such thing."

When Bridget looked at him with concern, he managed a very slow wink.

"Not funny, Clyde. You have a substantial incision down the middle of your chest. Laughing will hurt."

"Not until the drugs wear off, doll."

"The Kelly men are going to be the death of me," Bridget grumbled.

Clyde scanned the room. "Where is Blakey?"

"He's on his way back from Vegas." She glanced at the clock hanging over the door. "He'll be here soon."

"Maybe I'll rest until then," he said, his eyes drooping.

"The nurse wanted you to stay awake for a little while longer. How about one episode of *Diners, Drive-ins, and Dives*?"

He nodded and she knew that she'd be lucky to get another five minutes out of him.

. . .

Bridget startled at the sound of a familiar voice. She'd moved the chair next to Clyde's bed, per his request. Her fingers were still twined in his, but apparently, they'd both fallen asleep.

"I'm looking for my grandfather. Clyde Kelly?" the familiar voice said.

"He's in room 425. Your wife is in there with him."

"My wife."

Thankfully, he'd said it as a statement, not a question. She didn't have the emotional bandwidth right now to get called out on her lie.

"She's been here since the ambulance brought them in."

"Them?"

Bridget imagined the nurses were currently looking at him like he was a couple of pieces shy of a complete puzzle. She slowly slid her hand from Clyde's and stepped into the hallway.

She walked the six paces to station and placed a hand on Blake's arm. "I'm glad you're here."

Blake spun and gathered her in his arms, dropping his head to her shoulder. And not one part of it felt like play-acting.

"Hey," she said, pulling back. "He's alive and his prognosis, according to the doctor, is good."

"Thanks to your wife," the nurse said with a small smile.

Blake searched her face. So many emotions passed over his face, so quickly, she didn't catch any of them.

"Apparently, I'm quite skilled at dialing 911," she said.

"Do not make light of this." He pulled her a few steps away from the nurses' station. "I can only imagine how hard it is for you to be here. Hospitals and ambulances don't exactly have the best memories for you."

She dropped his gaze. This had been one of the hardest things she'd done in a long time. "It's not about me."

His gaze flashed to the open door. "Is he awake?"

"In and out. Anesthesia is still wearing off."

And his eyes were back on her. "Anesthesia?"

"How about we let him sleep a while longer and I'll bring you up to speed? And then you can go see him. He's been asking for you."

He fisted his fingers in his hair, making it stand on end. "He has?"

"Well, he asked for me and Destiny first, but you were a close third."

A small smile tugged at the corners of his lips. "If I didn't know his penchant for beautiful women, I'd be offended." His smile slipped away as quickly as it had appeared. "I didn't know my mother was going out of town. Why didn't I know that?"

Bridget followed the non sequitur, fully aware of the way thoughts jumped and jumbled in high-stress situations. "Because you're not her keeper? And before you go blaming yourself for anything else, no one could have predicted this."

"He has regular check-ups, walks every day, eats mostly healthy," Blake said, following her into the small family room behind the nurses' desk. "I don't get it."

She smiled, squeezing his hand. "That's exactly what I said to the surgeon. She told me it was probably genetic, and Clyde likely blamed any unusual symptoms on aging."

He leaned forward and she brushed back the hair that fell over his forehead. He closed his eyes at her touch. "I know he's not a young man, but I'm not prepared for this."

"Blake," she said, sliding next to him and placing her hand on his thigh. He quickly covered her hand with his own. "No one is ever prepared. And it's normal to be scared."

"Mr. Kelly," a man with stethoscope and heart-patterned scrubs interjected from the hallway. "Your grandfather is awake and asking for you."

"Love your scrubs," Bridget said, knowing Blake needed a minute.

"If you like these," he said, "you should see my socks." He lifted a pant leg to expose black and white socks covered with EKG lines and dancing hearts.

Bridget laughed. "You are exceptionally on-brand."

He shrugged. "No one ever knows what to get me for Hanukkah or my birthday. I don't know where they find them, but I have an entire drawer full of these things." His gaze landed on Blake, still bent over his knees, weight braced on his forearms. "I'll tell Mr. Kelly you're on your way."

Bridget ran a hand down Blake's back. "You ready to go see him?"

Blake drew in a breath and nodded.

"Then I'll be on my way."

"No!"

Her eyes went wide.

"Stay with me. Please." He grabbed her hand, holding on tight.

Her eyes dipped to their entwined hands. "Okay. I'll come in for a little while."

They rounded the corner, and Clyde's eyes drifted to the door. And then to their joined hands.

"Hey Gramps, you're awake." Blake said, stopping inside the door.

Bridget nudged him. "Have a seat," she said, pointing at the chair she'd been sitting in.

"Blakey," Clyde said, "you look like hell. What happened to your hair?"

Blake laughed, running a hand over his face. "You've aged me ten years, Gramps."

"You?" Clyde said. "Look at me. Good thing the ladies at bingo can't see me now. Sharon likes me because I'm the young, virulent one."

"Wait until she realizes Dr. Singh just improved your blood flow," Bridget said with a wink.

"I'm not ready for jokes," Blake said. "And I may never be ready for jokes like that one," he added, pointing a finger at Bridget.

"Now, Blakey, don't be talking to my granddaughter-in-law like that," Clyde said with a grin.

"Didn't you just have open heart surgery?" Blake asked, shaking his head. "Shouldn't you be more sedate?"

"It's actually a great sign that he's alert," a nurse said, entering the room and washing her hands at the sink. "I'm Peg Morrison," she said, "and I'll be taking care of Mr. Kelly for the rest of my shift." She moved to Clyde's bedside and checked the myriad of hoses and tubes connected to him.

"If it hasn't already, the anesthesia will wear off soon," she said, directing her comments to Clyde. "We want to keep you comfortable. If you need some medication for pain, punch this button," she said, demonstrating to Clyde.

"Can he take too much?" Blake said, watching the nurse's movements.

"No," Bridget answered without thinking. "It only allows a certain amount over a designated span of time."

"That's right. Are you in the medical field?" Peg asked, spinning to face Bridget.

Bridget forced out a small laugh. "No, just an experienced hospital visitor."

She nodded, not probing for more information. "I realize you just arrived, and you are free to stay, but I'd recommend going home and getting some rest. The best thing for Clyde right now—and both of you—is sleep."

"You okay with me leaving, Gramps?" Blake asked, clearly torn between wanting to stay and in desperate need of some rest.

"Peg looks qualified," he said, his usual smirk playing at his lips.

"You'll call if anything changes?" Blake asked the nurse.

"Absolutely. And they'll want to get him up tomorrow" — she flipped her wrist, checking her watch— "or rather later today. You can come back and help with that."

"Bridget," Clyde peered around Blake. "Will you come back too?"

She stepped up to the bed and placed her hand over Clyde's. "If you'd like that, yes."

"Yes?" Blake whipped his head in her direction. "What about work?"

"I texted Kristina about an hour ago, letting her know that I'd be available by phone, but that I'd be out of the office for a day or two."

Blake stared at her. "You're taking time off work? *And* willingly coming back to a hospital?"

She nodded. "Apparently, the Kelly men make me do a lot of things I normally wouldn't."

"Like?" he asked, clearly testing her.

"Like fostering a dog, riding in an ambulance" —she stepped closer and placed her hand on his chest— "unexpectedly get married," she whispered. His pulse jumped under her fingers, and he held her gaze, a surprising flash of heat flaming in his eyes. She waited for a pithy response but got none—at least not from the junior Mr. Kelly.

"Blakey, why is it that this beautiful, capable woman does not have a ring on her finger? You married her without a ring?" Clyde said.

Blake gave his head a little shake and pulled his gaze from Bridget. "Seriously, Gramps, you should not be this spunky right now."

Clyde's smile drooped a little and he blinked like he was

fighting sleep. "I still have Norah's ring, if you'd like to give it to Bridget."

Bridget's stomach flipped. She'd like to blame Clyde's comment on age or anesthesia, but he'd clearly proven he was one hundred percent cognizant. This little charade slid even further outside her comfort zone. A little white lie was one thing. Dead grandmother's rings were another thing entirely.

She turned to the nurse, grasping for a subject change. "What's your pet policy? Can I bring Clyde's granddog for a visit tomorrow?"

The nurse winked. "I'm assuming she's a therapy dog."

A genuine smile crossed Bridget's face for the first time in many hours. "Of course."

"Then I don't think it should be a problem. For a brief visit."

"Get some rest, Clyde." Bridget leaned down and placed a small kiss on the older gentleman's forehead. "I'll see you later—if you promise the major drama is over."

He yawned and settled his head against the pillow. "I'll be back to boring old me."

Bridget laughed. "The last word I associate with you, Clyde, is boring." She turned to Blake. "I'll wait outside for you."

He nodded. "I'll be out in a minute."

Bridget stepped outside the room and collapsed against the wall. Clyde was going to be okay. Blake was here. She managed something that before a few hours ago, she would've thought impossible—returning, and staying, in a hospital. Exhaustion swept through her, and she miraculously made it the six feet to the closest chair before crumpling.

"Hey," a soft voice said. Blake was crouched in front of her. "You are fucking amazing. You know that, right?"

"I think you meant, 'Holy *Suzanne Brigit Bird*, you are amazing, Bridget Hayes,'" she said, mustering a small smile.

"That is what I meant," he said, matching her tired smile. "Or would have, if I knew Sue Bird's full name."

She waved a hand in front of him. "Details."

"Two amazing point guards with the same name, huh?" he said, offering her a hand and pulling her into a standing position.

"Well, first name versus middle, and spelled differently. And hers is probably said all fancy French style, Brie-zhigt."

"Details," he repeated back to her. "And speaking of amazing, where is Destiny?"

"With Kal and we agreed it would be easier for me to pick her up mid-morning. She's working from home until at least 10 am."

They walked toward the door, Blake pulling his suitcase. She'd forgotten he'd gotten off a plane a few hours ago. The cool May air hit them as they stepped outside the hospital and Blake collapsed on a bench right outside the door, dropping his head into his hands.

She sat and put her arm around his shoulders. Personal experience taught her that no matter how difficult the road for the patient was, it was equally difficult for their loved ones. Her mother had told her on several occasions that the sense of helplessness was overwhelming.

"Blake?"

He turned and wove his arms around her waist, laying his head on her shoulder. It wasn't long before wetness soaked through her shirt. She held him until his breathing returned to normal.

"My apartment is only a few blocks away. Why don't you come there with me?"

He looked up at her questioningly.

"You can get some sleep and you won't have to be alone."

"And you're okay with that?"

She lifted a shoulder. "That's what friends do for each other."

"Friends," he said, searching her face.

"Friends," she whispered, knowing deep inside that whether they acted on it or not, they were much more than friends.

"Okay," he said, standing.

She grabbed the handle of his suitcase. "Are you okay walking?"

"Are you?" his gaze settled on her leg.

"I sat a lot today. My body could use a stretch."

They walked the first two blocks in silence.

"Thank you," he breathed out as they neared her apartment.

"No worries" —she smiled at him— "I've rolled my share of suitcases."

He stopped on the sidewalk. "No, thank you for everything you did for Gramps today. Yesterday. I can't even think about what would have happened had you not been there."

"But that didn't happen. What-ifs are not a good use of your energy." Or so she kept trying to tell herself. This was clearly the perfect example of "do what I say, not what I do."

Bridget buzzed into her building, holding the door for Blake. "I know, but . . ." he protested.

"No buts," she said, pushing the button for the seventh floor. "It'll all seem better after some sleep."

Stepping inside her apartment, she wheeled his suitcase down the hall.

"Where are you going with that? I'll take the couch."

"No, you won't," she called down the hallway.

He followed her into her bedroom. "Bridget, I can't take your bed."

"I think we can handle both sleeping here. It's a big bed and it's not like we haven't done it before."

He looked from her to the bed and back. She didn't have to ask what he was thinking. She knew because she was thinking about it, too. Outside of the last few hours with Clyde, it had been hard not to think about it. It differed from any sex she'd had in the past and, much as she tried, she could no longer pass it off as a way to shake her crush, or even something she did to flaunt her self-imposed rules. Now, what to do about it? That was a much harder thing to figure out.

"Do you want something to eat? Or drink?" she asked, trying to draw their attention from the bed, taking up literal and figurative space.

He shook his head. "I could use a shower, though. Mind if I borrow your bathroom?"

"Let me get you a towel." She stepped into the bathroom, needing a moment, but when she turned, he was right behind her.

"Bridget," he whispered, cupping her cheeks in his hands. He leaned in and placed a chaste kiss on her lips.

She meant to step away, but instead stepped closer to him.

He met her lips again, but this time the kiss's purpose was not "thank you." It tasted of desire and breaking restraint. Of everything she'd been trying to shove to the back of her mind since the moment he'd walked away from that Minneapolis hotel room. He pulled her tight into his chest and her core clenched when his erection pressed against her belly.

"Blake," she stepped back, breathless. "If we do this again, I want to make sure it's not just a distraction from a stressful day."

"I think we both know it's not 'if' but 'when,'" he growled.

Parts of her howled when she moved back a step, but it was the right thing to do. "If or when, this is not the right time."

His chin dropped to his chest, but he nodded his assent. She left the bathroom and didn't exhale until she heard the shower turn on.

CHAPTER EIGHTEEN

Blake placed a hand on the wall and leaned into it, letting the shower spray wash over him.

This had been, without a doubt, the longest three days of his life. Two flights. An argument with Andrew. Gramps' heart attack. And he was about to climb into the bed of the one woman he couldn't stop thinking about.

Was there a word for what happens after exhaustion?

He stepped out of the shower, toweled off, and pulled on the sweats and t-shirt he grabbed from his suitcase. He preferred sleeping in a lot fewer clothes, but tonight anything less than a Kevlar snowsuit might not be enough for the situation that awaited him outside the door.

Propped up in bed, Bridget held a book, a small lamp casting her in a warm glow. She wore a sweatshirt and yoga pants—they'd obviously had the same idea.

"You're sure about this?" he asked, stepping up to the bed.

She nodded. "We're both exhausted. I'm sure that sleep is the only thing either of us is interested in."

Blake cocked an eyebrow.

"Fine," she said, closing the book with a snap and laying it on her marble-topped bedside table. "Sleep is the only thing either of us is capable of right now."

"That's not accurate either, but it's closer to the truth."

She picked up her phone. "I set up an alarm for nine so I can get to Kal's and pick up Destiny. Is that time okay for you, or should I set a second alarm? Is four and a half hours enough sleep for you?"

He knew now that the speed of her voice directly correlated to her anxiety level and it was comforting to know this wasn't easy for her, either. "Nine works," he said, sliding under the covers.

"Do you need to go back to Vegas?" she said, skimming a hand over her quilt, her fingers tracing the stitching.

"No, the last two concerts were tonight and tomorrow—or rather last night and later today. They assured me they could cover my parts. I feel terrible, but I'm needed here. Plus, a cooling down period might be good for everyone." *Shit*. He hadn't meant to share that. Yet.

Her eyes flashed to his. "A cooling down period?"

He needed to tell her about the fight, but he'd imagined a very different scenario. One that didn't include them in a bed together. He blew out a big breath. "You know how Andrew wanted to talk to you when you called about Gramps?"

"I wondered about that."

He stretched out his legs, trying to stay as close to the edge of the bed as possible. His fingers curled, bunching the sheet, the memory of the hours he'd wandered Vegas thinking he'd have to leave the band playing in his mind. "We had a big fight."

"You and Andrew?" When he nodded, she pressed her fingers into her temples. "Let me guess, you fought about me."

"Yeah. Mostly."

"And Andrew wanted to yell at me, too?" Irritation laced her voice.

"No," his eyes met hers and he squeezed her hand. "He wanted to apologize."

"Andrew, apologize? Are you sure you're not delirious from stress and fatigue?"

Blake slid down, his body heavy with exhaustion. "I'm not likely to forget that fight any time soon. So, no."

She chewed on her thumbnail, covertly looking at him from the corner of her eye. "I'm sorry. The last thing I ever want to do is disrupt something you both love so much. You know that, right?"

He pulled the thumb from her mouth, his eyes lingering a beat too long. He cleared his throat. "I do. And I respect how deeply he loves you. But I think from now on, he'll be a little less overbearing."

"Really? What did you say to him?" She scooched closer and he nearly fell off the bed, trying to move back. "I don't have cooties, you know."

A nervous laugh fell from his lips. "Did you get the treatment, too?"

"Blake," she tipped her head and peered over her glasses.

"It's just this" —he gestured to the bed— "situation would be so much easier if you did. Had them, I mean."

She inched closer, unable to hide her smile.

"Bridget, stop playing." She stuck out her bottom lip and he forced himself to look over her shoulder. "It is taking all my power to keep my hands off you."

She lifted her hands in surrender and scooted back to her side of the bed. "Tell me what you said to Andrew. Pretty sure that's a guaranteed fast-acting anti-aphrodisiac."

Blake barked out a laugh. "Truth. Among other things, I mentioned maybe it was time for him to see you for who you are now, not the woman you were ten years ago."

"Among other things . . ." she said, trailing off.

He shrugged. "We cleared the air a little. Still, it's probably not a great idea to tell him I ended up here." He patted the sliver of space between them.

"Shoot. I texted him while you were in the shower and said, 'Guess who's sleeping in my bed tonight?'"

"Where is all this sass coming from?" he asked, his lips curving into a smile.

"Clearly, I'm punchy. It's been a day and then some."

He needed to tell her that Andrew wouldn't stand in their way if they wanted to be together. But that was irrelevant if she wasn't interested. And that was a conversation he needed sleep for—and maybe a giant steel shield for his heart.

"It's time to sleep. We can't have an octogenarian who just had open heart surgery be spunkier than us. He'd never let me live it down. Or, worse, he'll ask a lot of pointed questions about why I'm so tired."

She laughed softly. "We can't have that."

He picked up her hand and placed a kiss in the middle of her palm. "Good night, TNR."

She switched the lamp off, cloaking the room in darkness. "Good night, Blakey."

Violins played in his dream. Sounded like "Fur Elise." Funny, Beethoven didn't regularly feature in his dreams.

"Blake," a soft voice called. "Lift your arm so I can turn that off."

Hmm, classical music and a woman? Maybe he'd stay in this dream. See where it went.

"Blake," the voice said again, this time louder. "Little trapped here."

He pried an eye open and jolted. Definitely Beethoven. But not a concert. A ringtone. Bridget's ringtone. His arm was draped over her torso and his leg laid across her thighs. Shit. He rolled away from her, and she silenced her phone.

"I'm sorry," he said.

"It's okay," she mumbled. "It happens."

He chuckled. "Really? Do you invite many men into your bed who inadvertently snuggle you after a family member's emergency surgery?"

Pink crept into her cheeks. "Um, I thought you were talking about your pants situation." She waved in the direction of his crotch.

Laughter ripped from his chest. "Pants situation?"

Her cheeks went from pink to fire engine red. "What would you prefer I say? Something like, 'What's with the giant erection you're sporting, Blake?' Would that be better?"

He couldn't stop laughing. The combination of utter exhaustion, the absurdity of this one-bed situation, and one of the most capable, polished professionals he knew using the statement "pants situation" had knocked him over the edge.

"Stop laughing," she said, slapping his chest, but it held little weight as she battled her own fit of giggles.

"Can't," he gasped, struggling for air.

She swatted him again before rolling toward the edge of the bed. "You're terri—" she started before a screech sliced through the air.

His laughter died instantaneously, and he was hovering over her in seconds. "What is it?"

Her face twisted in pain. "Leg. Seized," she wheezed. "*Domantas Sabonis.*"

"Can I help?" He brushed the hair from her face.

She shook her head, her skin paling by the second. "I'll do it." She drove her fingers into her thigh and pushed.

"Let me," he said, pulling her hands away. "Just tell me what to do."

"*Do-man-tas*," she gritted out a second time.

"Bridget, you don't have to do this all yourself. I'm here. And try *Arvydas Sabonis*, much easier to yell."

She laughed softly, but tears trickled from the corners of her eyes.

"Like this?" he pushed his fingers into her quad.

She nodded. "Use your other hand to rub my hip, where it meets my thigh."

"I thought you'd never ask," he said, winking at her.

She laughed again, and her body fractionally relaxed. "That's it. Take a deep breath. And another. Am I pushing too hard?" He worried he was going to push straight through her thigh.

She wrapped her fingers around his wrist. "That's good. It's releasing."

He sat back on his calves. "How often does that happen, Bridget?"

"Hardly ever. Now," she added, slowly levering herself into a sitting position. "It happened pretty often in the first few years, but maybe only once or twice a year now."

"Do you need to take anything for it? Pain killers? Do you want me to get anything for you?"

She wiped her forehead, clearing away a few beads of sweat. "No. I stay away from the hard stuff and ibuprofen doesn't touch the pain. The best thing for it is a hot shower."

"I'm happy to help you with that."

She rolled her eyes. "Such a giver."

He spread his hands wide and shrugged. "I do what I can."

She turned, no sassy comeback, and tentatively pressed her foot on the floor. She stood with only a tiny wince. "I'm sorry," she whispered.

Had she just apologized? "For what?"

"That" —she pointed to the bed— "what just happened, is too much for some people."

"For your family?"

She nodded. "That's me, snapped and shattered. Stitched together and bolted in place. Fragile and frail. At least that's what they think."

He jumped up and rounded the bed, placing his hands on her shoulders. "No one wants to see someone they love in that kind of pain, Bridget. I think maybe you've confused pity and fear."

"I'm going to shower now," she said, not looking at him.

"Bridget?" he said, placing a finger under her chin, lifting her face. "Want me to send them all a strongly worded email saying that you are badass and bionic, not snapped and shattered?"

She snorted. "You are an incredibly decent human being, Blake Kelly."

"You take that back, Bridget Hayes."

"I will not."

"Fine. But it stays between us," he said, with a smile. "It's taken me three and half decades to cultivate this image. Don't you go ruining it for me."

She searched his eyes. "I don't want to take a single thing from you. I only want the best things for you."

He leaned down and kissed her temple. "Same."

"I have an extra to-go mug," she said, when he rounded the island in the kitchen. "I made plenty of coffee. Want me to fill it for you?"

"So much."

"Cream and sugar?" she asked, holding up a carton and a small white cannister.

"Yes and no." He motioned for her to hand him the cream. "How's the leg?" he asked, keeping his eyes on his mug.

"Better," she said, glancing over the top of her glasses at him. "I'm going to Kal's to pick up Destiny. I'll bring her to the hospital for a brief visit and then, unless you or Clyde need something, I'll bring her back here. Give her some quiet time."

"Sounds like a good plan."

Bridget returned the cream to the refrigerator and dropped her phone into her handbag. "Did you hear from the guys? How did the concert go?"

Blake grunted. "Matt texted while you were in the shower, said the concert went better without me. No idea what he's doing up at this hour, though."

"Doesn't he still call in to Avery's show from the road?"

Blake snapped his fingers. "That explains it. Sometimes I forget about that."

"Because *you're* not up at this hour, perhaps?"

"It's 6:30 am in Vegas right now. I'd definitely still be in bed, especially the night after a concert."

Bridget pinned him with a look. "You know it didn't go better without you, right? They tease you because they love you. And if they're teasing you, they're not mad at you."

Yeah. He'd had the same thought. "I texted back asking if they had anyone show up at the signing table, what with the best-looking member missing."

She snapped a kitchen towel at his hip. "So humble."

He laughed, but he'd been relieved when Matt's text arrived. It confirmed Andrew's words. Fighting didn't change who they were, what they meant to each other.

"I hate to mention this," Bridget said, pulling him from his thoughts. She twisted Destiny's leash around her hand and added it to her bag. "But if you have energy left later today, we should probably talk about the event. It's a week away and we have a couple of loose ends."

He leaned back against the kitchen counter. "How about I meet you back here after Gramps has dinner? I'll bring takeout?"

"Take this," Bridget handed him a Flames key chain with a fob and key attached. "It'll get you in the front door."

"Wow. First inviting me into your bed and now a key to your apartment?" He put a hand over his heart with a gasp. "This is moving quickly, Bridget."

She topped off her coffee and motioned for him to remove the lid from his cup. "They're for the lobby door. You still have to knock on my front door."

"For now." He waggled his eyebrows at her.

Bridget rolled her eyes. "Don't you need to get to the hospital?"

He slipped the key in his pocket with a smirk. "See you soon."

"Look at you," Blake said, entering Gramps' room. The nurse had him on the edge of the bed.

"Yep. Sitting up. I'm a medical marvel," Gramps said dryly.

"Now, Clyde," a nurse Blake hadn't met chided, "you had open heart surgery yesterday. One step at a time."

"I brought a spinach and egg sandwich, if that helps," Blake said, holding the bag aloft.

"With bacon?" Gramps said, standing with the aid of the nurse and gingerly walking to the end of the hospital bed.

Blake gave Gramps a wide berth, setting the bag on the rolling tray, and dropping into the orange vinyl chair, causing it to squeak. "I think bacon might be on the contraband list," he said, looking at the nurse for approval.

She nodded. "Likely tomorrow, a dietician will talk to you about your diet going forward."

Gramps grunted and pivoted back to the head of the bed. "If you didn't bring bacon, did you at least bring Bridget and Destiny?"

Blake laughed. "They'll be here in a little while."

"Let's get you back in bed, Clyde. Do you want to lie down or sit up?"

"I'll sit up while my grandson is here."

"Very well." The nurse handed Gramps a large pillow shaped like a heart. "Wrap your arms around it like I showed you and then scoot your butt back." She looked at Blake. "This keeps his incision stable while he moves. He'll need to continue to use it when he gets home. When he stands or sits. Or sneezes," she added. "Sneezing can be quite painful."

"It's okay," Clyde said, shimmying back on the bed. "The only thing I'm allergic to is sandwiches without bacon."

The nurse laughed and shook her head. "They warned me you were feisty."

"It's the secret to a long life," he said, as she pulled the sheet up over his legs. "That, and bacon."

Blake laughed. "Maybe it's time to let that joke go, Gramps."

"Who's joking?"

The nurse typed a few things into the computer and placed a large remote next to Clyde's hand. Gesturing to it, she said, "Use the call button if you need anything, Clyde, otherwise I'll leave you to enjoy your grandson."

Blake watched her leave before turning back to his grandfather. "Clyde, huh? Yesterday they were calling you Mr. Kelly."

Clyde snorted. "Calling me Mr. Kelly makes me sound like an old man. I nipped that in the bud."

Blake laughed. "Yeah, you're not an 'old man' for at least another three years."

"Exactly."

Blake scooted the recliner closer to the bed, assessing his grandfather. "How'd you sleep?"

Clyde sighed. "Not great. They're in here all the time, poking and measuring."

"But you rested?"

"Yes. Did you?" Clyde waggled his eyebrows.

The thought of his body wrapped around Bridget's, the softness of her skin, the smell of her shampoo, sent heat up his spine. A better man would have insisted on sleeping on the couch. Or would have returned to his own apartment. But Bridget Hayes had a gravitational pull he couldn't resist.

"A little," he answered.

"By yourself?"

Blake raised his eyebrows. "Gramps."

Clyde's smile fell and he reached for Blake's hand. "She's a good woman, Blakey. Maybe you don't push this one away. Maybe you hang on to this one."

He wanted that, he did. But even if he felt more secure about his place in the band, there was still the fact that he wasn't commitment material. Plus, shouldn't he talk to Bridget about all of this before his grandfather? "We're friends, Gramps."

Clyde snorted. "I might be half dead, but I still got my marbles and I see the way you two look at each other. I don't look at my friends like that."

"Except Sharon?" Blake waggled his eyebrows.

"What are you afraid of, son?" Clyde asked, ignoring Blake's blatant attempt at changing the subject.

So much for not talking about it. "I'm not built for commitment, Gramps. And I'm sure we can agree, that's what Bridget deserves."

"What's wrong with commitment? I won't say it's easy. But with the right woman, the right *person*—I'm trying to learn that inclusivity thing—it's worth it, Blakey. I wouldn't trade one day of my fifty-three years with your grandmother. Not the hard ones. Not the days we drove each other crazy. None of 'em."

Blake stood and paced at the edge of the bed, scratching his beard. "How did you know Grams was the one?"

Clyde shifted in the bed, and Blake stepped forward to reposition his pillows. "I'm not sure I believe in the idea of The One or a soulmate, but after I met Norah, dating other women lost all appeal and when we were apart, I constantly thought, 'I wish Norah was here to see this, do this,' and so on. With her, the good things became great things."

Blake leaned against the footboard, his fingers digging into the metal. He didn't want to date other women. He'd stood on the path at the desert botanical garden and thought about how Bridget would love it there. He dreamed of taking *their* dog for a walk in Central Park, together.

"Blake."

His eyes flashed to his grandfather's. He never called him Blake.

"What's the real problem, son?"

He blew out a tremulous breath. Time to come clean. "What if I give her my heart and she doesn't want it? What if she pushes me aside? Rejects me?"

Clyde lifted a shoulder, wincing a little. "What if she does?"

Blake bumped a fist against the corner of the bed and smirked. His practical grandfather. No mincing of words here. "Great pep talk, Gramps."

"It wasn't a rhetorical question, son. What if she leaves you? Will you disintegrate into nothingness?"

A mirthless laugh fell from Blake's lips. "No."

"But what if she stays? What happens then?"

"I spend every day waiting for her to leave?"

"Or you get to spend every day with an amazing woman. A woman who laughs with you. A woman who challenges you."

"I'll think about it." He didn't need to tell Gramps he'd been thinking about it—and trying not to think about it—ever since that night in Minneapolis. Likely longer.

Clyde patted the bed, gesturing for Blake to sit next to him. Blake sat and grabbed his hand, settling it next to him.

"I love Lizzie with all my heart—and she loves you. But I know she's not been the best role model. Or even around when you needed her. But your mother is not representative of every woman. A woman like Bridget loves with her whole heart."

"How do you know that? You've only known her for a couple of weeks."

"She watched Destiny despite her crazy schedule, and she stayed with me when I wasn't feeling well and wouldn't leave this room until you got here. I don't need to know more."

Blake rubbed the back of his neck, his gaze dropping. "What about that crazy schedule, Gramps? She works a lot. Just like Mom."

"Please review my previous argument. She made time for a dog. She made time for me. She'll make time for you. And in return, she deserves all of you. Not just what's in your pants."

Blake's eyes flew wide. "Gramps!"

"Think about it, Blakey. You can't ask for her time if you're unwilling to give her your heart. Your whole heart. You can't hold pieces back because you're afraid of getting hurt. It doesn't work that way." Clyde's eyes fluttered and he yawned.

"Why don't you take a nap? I'll wake you when Bridget and Destiny get here." *And after I let your comments digest a bit.*

Clyde nodded, and his eyes fell shut.

"Knock, knock," Bridget called from the doorway.

Blake looked away from the 2016 season of *Spring Baking Championship*, unable to hold back his smile.

"Sorry, I'm a little later than I planned. I stopped by the office, and of course, everyone wanted to meet Destiny." She pointed at Clyde. "Should I come back when he's awake?"

"No, stay. They'll be waking him soon for lunch," he said, meeting her at the door and planting a small kiss on her forehead. When she raised an eyebrow, he said, "Can't have the nurses think I'm not excited to see my wife."

"Destiny?" Clyde said groggily.

Hearing her name, the dog squirmed in Bridget's arms. "Hold on, little girl," Bridget said with a chuckle. Bridget walked to the side of the bed and sat down gingerly, settling Destiny in her lap. "How are you today, Clyde? Your color looks much better."

"I'm considerably better now," he said, scratching Destiny's head. He leaned toward the dog and whispered, "Lunch is arriving soon, Destiny. Want to share it with me? I have to warn you, though, there won't be any bacon."

Destiny barked a soft woof.

"Agreed. Bacon makes every meal better," Clyde said with a laugh. "And how about you, Bridget? Did you get some sleep?"

"A little," she said, setting Destiny on the bed, firmly holding her collar.

"Huh," Clyde said, with a slight tilt of his head. "That's exactly what my grandson said."

"Gramps!" Blake said, shaking his head.

"What?" A look of innocence pasted on his face.

"How about some lunch, Clyde?" a chipper voice asked from the doorway.

"Welcome back, Peg," Clyde said to the nurse who'd been with them yesterday. "You didn't get much time off."

"I asked to come back just to see you," she said with a smirk.

Bridget laughed. "You may have met your match, Clyde."

"Dad!" a voice interjected from the hallway.

Blake assessed the woman in the doorway. No one would guess she'd just gotten off an eight-hour transcontinental flight. Not a wrinkle on her understated but perfectly tailored Alexander McQueen ebony blazer. Her silver hair pulled tightly into its customary chignon, not one hair out of place. As if it would dare defy her.

"Lizzie," Clyde said. "I thought you were in Paris."

"I booked a flight as soon as I got Blake's message. It was a bit of a nightmare getting out, but I'm here." She approached the bed. "Are you okay?"

"I'm fine," the older man said gruffly. "You didn't need to come."

"Of course, I came. Where else would I be?"

Peg cleared her throat, clearly sensing the tension in the room. "Mr. Kelly's had great care. Your son and his wife have been here nearly the entire time."

Bette blanched. "My son. And his wife." She looked at Blake. He stared back at her, daring her to contradict the nurse, knowing she wouldn't. Bette Kelly never made a scene.

"Yes," Peg continued, "Bridget's the one who brought him to the ER."

"Bridget?" Bette's eyes floated over to Bridget and assessed her—from head to toe.

"The ambulance brought him to the ER. I just rode along," Bridget said with a weak wave and a garbled laugh.

Bette pulled at the hem of her jacket. Did anyone except Blake know that was her tell? Likely not. No one else had needed to pay attention to every detail hoping to find a way to get her attention.

"Well," she said, "thank you, Bridget." Her eyes flitted from his "wife" to the dog to him.

Bridget cleared her throat and stood from the bed. "It's been a long couple of days for Destiny. I should take her home. Let Clyde be with his fam—let him catch up with Bette," Bridget said, catching herself.

"I'll walk you out," Blake said to Bridget, before turning his attention back to his mother. "He needs a lot of rest, Mom. Don't tire him out."

Bette cocked an eyebrow. "I think I know what my own father needs, Blake."

"Do you?" He held her gaze and something almost vulnerable passed over her eyes. No, he must be mistaken. Bette Kelly didn't do vulnerable. Didn't know the meaning of it. "I'll be back shortly, Gramps."

Blake met Bridget at the door and lifted the dog from her arms, nodding his head toward the hallway. They walked in silence until they entered the elevator.

"So that was your mother."

"Yep," he said, popping the P.

"She didn't blow our cover."

Blake nodded. "Bette Kelly does nothing that might make her look foolish."

Bridget laid her hand on his arm. "For what it's worth, she seemed genuinely concerned."

Blake hummed and handed Destiny over when the elevator doors whirred open. "What food should I pick up for our meeting later?"

Bridget searched his face. "If you'd rather spend the time with your mo—"

"No," he said, a little more forcefully than he'd planned. "We need to get things wrapped up. As you said, our timeline is shrinking rapidly."

"Okay," she nodded. "Pizza works, if you like that."

"Toppings?"

"You pick. I'm easy."

Blake shook off the surprise of seeing his mother and waggled his eyebrows. "Stop throwing yourself at me, Bridget. It's embarrassing."

She pulled a face. "I get the feeling that a lot of women have thrown themselves at you, Blake Kelly."

"I meant embarrassing for you," he whispered.

"In-core-gerbil."

"What?"

"Nothing." She waved a hand in the air. "It's something that Grace says. I'll see you later. Text me when you leave here."

"Yes, dear."

She tipped her head and peered over her glasses.

"Yes, wife?"

Bridget snorted. "Destiny and I are leaving now."

He watched her exit the hospital. Tight ass. Ponytail swinging. A slight limp you'd never notice unless you were looking for it. And, he was pretty sure, no matter what Gramps thought, the owner of a sizeable chunk of his heart.

He'd figure out what to do with that knowledge, but right now, he had a different woman to deal with. It was time to have a conversation—a real one—with Elizabeth Kelly. He confronted Andrew and still had his job and his found family. He could do it with his mother, too.

CHAPTER NINETEEN

"So you got married?" his mother said when he stepped into the room. Her head was bent over a small laptop and Clyde snored lightly, his head listing toward her. Like he'd fallen asleep talking to her.

He leaned against the wall, the long days making every muscle and joint ache. "Do you honestly think I would get married and not tell you?"

She snapped the lid of her laptop shut. Clyde rustled at the sound but didn't wake. "Honestly? Yes."

"A wedding *would* require you to take a day off work," he said dryly.

"The work I do to support you," she hiss-whispered back.

"Mom, I'm thirty-five years old. I've been supporting myself for a while."

"Says the man who pays no rent and has no mortgage."

Enough. They needed to clear the air. He'd let too much time pass, too many feelings fester. Buoyed by his conversation —or yelling match, to be entirely honest—with Andrew, he motioned to the door. "Can we talk in the lounge?"

He walked out of the room, and surprisingly, his mother

followed. He dropped into a chair in the empty waiting room and scrubbed a hand down his face. Was he mildly terrified to have this conversation? Yes. Did it still need to happen? One hundred percent.

Bette carefully folded herself into the chair across from him, draping one leg over the other. "So, if you're not married, who is Bridget?"

Did he give her the easy answer or the complicated one? He steepled his fingers, staring down at his hands. Probably better to start small. "Her name is Bridget Hayes—"

"Hayes, like in Andrew Hayes? The man in your band?" she interjected.

His head popped up. "How did you know that?"

She sighed. "I pay attention to your life, Blake. Give me some credit."

He blinked a few times and scratched his head. "Yes, Bridget is Andrew's sister. And in some weird small world thing, we ended up co-chairing an event for Woof Watchers."

She snapped her fingers. "That's the foster group you work with, right?"

Okay, now she was seriously freaking him out. His mother knew the guys in the band and his favorite charity? He supposed he mentioned both at their stilted dinners, but it never seemed like she was listening.

"How did she go from Storyhill sister and co-chair to wife?"

Wife. It should sound ridiculous since he'd never once considered getting married, but somehow it didn't. And wasn't that alarming? Blake swallowed the panic climbing his throat and turned his attention back to his mother. "Quick version. I was serving as an emergency foster for Destiny—the dog she held—and my replacement backed out. So, when I went on tour, Bridget took the dog. She'd been taking her to Gramps' during the day and picking her up for overnight duty. That's what she was doing when Gramps collapsed. He told the paramedics she was family, so she could ride in the ambulance. And the surgeon said if she hadn't been there, Gramps likely would have died."

The same look of vulnerability from earlier washed through her eyes. Was he imagining it? Just seeing what he wanted to see?

Bette smoothed her hair, her fingers trembling nearly imperceptibly. "We should thank her somehow. Is there something she wants? Something I can buy her?"

And just like that, irritation rose like bile in his throat. "Mom, no. She's not like that. She doesn't want your money."

Bette nodded and her breath audibly caught in her throat. "I'm not ready to lose him."

Something they had in common. "Me neither."

After an extended silence, both lost in their own thoughts, Bette lifted her head. "So she's not your wife, but is she your girlfriend?"

Blake pulled in a deep breath. "No." *Not yet anyway.*

"Why not?"

Really? They barely spoke to one another, and she wanted to get into this now? Here? He studied the laces of his Chucks. The "we're just friends" refrain sat on the tip of his tongue, but he'd asked her in here to pave a way forward, not repeat past behavior. Honesty, it was.

"I'm not comfortable with commitment," he said.

"Why not?"

"I don't know how," he whispered.

She scoffed. "You commit all the time. To Storyhill. To Woof Watchers. To Gramps."

"That's different," he said, suddenly feeling very much like that eight-year-old boy sitting in the kitchen trying to earn his mother's approval.

"Explain," she said, sliding into the chair next to him.

He took a fortifying breath. Honesty really sucked. No wonder he'd avoided conversations like this one for so long. "You wouldn't talk about *him*, and you were gone so much, so I grew up believing I had a dad *and* a mom who didn't want me," he blurted out. "As a kid, I thought maybe I just wasn't loveable, so I locked my heart away." He was amending his previous thought—honesty *and* self-awareness sucked. "And it stuck. Now, I'm not sure I can change it, even if I want to." And he wanted to. For Bridget. A plump tear dripped down his cheek. He wiped it away and lifted his head, surprised to see a matching drop falling over her cheekbone.

"Beak," she gasped out.

She hadn't called him that in two decades. As a little kid, he couldn't say Blake, and she'd adopted his mispronunciation as a nickname.

His confession still hung in the air as her phone rang. Of course, it did. She pulled it out of her pocket and swiped to answer it. Seriously? He'd just laid his heart bare and she was taking a call? If he wasn't so exhausted, he'd march out of the room.

She held up a single finger, signaling for him to wait. He didn't want to wait. He'd spent a lifetime waiting for her.

"Hi Emily" —she pushed a hand down the length of her thigh— "yes, I'm back in the country. I'm with my father and my son. If you could please pass your questions to Marc, I'm going off-grid for a day or two."

A feather could have knocked him over.

She ended the call and turned to him. "Sorry about that, but this way, they won't keep calling."

"Do you go 'off-grid' often?" he asked, his voice thick.

"Almost never. But then my father having a heart attack and my son accusing me of being a terrible mother—in less than twenty fours—is new to me."

"I didn't say you were a terrible mother. Just absent." The people pleaser had a hard time repeating his indictment, but he'd come this far. He wasn't backing down now. He opened his mouth to soften the blow—because old habits die hard—but she beat him to the punch.

"I am so, so sorry I made you feel that way." She slipped off her shoes and pulled her legs underneath her. He'd never seen his mother in anything other than a power position, and it was unnerving. The tears started again, tracking down her cheeks. "Yes, you were a surprise pregnancy, and yes, I'm not naturally maternal, but from the moment I heard your heartbeat, saw your tiny fingers on the ultrasound, I never wanted anything more."

"Not even that giant contract with CVS?"

A garbled laugh broke through the tears. "Not even that." She pulled a tissue from her pocket and patted under her eyes. "This is not an excuse, just an explanation. I knew I was going to be a single parent from day one, and the idea of housing and feeding two people terrified me. At first, I worked all the time to keep a roof over our heads."

"And then?" Blake asked.

She stared at the ceiling, quiet for several beats. "I gained so much comfort from seeing my bank account grow and I knew I wasn't the room mother, field trip chaperone kind of parent, so I made sure you had everything you could want or need."

He sighed and put an arm around her shoulders—just to try it out. "I would have traded every toy, every designer shirt for a couple of hours with you."

She leaned into him, and he tried not to flinch in surprise. "But not the piano lessons?" she said, humor lacing her voice.

She was trying to lighten the mood and the things he'd bottled up for decades wouldn't go away with a single conversation, but he could try to meet her halfway. "Nope. Not the piano lessons. Or the therapy."

She laughed softly. "I paid for therapy?"

"Your assistant helped me navigate your insurance. Very helpful."

Bette groaned. "Oh god." She squeezed her eyes shut. They sat in silence for a long time. Finally, she asked, "Where do we go from here, Beak?"

He stared at the painting of the Central Park bridge on the opposite wall. Where did they go from here? They couldn't change the past.

"How about a deal?" he said, swiveling to meet her gaze.

"I'm good at deals."

He smiled and opened the Notes app on his phone. "It's no cocktail napkin, but how about a contract of sorts?"

She stared at the blank screen. "What are your terms, Mr. Kelly?"

"Let's keep it simple. One" —he typed under the heading, Kelly & Kelly Agreement— "no more overpriced Cobb salads. Any joint dinners will be at home. Before you say anything, takeout is acceptable. Two, we are family, and as such, any shared activities are not to be labeled 'win-win' situations. Three," he continued, "we don't wait for someone to almost die to talk to each other. And last, we leave the past where it is and start fresh today. How does that sound?"

"You drive a hard bargain, Beak. I really love those overpriced Cobb salads. But I'll concede if you promise me one thing."

"Which is?"

She sniffed, wiping the tissue under her nose. "An invitation to your wedding. And a seat in the front row."

He laughed. "If that ever happens, you'll be the first to know."

"Sorry to interrupt," Peg called from the doorway, "but

Clyde is awake and asking for you. Something about not leaving the two of you alone?"

They laughed and he patted his mother on the leg. Clyde wasn't wrong, but maybe now it would be a little less dangerous. Baby steps, as Bridget would say.

"You go," he said to his mother. "Have some time with him."

"Because you have a wife and dog to check on?"

He smiled. "Something like that."

"Pizza delivery," he called through Bridget's door. Destiny barked, and he grinned. "I hear you, Destiny. Go get Bridget. The food is getting cold."

Bridget swung the door wide. "Someone forgot to put on his patience pants this morning."

"In my defense, a beautiful woman distracted me when I was getting dressed this morning."

She rolled her eyes and motioned for him to enter.

Destiny circled his legs, hopping, trying to get her snout closer to the pizza box. "Careful baby."

"Dear, wife, and now baby? Give a guy a key and he takes all kinds of liberties," Bridget said over her shoulder.

"I was talking to the dog."

"Right," she said, that gorgeous pink coloring her cheeks. "Is eating at the island okay?" she asked, motioning to the counter.

"Sure." He dropped the box and rounded the counter. "Where can I find plates?"

"Plates? Who eats pizza off plates?" She pushed a stack of napkins toward him. "Oh my god," she said, whirling on him. "You're not one of those snobs who uses a knife and a fork, are you?"

He gasped playfully, his hand covering his heart. "How dare

you? I am a native New Yorker. Forks and knives are for you froofy Garden District types."

"I haven't lived in New Orleans in a long time."

"I just thought with your love of the rules, TNR, you'd insist on plates."

She slipped around the counter and hopped onto a bar stool. "Maybe I'm changing my ways."

"Really? Do tell," he said, joining her at the island. "What is the cause of this transformation?"

She picked up a piece of pizza and took a big bite. "You," she said around her mouthful.

"Oh no, I will not be held responsible for your rejection of plates *and* talking with your mouth full."

"It's what happens when a TNR spends too much time around a certified Comic Sans-type." She shrugged. "Not my fault."

"You're the victim here?"

"Totally."

"I seem to remember someone begging to be led to the dark side," he said with a wink.

"I did not beg," she mumbled. "And if I did, it was because someone wasn't moving fast enough."

"Comic Sans living is all about enjoying the moment, not rushing through it."

She lifted her gaze and when their eyes met, the grand finale of a fireworks display exploded in his belly. "Comic Sans or not, I cannot let you carry on with tomato sauce dripping from your chin." He wiped a napkin under her lips and jolted from the raw need the gesture summoned. He needed a distraction. Fast. He balled up the napkin and launched it toward the trash can, missing by a foot.

She snorted, pulling some of the tension from the air. "It's a good thing you can carry a tune, Blakey. That was pathetic."

He balled up a second napkin and flipped it to her. "Care to demonstrate? But be careful, Ms. All-American. If you miss, the teasing will be merciless. Decades from now, I'll still be telling the story to our grandchildren." *Shit. Where had that come from?*

"*Our* grandchildren?" she asked, her mouth gaping, her eyes wide.

He shrugged, praying his Irish complexion didn't give him away. "Your grandchildren. I meant to say *your* grandchildren."

"Speaking of family, how was the time with your mother?"

He'd never been more thankful for her power to deflect. He held his hand down to Destiny, slipping her the tiniest sliver of pepperoni. "Clyde fell asleep, and we actually talked."

"Yeah?"

He nodded. "I think Gramps' heart attack made us both realize it's only the three of us. I don't want to get my hopes up, but I think we took some small steps toward being more engaged in each other's lives."

"Blake," she said, grabbing his hand, "that's great."

His eyes settled on where their hands joined. "Like I said, we'll see where it goes." He could deflect just as well as she could.

She flipped the pizza box lid closed and held up the forgotten napkin. "Now watch and learn." She tossed it in the air, and it arced perfectly, landing dead center in the bin.

"Impressive. Too bad you're not playing in the three-on-three tournament. Clearly" — he pointed at the trash can— "you still have skills. The comeback angle would sell a lot of tickets."

Her smile flattened. "I'm not playing. And I told you why." She stood from the counter, discarded the pizza box, and walked into the living room.

He wanted to help her. Give her the opportunity to combat her demons. Give her a taste of the relief he experienced after talking with the band and his mother. But it was her battle, not his, and he knew better than to push.

He stooped, grabbing Destiny around the middle, and joining Bridget on the couch. She laid out three color-coded spreadsheets on the table.

"That one" —she pointed to the left document— "is the list of completed items. The middle sheet lists the open items that Kristina, my assistant, is following up on. This one" —she tapped the sheet to her right— "is what's left."

"There are only four things on that list, Bridget," he said. "How did you get this all done?"

She shrugged. "You helped."

"Not much."

"Nine-point Times New Roman," she said, tapping a finger against her chest. A hint of irritation lacing her voice. "We might not be fun, but we get things done."

"Hey," he said, grasping her finger. "I think your ability to organize the shit out of anything is sexier than hell."

"You do?" She searched his face, and her tongue peeked out, moistening her bottom lip.

His entire body flinched.

And Bridget must have felt it because she jumped into a standing position. An ear-piercing squeak reverberating through the room. At the sound, Destiny barked, scrabbled toward the floor, painfully pushing her dog claws into his and, in a blink, Bridget landed in his lap.

"Sorry," she said, her voice breathy, her face inches from his. "Must be more mindful of dog toys." She attempted to right herself, but he held her in place.

"Bridget," he said, barely above a whisper. "Stay."

"Why?" Her voice trembled, but she didn't move.

"Because the crush that I've had on you for years has gotten worse. Because I spent a lot of time on tour, despite my fears about causing an issue with the band, thinking about you, wanting to be right here, talking to you, holding you just like this."

She ran her hands down his arms and placed a soft, barely there kiss on his lips. "When," she said, pulling back and holding his gaze.

"When I was on stage. When we texted—"

She silenced him with a finger to his lips. "You misunderstood me. Last night you said, 'It's not a matter of *if*, but *when*.' When," she repeated.

"You're sure?" he asked, barely able to restrain himself once he'd understood her meaning.

Bridget nodded, her fingers tracing his torso.

He placed a hand on either side of her face and kissed her. A testing kiss. Forcing himself to be slow, gentle, when all he wanted was to tip her back on the couch and plunder her mouth like a pirate who'd finally found treasure after years of searching.

She arched into him, her breasts pressing into his chest, pinning him against the couch. He tugged at the hem of her t-shirt, running his fingers over the strip of exposed skin above her waistband. She gasped and wiggled in his arms.

"Ticklish?" he said against her lips.

"Dog tongue," she said, a giggle escaping her lips. She jumped again. "*Stephen Curry*, that is cold."

"Destiny," he said. The dog yipped at the sound of her name. She scrambled up the sofa and dropped the squeaky toy in the space between their bodies. He laughed and scratched the dog's head. "So far you've been a decent wing woman, but right now, you're ruining the mood."

"How about you take her out and I'll meet you in the bedroom?" Bridget stood and walked toward the hallway, looking over her shoulder and a giving him a tiny wink.

"Deal," he breathed out, mesmerized by the sway of her hips. She disappeared around the corner, and he shook his head, attempting to dislodge the lust fog hanging around him. "Now, as for you little girl," he said to the dog sitting in his lap, staring up at him, "if that was your plan to get us into the bedroom, thank you. But next time, maybe do it *before* I have to take you to Central Park with this, ahem, pants situation."

CHAPTER TWENTY

THE FRONT DOOR OPENED AND CLOSED, AND BRIDGET collapsed on her bed. She fought through the explosion of need coursing through her body, trying to find rational thought. The night of the wedding, she'd been trying to forget her normal life *and* to put an end to a persistent crush. Both things that no longer rang true.

A gentle knock sounded on her bedroom door.

She looked up. The handsome man she'd been thinking about for so many years stood, leaning against her doorframe, one ankle crossed over the other, hands stuffed into his pockets.

"Destiny?" she asked, rising from the bed and crossing the room.

"In her crate. Walked in unprompted." He glanced down the hall. "I can get her, if you'd like."

She slid her palms up his chest, dipping a finger under the collar of his shirt. He sucked in a ragged breath and went still. She placed a soft kiss in the hollow of his throat, and his pulse jumped against her lips. "I don't think Destiny should see all the things I'd like to do with you tonight."

He growled and traced a finger along her jaw, down her

neck. "You're absolutely sure about this? This isn't play for me anymore, Bridget. Likely never was. No matter what I told myself." His gravelly voice dipped on the last words.

"Absolutely sure," she said, slowly unfastening the top button on his oxford.

He dipped his head and sucked her bottom lip into his mouth. She leaned into him, and he ran his hands under her shirt, sliding a finger under her bra, teasing the underside of her breast. The simple touch lighting a fire in her veins that spread through her body in seconds.

She stepped backwards toward the bed, pulling him with her. "Too many clothes," she mumbled, unfastening his belt and yanking his shirt free.

He grabbed the hem of her shirt and stopped. "Do you want me to turn off the light?"

She sucked in a small breath. *He'd remembered.* A part of her heart cleaved off like an iceberg falling into the ocean. "No," she said, and stepped back, putting a hand to his chest, stilling his movement. She didn't want the light off. She wanted to be seen. She wanted to be seen by *him.*

She sucked in a deep breath, giving herself a moment to calm the tremor in her hands. She pulled her shirt over her head and unclasped her bra, letting it fall to the floor.

He stepped forward, resting his fingers on her waist. "Can I help?"

She blinked and met his gaze, shaking her head. "I think I need to do this myself."

He nodded and dropped his hands to his side, moving to create a few inches between them.

She unbuttoned her pants and shimmied out of them and her underwear. His eyes drifted over the length of her body, and she forced herself not to flinch as his gaze passed over her scar.

"Beautiful," he said on a whisper of a breath.

"Your turn," she said, fighting off the urge to dive under the covers. She wouldn't hide tonight. No matter the internal battle. She laughed as he shucked his shirt and pants in a blur of flying fabric.

"That was impressively fast," she said, grabbing his hands and reeling him in until their bodies met from chest to knees.

"Like you said earlier, I didn't wear my patience pants tonight." His hands trailed down her spine, cupping her backside and giving it a squeeze.

She held his gaze, walking backward until her calves hit the bed. He guided her down, kissing her cheeks, the corners of her lips, before covering her mouth with his own. He ran his tongue over her bottom lip, and she parted, granting him access.

The kiss was slow, searching, languid, the opposite of the frantic tangle of lips and limbs in Minneapolis. A tremor of fear mixed with anticipation. She knew what this was. This wasn't sex. It was making love.

Love.

The word rattled through her. Was she in love with him? Love was messy. Something she couldn't control. She stiffened as an icy shiver snaked down her spine.

He ended the kiss and searched her face. "Where did you go? Do you want to stop?"

She shoved the unease from her mind. She wanted this. She wasn't missing out on this because she couldn't settle her thoughts. She wrapped her hand around the nape of his neck and nipped his earlobe.

A deep groan rumbled in his throat. "I like the way you answer questions, TNR."

She smiled against his jaw and dragged her teeth down his neck, biting lightly when she reached his shoulder.

Another groan. "Please tell me that this is not the last time we're doing this," he said, his hands roving, and his pupils blown black.

"I guess that depends on how good it is," she said, trying to slow her racing heart.

"Challenge accepted," he said, sitting back on his heels and easing himself to the foot of the bed.

"Wait," she said, instantly missing the heat of his body. "Where are you going?"

He didn't answer, digging his fingers into the arch of the foot on her injured leg. She moaned at the delicious pressure. "Who needs sex when that feels so amazing."

He snorted. "We're going to be here for a while. I need you relaxed." His fingers moved to her calf. "So strong," he said, dragging his hand over her lower leg.

"Not as strong as it once was," she said, shuddering under his touch, bracing herself for the moment he touched her scar. She jolted when instead of his fingers, his lips kissed along the pulled and pinched red skin.

"Is this okay?" The question vibrated against the sensitive skin.

"Yes," she whispered, surprising herself.

His soft lips continued to move upward, tracing the jagged boundary between red and pink skin. "One kiss for every step they said was impossible. For a body that was battle tested and victorious."

"That's just stubbornness," she said.

"It's strength," he said, looking up at her with hooded eyes.

"Thank you," she whispered, her voice thick with unshed tears.

"Don't thank me yet. I'm just getting started." He dipped his head and drew his tongue over her core. She arched up off the bed and he settled a hand on her hips, nudging them back down

269

and pinning them in place. Her fingers found his hair and she scraped her nails over his scalp. "That's a p-p-pretty good start," she wheezed out.

He pulled back, replacing his mouth with his fingers. Rocking the heel of his hand against her center, he blew a stream of air over her wet flesh. The sensation rocketed through her body and pulled a scream from her lips.

He inched back up, the delicious drag of his body against hers nearly painful. He threaded his fingers through hers, bringing them together over her head. She lifted her knees, wrapping her stable leg around his waist, her other pressed into his ribcage, encouraging him to continue.

"I want all of you," she said, pulling her hands free and trailing her fingers along his length.

"Condom?"

She pointed to the drawer in her bedside table, and he kneeled between her legs, grabbing one, and opening the package—or trying to.

"You're shaking," she said, surprise filling her voice.

He met her gaze, his eyes soft, and nodded. "I've had plenty of sex, but this is the first time I've made love to someone."

Her breath caught. This was more than sex to him, too. Before her mind jumped the tracks like a runaway train, she stilled his hands and took the foil packet from him. "Let me help," she said, tearing it open and rolling it on.

Wordlessly, he shifted forward and in a single heartbeat, he filled her and started moving. When his breathing changed, she reached a hand between them, wanting to come with him. He gently pushed her hand aside, replacing it with his own. He circled her with the pad of his thumb. A second scream climbed up her throat and he caught it, slamming his mouth over hers as they toppled. Together.

When her pulse neared a normal rate, he rolled off her and

pulled her into his chest. He traced concentric circles across her shoulder blades, down her spine. She pulled the sheet and blanket over them, suddenly feeling very vulnerable.

"I can hear you thinking," he said. "Want to share?"

She forced a laugh. "Just mentally going through my calendar, blocking out time to do this again."

He didn't laugh. Didn't make a joke about her allegiance to her calendar. Instead, he called her out. "Liar." He scooted back and tipped her chin up so that their eyes met. "Did my comment about making love freak you out?"

"A little," she admitted.

He cocked an eyebrow, challenging her.

"Okay, a lot."

He rolled away from her and out of the bed. Picking up his clothes from the floor.

"Wait." She reached for him, her heart thumping against her ribcage. "Don't leave. Aren't you a little freaked out, too?"

He pulled on his boxer briefs and slipped his shirt over his shoulders. "I am, and much as I hate it, I think this conversation warrants clothes." He picked up the robe strewn across her reading chair, laid it on the bed and disappeared out the door.

Slipping her arms into the robe, she propped herself up against the headboard. She was about to ask if she should follow him when she heard nails scrabble over the hardwood and two black paws and a head popped up over the side of the bed. Blake appeared behind Destiny, his shirt still hanging open.

"Did she get out, or did you let her out?" Bridget asked, pulling the chunky girl up on the bed.

"Miraculously, she stayed in the crate." He scratched between his pecs and her eyes followed the movement. "Bridget?" He waved a hand in front of her. "Did you hear me? She stayed in the crate."

"Yeah, I think your words were drowned out by all those abs," she waved in the direction of his chest and forced her eyes away. "Have you always had those? Wait, don't answer that. You'll tell me you don't even have a gym membership and it'll make me angry. And those relaxing orgasms will all be for naught."

He grinned at her.

"I'm babbling again," she said, squeezing her eyes shut. She felt the bed depress as he lowered himself to it.

"Yes. But it's cute." He brushed a strand of hair behind her ear and kissed her temple. "I don't have a gym membership. I'm gone too much. But I carry resistance bands with me, use hotel gyms when available, and do *a lot* of sit-ups." He turned her face toward him and when she opened her eyes, he said, "And if those orgasms wear off, I know where we can find more."

"Ugh. If you want to have a clothes-on discussion, please button your shirt, and stop saying orgasms. Please," she repeated.

His face sobered and he buttoned his shirt. "To answer your earlier question, yes, I'm freaked out, too. But likely for different reasons."

She bit her thumbnail. "We should talk about it, right?"

"That would be the adult thing to do."

She let her head drop against the headboard. "Ugh. Adulting is hard."

He laughed. "Says the woman who successfully manages an army of people and millions of dollars."

She wrinkled her nose. "Proving a person can be a superstar in one area and a complete mess in another. Every time my personal life came calling, I said, 'I already gave at the office.'"

He chuckled and tipped her chin down with his thumb. "I think talking it out will help that."

She rubbed her eyes. "And how do you propose two master deflectors do that?"

He pulled her hands from her face, threading his fingers through hers. "We got pretty good at the one question game. What if we started there?"

Destiny rolled over with a wheeze and a snort, making them both laugh.

"Clearly Destiny thinks it's a good idea," he said, stroking the pup's belly.

"Well, if the dog thinks it's a good idea, it must be," she said, with far more confidence than she felt. She pulled her knees up to her chest, wrapping her arms around them. "Who's going first?"

He pointed at her, and she didn't know if being the one to start this game was good or bad. "This would be a lot easier if I had a spreadsheet or flow chart to reference. But here goes. Am I right in assuming that you'd like to give this thing between us a real go? Not just friends or friends with benefits, but a proper relationship?"

"Yes."

She lightly punched him on the thigh. "Whoa there. Don't get crazy with all the words. Based on your effusive answer, am I allowed a follow-up question?"

He smirked, a single dimple popping. "I'll allow it."

"Why?" He opened his mouth, but she held up a finger, stopping him. "You've stated, frequently, that you're not a relationship guy. Has that changed?"

"Yes," he said again, a full smile popping both dimples this time.

"Stop that." This time, she punched his thigh with more force.

He squeezed her hand and gave her a tiny peck on the cheek. "A conversation with Gramps, and the one with my mother, forced me to take a hard look at my stance on relationships. Long story short, I'm willing to brave the deep end if you're willing to jump in with me."

Was she brave enough to dive in with him? She'd like to think so, but something tugged at her, holding her back. "Okay," she said lamely. She knew he wanted more, but it was all she could give in the moment. "It's your turn to ask a question."

His face fell. Just for an instant, before he replaced it with something neutral. "That night at Sid's, before dinner with Grace and Andrew, you asked me why I didn't want Andrew to find out about the night in Minneapolis. I told you my reason, but you didn't tell me yours. Tell me now?"

She drummed her fingers on the blanket, trying to find the right words. "After the accident, I made a promise to myself. If I couldn't have my dream, I would do everything I could to make sure other people got theirs." She stared at her toes, unable to look at Blake. She'd never said this aloud before. "It's why I've started a lot of initiatives at work and it's why I didn't want Andrew to know. If my actions caused issues in the band, if anything I did caused Andrew, or you, to lose your dream, I couldn't live with myself."

He pulled her into his chest, tipping his head against hers. "That's admirable, but it's a lot of pressure to put on yourself. You can't take someone's dream away, Bridget. And you can't hold it for them either." Silence slipped between them as if they needed a moment to digest the things they'd shared.

Minutes later, he said softly, "Do you think we've both been using Andrew as an excuse?"

"No," she said a little too vehemently. "He's never liked the idea of us together, you know that."

"I would have agreed before the fight in the desert." A small laugh trickled from him. "Coming soon to a theater near you. Andrew Hayes and Blake Kelly star in 'Fight in the Desert.'

Will it be a full-on sandstorm or just a dust up between friends?"

"Blake, this is serious. Quit joking around."

He ran a hand over her hair, pushing it behind her shoulder. "Andrew and I talked it out. He wasn't exactly joyful about it, but he acknowledged that anything happening between you and me isn't any of his business."

"That's not really an endorsement."

"True. But does it really matter? I know this is ironic coming from me, but letting Andrew have a say in our relationship is giving him way too much power. I was so afraid of losing Story-hill, of losing my job, that I lost sight of that."

"He's my brother," she whispered. Even her voice was running out of steam with this argument.

"I know it's not exactly the same, but he's mine, too."

She rolled out of bed and paced beside it. "I need to talk to him myself."

"Right now?"

She snorted. "No, but soon. And in person."

His eyes went wide. "In person? How long before you see him again?"

"He texted this afternoon. With everything going on with Clyde, I forgot to tell you. Grace has a meeting with the label next Thursday and since you guys are on break, he's coming with her. We're meeting for drinks. I'll talk to him then."

"Thursday. What happens until then?"

She stopped pacing. "You'll be busy getting Clyde settled back at home. You won't have time to even think about me until the event."

"Bridget, is this your way of letting me down easy?"

The crack in his voice nearly killed her. "No. But this is something I have to do." She was running and she knew it.

Running from her big, scary, messy, uncontrollable feelings. "I'll see you at the event. We'll talk then."

"If that's what you want," he said, his voice resigned.

What I want is to climb back into bed and let you hold me. I want to trust that everything will work out. I want to let you be my new dream. But I can't.

"It is," she lied.

CHAPTER TWENTY-ONE

FOUR DAYS. IT HAD BEEN FOUR DAYS SINCE SHE'D ASKED Blake to leave her apartment. Four days of trying to block out the expression on his face when he leaned in, placed a kiss on her cheek, and said goodbye. She'd never been more distracted at work, and she'd lost count of how many times she'd picked up her phone to text him, only to set it back down.

It'd been two days since she'd leashed Destiny and they'd walked through the park, and she'd found herself standing on the sidewalk across from Blake's brownstone. Recognizing the location, Destiny pulled her leash taut, trying to cross the street. The dog missed Blake and Clyde. And Bridget longed to know if Clyde was back, snug in his recliner, recuperating. Neither thing was enough to propel her across the street.

"Knock, knock," Kristina said, walking into Bridget's office, providing a much-needed break from her thoughts. She placed the Woof Watchers folder on Bridget's desk with a flourish. "Done. Four corporate sponsors and ninety-eight auction items."

"Wow," Bridget said. "Great work. You must be very persuasive."

Kristina waved a hand in the air. "Not me. You."

Bridget's brow furrowed. "Me?"

"If mentioning homeless dogs didn't immediately do the trick, all I had to do was drop your name, and people signed on the dotted line. The common refrain was, 'Bridget has done so much to help us' or 'Bridget makes working with the Flames so easy.' Yada, yada, yada."

"Really?"

Kristina nodded. "Flawless reputation," she said with a wink.

And another sign that maybe it was time to ease up a bit. Congratulate herself on everything she'd accomplished instead of constantly pushing for more. Consider the debt paid.

"Do you need anything else, boss?" Kristina asked. "If not, I'm off for the rest of the day. Kindergarten graduation."

She smiled and shook her head. "Thanks again. You did an amazing job." And to think Bridget almost hadn't asked for help.

"Thanks for trusting me with it. I really enjoyed it."

"Tell Gabby congratulations from me."

Her assistant gave a quick wave, and Bridget flipped open the folder. "Whoa," she exhaled, running her fingers down the final column. The corporate sponsor total was more than Woof Watchers' entire fundraising goal. All the auction items and ticket sales would be cushion. Blake was going to be so excited. She picked up her phone to text him and set it back down. For the zillionth time.

She could email him. He'd sent her one earlier in the week, confirming he'd completed the final tasks on the list. Even found a bakery to create specialty dog treats—for any dogs in attendance and bagged to sell to attendees. She smiled, thinking about him eating the treat in her apartment. The thought made her lungs hurt. And her heart ache. She battled them back with an Andrew-shaped bat. He'd be in New York in twenty-four hours and until then, she needed to push all thoughts of Blake Kelly into the background. *Good luck with that.*

Her phone vibrated in her fingers, and she jumped, her hand flying to her heart. She slowly turned her phone like she was diffusing a bomb. She blew out a breath. The text was from Kal, not Blake.

Kal: You going to the game tonight?

Bridget: Not tonight. Hanging out with Destiny and watching it on TV.

Kal: Blake can't watch her?

Not a good sign when even the mention of his name made her stomach threaten to empty its contents. She placed one hand on her stomach and used the other to thumb in a response.

Bridget: Want to stop by my apartment for a beer after the game?

Kal: That's not too late?

It might be if she remembered how to sleep. But it seemed her ability to do that left the same night Blake did. *Nope,* she typed, *bring your PJs. You can head home in the AM.*

Kal: A school night slumber party? Someone's feeling naughty.

Bridget: xo – see you later. Text me your rideshare details when you leave the arena.

A weeknight slumber party probably wasn't the best idea. Maybe the time to start easing up was right now? Take the next couple of days off? She navigated to the Flames internal website, clicked on the PTO link, and entered her password. The banner across the top told her she had 139 days of unused vacation. She did the quick math. That meant, outside of the one day she'd taken for Grace and Andrew's wedding, she hadn't taken any vacation in *four years*? Was that true? She scoured her memory and couldn't come up with anything except the week between Christmas and New Year's she took off to visit her family, but that didn't count because they closed the offices that week. Wow. One day of vacation in four years.

She entered the next two *and a half* days into the system—if she was doing this, she was starting right now—and emailed her team before she could talk herself out of it. And, if she was making changes, there was one more thing she'd been thinking about for a couple of weeks now. She'd fallen in love with Destiny. Her snorts, her demands for food, her laundry thieving, *and* the way the little love muffin made her leave work at a reasonable hour.

She dialed Woof Watchers, spoke with Camila, and ten minutes later had filled out, signed, and emailed the adoption paperwork. Camila had assured her that unless something unexpected came up in her background check—she assured Camila she was not that interesting—she could consider Destiny hers.

Last step, to set up an out-of-office email message. Something she'd never done before. She buzzed Kristina before remembering she was gone for the day. She felt foolish but typed "auto reply email" into Google. Seemed easy enough. Seven steps and she'd be on her way to pick up *her* dog.

She clicked Save Changes, and her phone vibrated again. "Bring it on," she said with renewed vigor. That lasted all of twelve seconds. The text was from Andrew. Right. There was still one more challenge in front of her.

Andrew: Still available to meet tomorrow night?

She exhaled a slow, tension-filled breath. Her request was likely to ignite a firestorm of questions, but she needed to ask it.

Bridget: Yes, but can we meet just the two of us?

Andrew: Everything okay?

Let the questions begin.

Bridget: Just need to talk to you about something.

She really was getting good at this whole "not a lie, but not the whole truth" answer game.

Andrew: We land at noon. When are you finished with work?
Bridget: I took the day off.
Andrew: Now I know you're not okay.
Bridget: Took it off to finish prepping for WW event on Saturday. Another half-truth. *How about 4pm? Drinks at Sid's?*
Andrew: Text me the address.

In the end, far fewer questions than she was expecting. She'd take it as a win. She dropped her phone in her handbag and headed out the door. First stop, slumber party supplies. Chips and beer should do it. Second stop, pick up her pooch.

"So let's get the niceties out of the way, so we can talk about the good stuff," Kal said without preamble, sliding onto an island barstool. "Good game. The broadcast went smoothly. And how are Destiny and Clyde?"

Bridget uncapped a bottle and slid it toward Kal. "Thank you. Glad to hear it. Destiny is good. Enjoying her days at doggie daycare. I don't know."

Kal spun the label toward her and nodded approvingly. "You don't know what?"

"I don't know how Clyde is doing." Bridget uncapped a second bottle and opened the bag of chips, joining Kal at the island. "I'm assuming no news is good news. He was supposed to be released from the hospital yesterday."

"You don't know for sure?"

Bridget sighed. Her high from adopting Destiny was quickly wearing off. "Are you repeating 'you don't know' just to irritate me? Because it's working."

Kal laughed. "Wow. The niceties didn't last long."

"Sorry. It's been a week." Bridget grabbed a couple of chips and popped them in her mouth, letting the salt dissolve on her tongue.

Kal gestured to the bottle in front of Bridget. "That explains the beer on a school night."

"Not a school night. I'm officially on vacation until Monday."

Kal stared at her, her mouth hanging open. "Are you sick? Have you recently bumped your head? Blink twice if you're being held against your will and being forced to take time off."

Bridget rolled her eyes. "None of the above. I have the Woof Watchers event this weekend and some last-minute things to wrap for that. And I've decided it's time to make some changes in my life. Starting with getting some perspective about the hours I work."

Kal was still staring at her. "We just talked last week. What caused this . . . this . . . okay, the only word for it is, *epiphany*?"

"I applied to adopt Destiny," Bridget said. "Can't work eighty hours a week with a dog at home."

Kal drummed her fingernails on the counter, her eyes narrowing. "Why does that not feel like the entire story?"

Bridget shrugged.

"Blake must be thrilled."

"I wouldn't know," she said around the handful of chips she'd (intentionally) shoved in her mouth.

"And now we're getting to the truth of the story. What happened?"

Bridget swallowed and propped her head in her hands, Destiny buzz fully gone. "Do you want the 'made-for-big-basketball-deals-Bridget' answer or the 'personal-matters-confuse-me-Bridget' answer?"

Kal curled her fingers, motioning back to herself. "Give it to me straight."

"Abridged version." She covered her face with her hands, peering out between her fingers. "After another round of mind-blowing sex, I asked him if he wanted to give a proper relationship a go and he said yes. Then I freaked out."

Kal set her bottle on the counter with a loud clunk. "*You* asked him and then *you* freaked out?"

"I know. What is wrong with me? It just seems so fast. And rash decisions haven't worked so well for me in the past."

"One rash decision didn't work for you. One. And fast, Bri? You've been in love with him for years."

Bridget spun on her stool, stood, and walked to the living room, collapsing onto the couch next to Destiny. "I've had a crush. I've not been in love with him."

Kal pulled a face and shook her head. "Crushes are fleeting. This thing with him has always been more than that, and you know it."

"Maybe," she mumbled.

"Not maybe," Kal said, pointing her beer bottle at Bridget. "What happened after the freak out? Did you talk it through?"

"No. I literally kicked him out of my bed," she whispered. "I told him I needed to think and . . ."

"And?"

She grimaced. "And talk to Andrew about it."

"Bri."

Bridget slapped her forehead. "I know."

"You are a strong, independent, feminist-as-fuck woman. You don't need Andrew's permission. For anything."

Bridget tipped up her chin. "I still think I should talk to him about it."

Kal snorted. "Disagree. But not my life. When is this 'talk' supposed to happen?"

"Tomorrow afternoon."

Kal flopped next to her on the sofa, throwing an arm around her shoulder. "So what will you do until then?"

"Con my best friend into a sleep-over with me and my dog and ask her not to judge me too harshly."

"I love you, Bri. I'm not judging."

"Kal," Bridget said, giving her bestie the side-eye.

"Much. I'm not judging much."

The next day passed in a blur. She cleaned the apartment. Took a shower. Did three loads of laundry. Finished up the last email for the event. And spent the last three hours, Destiny asleep at her side, binging old episodes of *Barefoot Contessa*. She got why Clyde was hooked, but she didn't understand how one woman could have so many recipes for chicken.

She rubbed Destiny's belly. "You ready to spend the night with Auntie Kal? I know I promised to be home more, but tonight your Uncle Andrew is in town and I have to talk to him about . . . something."

Kal was right. She didn't need Andrew's permission or blessing. What she needed was to locate her backbone. And loosen her vice grip on her life. The scheduling and the planning started as a productive way to heal from the accident—physically and mentally. But somewhere along the line, it morphed into an unhealthy need to control . . . well, *everything*. She'd known it for a long time, but fear and its venomous little fangs had stopped her from doing anything about it.

Her phone chimed, telling her she had an hour before she was due to meet Andrew. If she was going to leap without a net, it started with him.

"Get your leash, little girl. Our new adventure starts now."

"Hey Stockton," Billy called from the bar as she entered the dim space. "Malone coming?"

She smiled. Billy was nothing if not consistent. "Sorry to disappoint, but I'm meeting my brother tonight."

His face fell and he offered a less exuberant, "The usual?"

She started to say yes, but stopped. New adventure, she reminded herself. "No, give me something new, Billy. Something fruity with an umbrella."

"Stockton, you forget this is a sports bar? We don't do fruity and the only umbrella around her is the one in the lost and found."

"Fine, give me a long island." She waved her hand toward the towering display of bottles behind the bar.

"Whoa, going big," he said with a chuckle.

"Go big or go home, I always say." She'd literally never said that.

"And I'll have a Guinness," said a deep bass voice behind her.

"Hey," she said, turning to greet Andrew.

"Hey," he said, grabbing their drinks from the bar. "You look—"

She held up a hand. "Don't say it. I know I look like shit."

"*Shit?* Did I finally win the bet, Bridgie?"

She rolled her eyes. "Put his drink on my tab, Billy. My brother finally cracked me."

He followed her to a booth in the corner and slid in. "Why do I get the feeling it's not me that cracked you? What's up, Bridget?"

Wasn't that just the question? What *is* up? Every book she'd ever read about managing tough conversations says to start with something positive. "I adopted Destiny. The dog I was fostering."

"*O-kay.*" Andrew wiped a strip of Guinness foam from his top lip and squinted at her. "You mean the dog Blake was fostering?"

Bridget waved a hand in the air. "We shared the duties. As of this morning, you're looking at an official dog mom." She pinned her shoulders back and gave him her best business executive smile.

"You sure you have time for a dog?"

Her shoulders slumped. "Yes! Why does everyone keep asking me that? I wouldn't have adopted her if I didn't."

"Okay," he said, hands up in surrender. "Just a question. Where is she now?"

"She's spending the night with auntie Kal."

"She's not with Blake?"

Bridget dropped her eyes to the table. "No."

"What's going on, Bridgie?"

She took a long pull off her long island. *Holy Richard Hamilton*, these drinks were no joke. She dropped her head into her hands and groaned. "I don't know."

He gave her ponytail a little tug. "Don't know or won't say?"

"Both," she said through her fingers.

"Bridget, seriously, what is going on? You're freaking me out."

"I'm a mess. And you called me Bridget. You never do that."

He laughed. "You're the least messy person I know. And I figured a 'can we meet alone' meeting called for your actual name."

"I think that's the problem."

His brow crinkled. "I'm not following. What's the problem?"

"That I'm not messy. That I've forgotten how to be messy." She drew in a breath. "That I'm *afraid* to be messy."

He circled his hand. "Start at the beginning."

"You're aware of the little crush I've had on Blake."

He sighed. "What did he do?"

"I think the crush turned into love."

He spit, a trickle of beer cascading over his lower lip, catching in the scruff of his beard. "*Love?* When did that happen?"

She cringed. "Since I slept with him at your wedding."

He beat his fist against his forehead and squeezed his eyes shut. "No, no, no, just no. Thanks for that image that I'll never be able to unsee now."

She laughed, some of the tension finally melting.

"Is this why you asked to meet me? To tell me you're together?" He pointed at her tall glass, condensation dripping down the sides. "With the strongest drink you could think of?"

"Not exactly. Blake told me about your fight. Said you agreed that anything that might happen between me and him is none of your business."

"Mostly," he interjected. "I said it was *mostly* none of my business. If he hurts you, he's still going to answer to me."

"See, that's why I told him I needed to talk to you before anything more happened between us. I can't risk . . ." The bells and whistles of the At The Buzzer arcade game rang out, cutting off her sentence.

"You can't risk what, Bridgie?" Andrew asked, after the game stopped howling and the bros playing it stopped whacking each other on the back.

"I can't risk doing anything to jeopardize your dream. Hurt the band. Hurt you. I know what it's like to lose your dream, and I don't want you to feel that. Ever."

"Hold up." He held up his hands. "You've had feelings for him for years and stayed away from him because you worried how it might affect me? Affect Storyhill?"

"Don't act so surprised. You always told me not to hook up with any member of Storyhill."

Andrew fisted his fingers in his hair. "Grace is right. I am a world-class dick."

Bridget looked up, eyes wide. "Grace said that?"

"Well, not in those exact words, but that was essentially the meaning. Bridgie," he said, staring down the guy about to drop quarters into the game right next to him, "that was just me being an overprotective brother. If you'd have come to me and told me it was more than a hook-up, I would have—"

Bridget laughed, the sound thick through the tears clogging her throat. "You would have blown a gasket."

He laughed. "Okay, you're right, I probably would have. But I don't want to be the one keeping you from your dreams, either."

She shook her head, staring at her lap. "I don't have dreams anymore."

"That's not true. Everyone has dreams."

"Not me. I have goals—a lot of them—but not dreams."

A look of recognition flashed across his face. "Because if you don't have them, they can't be taken away? Like your basketball career."

The tears finally fell. She nodded.

"Bridget, if you don't have dreams all you're left with is nightmares."

She sniffled and wiped her eyes on a bar napkin. "Wow, that is profound, big brother. Sounds like the bridge to a country song."

"Uh, uh, you will not joke this away. This is the real reason you're not with Blake. All the stuff about me not approving is just a smokescreen. I should have seen that right away. You've never given a shit about my opinion on anything else. I'm right, aren't I?"

She started to shake her head no, but she was too tired, too sad, to deflect, to lie.

Billy rushed over, a massive stack of napkins in his hand. "Stockton, oh my god." He rubbed his hand on her back.

"What did you say to her?" he said to Andrew. "She never cries. She has terrible taste in drinks, but she's the toughest bitch I know."

Bridget raised her head, grabbing a fistful of napkins. "It's okay, Billy. Sometimes the truth hurts." He looked at her skeptically. "It really is okay." She held up her glass. "Think you could exchange this for my regular?" Billy nodded, pointed his fingers at his eyes and then at Andrew's, and walked backwards to the bar.

"Kal and I come here a lot," she said, reading Andrew's puzzled expression. "And he has a little" —she held her thumb and finger close together and then opened them wide— "thing for Kal. I think he's protecting me by association."

He ran a hand over her arm. "Or it could be because you're an amazing person and everyone in the world seems to know it but you."

"Stop," she said, waving her hands in front of her face. "Stop saying nice things about me. It's too shocking. I'll cry again."

"Okay, tough love it is," he said. "Sounds like you made one hell of a mess with Blake. Do you need my help cleaning it up?"

She smirked through the tears. "Only the first half of that qualifies as tough love. And, no, I created this steaming pile of shit. I'm the one who needs to clean it up."

"Whoa. Two curse words in" —he rotated his wrist, looking at his watch— "less than thirty minutes. Pace yourself, Bridgie."

"You know what, Andy? I'm so fucking tired of pacing myself, of believing I need to control every damn thing. I'm turning over a new goddamned leaf and leaving that shit behind."

A laugh rumbled from Andrew's throat. "Easy there, champ. Can't turn over a new leaf if you go into full-blown system failure by overloading the circuits. Maybe start with one curse word a day."

She pushed a finger into his chest. "You think I'm not up for the challenge?"

"I think my baby sister has yet to meet a challenge she can't conquer."

She sniffed again. "Thanks."

"And I promise to remind myself of that every time I start feeling the need to protect you."

"Or I will."

He laughed and nodded. "Fair. So, you've gotten the cursing out of the way. What's next up on the leaf-turning front?"

"I think it's time I find Blake Kelly and tell him I love him."

CHAPTER TWENTY-TWO

BLAKE PULLED A WOOF WATCHERS VOLUNTEER T-SHIRT over his head and looked in the mirror. His beard was longer than usual, and a deep purple stain hung under his eyes. Five days. He'd only heard from Bridget once in five days. A brief acknowledgement of an email he'd sent her. Any other communication about the event had come through Lucy at Woof Watchers. Including the fact that she'd applied to adopt Destiny.

On Thursday, Andrew had texted, asking Blake to meet for lunch. He'd declined, saying Gramps wasn't supposed to be left alone for one to two weeks after his surgery. He could have invited Andrew to the brownstone, but he wanted to let Bridget talk to him first. And he could only imagine the questions Gramps would have for Bridget's older brother. He hoped that she'd reach out after Andrew's visit, but she hadn't. He shouldn't be surprised. Bridget said they'd talk at the event. And Bridget followed the rules.

Today was the day. No more avoiding. Today, they had to work together to pull this thing off. He knew she'd be professional, but that almost made it worse. He didn't know if he could handle the woman he'd fallen in love with, being cool and distant.

He wanted her smiles, her touch. Not all-business version of Bridget Hayes.

After the welcome distraction of staying with Gramps this week, his mother was on duty today, leaving him with several empty hours before the event. Hours that could too easily fill with worrying and obsessing about Bridget. He shook his head. He'd spent the week waiting for her to reach out, jumping every time his phone pinged with an incoming text, and ignoring Gramps' suggestions that he "take initiative, young man." It was time to take Gramps' advice—and Bridget's. She always said that the best defense is a good offense. But how to do that?

He needed help. He didn't have time for a full band Bat Signal. Plus, Andrew might be coming around, but he didn't know what Bridget told him. He ticked through the remaining band members and Nick felt like the best option.

He opened FaceTime and hit Nick's name. In less than two rings, Nick's mini-me appeared on the screen. "Hi, Uncle Blake," the little dude said, his smile revealing a couple of missing teeth.

"Hi Henry. It looks like the Tooth Fairy might visit soon."

"They've already been here. I got two dollars."

"Wow. The Tooth Fairy is much more generous than when I was a kid."

"Yeah," he said, nodding his head sagely. "Inflation."

Blake bit back a smile and nodded. "What are going to do with the money?"

"I wanted to open an IRA, but Dad said it wasn't enough money, so I put it in my savings account."

Like father, like son. "Smart choice. Is your dad available?"

"He's doing laundry. I'll get him."

The phone bounced as Henry ran down the hall. "Dad!" he

yelled, causing Blake to wince. "Dad! Uncle Blake wants to talk to you."

The screen blurred and when it cleared, Nick was looking back at him, a couple of clothespins hanging from his mouth.

"Laundry, huh?"

"What can I say? I live a glamorous life. You got that event today?" he asked, pointing at Blake's t-shirt.

"Yeah. Thanks for sending a donation."

"Sure. Gave me a chance to talk to Henry about responsible pet ownership. And since you already emailed me a thank you, I'm guessing that's not why you called."

"Ah, no." Blake pushed his fingers through his hair, rubbing the base of his neck. "I need to talk to someone, and a full-on Bat Signal was not appropriate. You got time?"

"I've actually been waiting."

"For what?"

"You to call me about Bridget Hayes."

Blake's mouth dropped open. "Wait. Seriously? I thought Grace was the clairvoyant in this group."

"Not taking anything from Grace, I just pay attention. You might think you're stealthy, but your attraction to her has been pretty apparent. The dust up in the desert was all the confirmation I needed." He bobbed his head side-to-side. "That and I might have seen you leaving her room the morning after Andrew's wedding."

"And you didn't say anything?"

He shrugged. "Figured it wasn't any of my business. So, are you looking for advice on telling her how you feel, or did you already do that and screwed it up?" His hand covered the screen as he propped the phone up.

"I think I told her how I feel, and I don't *think* I screwed it up."

"You think? Clarify."

That's what he loved about Nick. Never said ten words when three would do. "I told her I'd like to date her. See where things went."

"And what did she say?"

"She said she needed to talk to Andrew."

Nick dropped one of Henry's t-shirts into a laundry basket and looked Blake square in the eye. "She said what now?"

"Right?" Blake paced from his kitchen to his living room and back. "I told her about the conversation Andrew and I had in Vegas, and she said she needed to talk to him herself. And that we shouldn't talk until she did so."

Nick lowered his voice. "Were you naked during this conversation?"

Blake stopped moving. "What does that have to do with anything?"

"Nakedness changes what you say *and* what you hear. Answer the question."

"No."

He tapped a finger on his lips. "Did either of you use the words, I love you?"

Blake groaned. "Not exactly. I told her it felt like we'd made love."

Nick pursed his lips, disappointment flashing across his face. "So you were naked."

"No." Blake pinched the bridge of his nose. "Nick, seriously, I am going to see this woman in a couple of hours and need some advice on what to do."

"Has she talked to Andrew?"

"I think so. He was in town a couple of days ago."

"And you didn't hear from her after that?"

"No." Blake was getting annoyed. "Just tell me what you think."

Nick carefully folded t-shirts on some sort of blue plastic

contraption and silence stretched between them. Knowing Nick was thinking, not ignoring him, Blake tried to wait patiently for his response. It was sort of working.

"How's she with risk?"

Blake inwardly groaned. "Terrible."

Nick nodded. "Then what I think is that Andrew is an excuse," he said, his words forming slowly. "She's scared." He pulled another kid-sized t-shirt from the washer and flipped it into the dryer. "It's your turn to be the strong one. Lay all your cards on the table. Tell her how you feel. Clearly. She needs to know for absolute certain that you are all in—if you are."

"I am. I haven't felt this before, but I either have the world's worst case of heartburn or I'm in love with her."

"And Blake" —Nick turned and looked directly into the camera— "after you tell her, you need to make sure she's all in. It serves no one for you to do all the heavy lifting. That never works."

Blake dropped his head to his chest. "How do you know all this?"

"Because I've made all the mistakes, buddy. And had a lot of time to think about how I should have done things differently."

"Any other advice?"

"Be clear, but since she's a little skittish, maybe don't come on full frontal. Sneak in from the side."

Blake wasn't sure what that meant, but he had an hour and forty-five minutes to figure it out.

"Thanks man."

"Go get her, tiger."

Laughter erupted from Blake's chest. "Tiger?"

"Sorry, that's what I call Henry." Nick cleared his throat, his brow dropping. "Let me know how it goes."

Blake nodded and disconnected the call. Lay all his cards on the table. Sneak in from the side. He may not know exactly how to do that, but there was a guy downstairs who claimed he'd once been the best wooer in the land. Time to pay Gramps a visit.

Blake walked into the arena and made his way to the volunteers' table. Lucy was directing the caterers to their appointed location. Camila was wrangling two exuberant yellow lab puppies into a cordoned-off pen lined with AstroTurf. And Bridget was placing auction items on long tables draped with white tablecloths.

"Blake," Camila yelled over puppy yips. "We need you to welcome the guests out front—they're not due to arrive for another 40 minutes, but there are always early birds, as you know. There are packets of tickets on the table, each marked with a name. Give them their envelope, direct them to the appropriate event, and encourage them to bid on the auction items until it's their turn at one of the games."

Blake smirked. He knew the drill, but the staff was always amped up on event days. He picked up the boxes of envelopes, carefully stacking one on top of the other. His eyes drifted over to Bridget. She'd heard his voice, heard Camila call out to him, but she kept her head down.

He walked up behind her. "Hi," he said—because he was a certified smooth talker. He rolled his eyes. "All good here?"

She turned to him. "Everything's in order. You?"

He lifted the boxes in answer to her question. "Guess it's time to turn on the Blake Kelly charm."

She smiled and he felt like he'd just won the lottery.

"Remember to set it to stun. We don't need any casualties today. I know how deadly it can be."

"Bridget," he said.

"Let's get this up and running first," she said, answering his unspoken question. She pointed to center court. "See you in the stands?"

He nodded and turned to go. She hadn't frozen him out or walked away. He'd take that as a win.

"Blake," she called after him.

"Yeah?"

Her lips curled. "A reminder. Those bags of cookies in the lobby are for dogs, not people."

"Got it," he said, spinning back toward the entry doors, smiling like an idiot. A joke was a good sign.

When everyone was checked in, he grabbed a soda and headed to the stands. With capable volunteers covering each station, he could take a short break. He needed to talk to Bridget. Being in the same building with her and not talking to her was driving him crazy.

He climbed the stairs. She was sitting in the third row with another familiar face. He dropped into the seat at the end of her row, waved at her, and pulled out his phone. He copied and pasted from his Notes app and hit send.

Bridget pulled out her phone. "A text?" she called down the row, lifting an eyebrow.

Gramps had helped him with the idea, but the execution was all him. He'd kept turning over Nick's advice about sneaking in from the side. Bridget was the most open over text and it was in those moments that he'd fallen in love with her. If face-to-face conversations were too hard, he'd start with a text. Sneak in from the side.

He shrugged. "Why mess with a winning formula? Read it."

She narrowed her gaze but lifted her phone. Her eyes widened, but remained glued to her screen.

He'd read and re-read the contents of the text so many times that he'd memorized the message.

You caught my attention from the start
Since that day, you've had my heart
I held you in my arms half a country away
On the dance floor and with the sun's first rays
I thought that was my only chance, my only taste, my one date
But it turns out, I'd underestimated fate
Your life knitted itself in mine
Through texts and truths my life started to realign
The beat of my heart could no longer be ignored
Its faith in love restored
You saw through my pain to the real me
Our connection, a true date with destiny
Now my heart craves only one thing
A chance to love you my whole life through
A chance to walk hand in hand with you

Her fingers moved over her phone, but she still didn't look at him. His phone buzzed and he jumped.

Bridget: You couldn't find anything to rhyme with thing?

He chuckled. *That's what you took from all that?* he typed back.

His phone buzzed again. Was she ever going to look at him?

Bridget: Do you mean all of this?

He stood and moved to the seat next to her. "That and more."

The familiar face sitting next to Bridget woofed.

He laughed. "How'd you get her in here?"

"I know people at the top. And I told security she's the organization's mascot. Really, she's my emotional support animal."

His smile dipped. "You needed her to face me?"

"That and" —she stared out at the court— "other things."

298

Destiny barked again and hopped up and down in Bridget's lap.

Blake rubbed the pup's head. "I think she's telling you to give us a chance."

"She *is* much better at love than me."

He tucked a hair that had come loose from her ponytail behind her ear. "You're better than you think."

She smirked. "Maybe that's true. I did get Mr. Commitment Phobe to open his heart."

"And write poetry."

"And that. Was that Clyde's idea?"

He laughed. "How did you know?"

She shrugged. "Best wooer in the land. Or so he says."

Blake laughed again and then sobered. "Did you talk to Andrew?"

She nodded, her eyes on Destiny, where she was absently scratching her head. "I did."

He lifted her chin with a finger and turned her head to meet his gaze. "And?"

"And you were right. Andrew is, was, always has been, an excuse. I realized quite a few things in that conversation, including that only a guy who loves me would give me the space to do what I needed to do. Even if it sounded crazy."

Blake took her hands. "I do love you, Bridget Hayes."

The buzzer sounded, announcing the start of the three-on-three tourney. Bridget's face drained of color, and she stood, handing Destiny to him. Who he'd just noticed was wearing a jersey. He looked up at Bridget. "She's wearing a Hayes jersey."

Bridget unzipped her warm-up jacket and let it fall to her seat. "So am I."

He couldn't have been more surprised if she had stripped naked. "You're playing?"

"I'm playing. I'm sure very poorly, but no worse than the rest of those geezers out there."

"What? Why? How?" he stumbled.

She smiled, still green around the gills. "While you were writing poetry, I was trying to figure out a way to show you I'm not running and hiding anymore. Not from my past. Not from the present. Not from you. I could've told you, but playing in the tourney seemed like the perfect way to *show* you."

Unshed tears burned behind his eyes. "I'm so proud of you."

A nervous laugh fell from her lips. "Don't be proud yet. I haven't made it to the court. There's a very real possibility I'll pass out."

He placed a hand on her waist. "Do you want my help?"

She shook her head. "Thank you, but no. I need to do this myself. So that we can start doing everything else *together*."

She descended the stairs and met Camila at center court, taking the microphone from her. "Thanks to everyone for being here today. I'm Bridget Hayes" —a cheer went through the crowd, and she looked surprised— "I'm the President of Business Operations for the New York Flames and co-chair of this event. Along with Blake Kelly. Stand up Blake."

He tucked Destiny under his arm like a football and waved. A few whistles rang through the air, along with a lot of applause.

"Blake and I knew each other a long time before we became co-chairs. But it turns out it took a date with Destiny to make us realize that we're a perfect team. Thanks for doing all this." She gestured to the arena. "I love you, Blake Kelly. For loving dogs. And for loving me."

"Does this mean I've got a date for after the event?" he yelled from the seats and laughter erupted around him.

Destiny barked three times. "If *we've* got a date?" he corrected, lifting the dog in his arms.

She nodded, her bright smile lighting up her face. "I think it's a pretty safe bet that you've got yourself a date for every event, from here on out."

"So, would you say that's a new *rule*?"

"Yes," she said with a soft laugh. "One that I don't plan on breaking."

The crowd cheered, and Bridget turned to Camila. "I think it's time to play some basketball."

EPILOGUE

EIGHTEEN MONTHS LATER

A black blur raced around the tables, skidding to a stop at Bridget's feet. The dog's tongue hung out, lolling to the side. Bridget laughed and scratched the world's cutest escape artist on the head.

"I'm sorry, Coach," a long-legged teenager said, slightly winded. "I wanted to say goodbye before we went home. When she saw you . . . I guess I wasn't holding on to the leash tight enough. I'll be more careful from now on, I promise," Ruby said.

"I know you will," Bridget said, reassuring the girl. "Thanks again for watching her while we're gone."

"Thanks for letting me," the young woman said enthusiastically. "Dad said if this goes well, maybe we can get a dog."

"Make sure to get it at Woof Watchers," Bridget said, wagging a finger.

"Can't wear their name on our jerseys and not adopt there," Ruby responded with a smile. She wrapped Destiny's leash tightly around her hand and spoke to the dog. "Come, Destiny."

When the dog didn't move, still staring adoringly up at Bridget, Ruby tried again. "Do you want a treat, Destiny?" The dog spun; all thoughts of Bridget gone. "I've got some in the car."

The dog happily trotted after the teenager. "See ya in a couple of weeks, Coach!" she said with a wave.

"I'm still not used to hearing them call you 'Coach,'" Kalisha said, bumping her shoulder into Bridget's.

Bridget smiled. After stepping onto the court at the Woof Watchers event a year and a half ago, she quickly realized two things: one, her leg wouldn't hold up to the punishment of running up and down the court and two, she needed to find some small way to get back on the court. In an ironic twist of fate, Ruby's dad—the man sitting across from her on the flight to Andrew's wedding—had tracked her down and, after explaining that the coach on Ruby's youth basketball team had to step away for medical reasons, asked if Bridget might consider coaching the team.

And for once in her life, she didn't over-analyze the decision. She'd immediately agreed to the volunteer position and hadn't once regretted the decision. Of all the new things she'd added to her life, coaching those young women ranked among the best.

Bridget threaded her arm through Kal's. "It is strange, but it feels great."

"I'm proud of you, Bri," Kal said.

"So proud you'd be willing to be my assistant coach? I could use an elite defensive mind."

Kal laughed. "You sure it's not an extra cat wrangler you're looking for?"

"I didn't say what kind of defense I needed," Bridget said, matching her best friend's laugh.

"Hey Coach," a familiar voice said just over Bridget's shoulder, joining their group of two. "Fancy meeting you here."

She turned and smiled at the man. "You shouldn't be surprised. I specifically remember telling you I'd see you at the next Storyhill wedding."

He chuckled. "I do recall that, but at the time, I was pretty certain there'd be no more weddings."

She brushed a small green leaf from his lapel and straightened his tie. "What changed your mind?"

"It's a long story."

"I've got all night, but maybe start with the abridged version. I do owe a man a dance."

"Short version, huh? He tapped a finger to his chin. "I'd say it was a woman, her lists, and her dog that made me reconsider."

Bridget cocked an eyebrow. "Lists, huh? Sounds like a woman with a plan. I think I'd like her."

He shrugged. "She's mostly okay."

She swiped at his chest. "Mostly?"

He leaned down, brushing off the hem of her dress. "Well, she does have dog hair all over the bottom of her wedding dress."

"The savage."

He laughed. "Right?"

"Gathered guests, may I have your attention please?" the DJ called from behind his monstrous set-up. "Please put your hands together and join me in welcoming the bride and groom to the dance floor."

"You ready to take this back to where it all started?"

Her gorgeous new husband met her gaze and winked. "I think we both know it started way before that dance, TNR. But I certainly liked where that dance led."

She bit back a smile. "A lifetime of love?"

Blake drew a finger over her bare shoulder and down her arm. "I was thinking more about what happened right after that first dance. Think we could recreate that, too?"

"I might struggle to find another Gladys to take us to the hotel, but the rest I can manage."

Blake waggled his eyebrows. "Still a top five memory." He offered her his arm and they stepped onto the dance floor. "Thanks again," he said as he wrapped an arm around her waist, moving them in time with the music.

Her brows pulled together. "For what?"

"Agreeing to be my wife. Traveling this road with me."

She shrugged and twirled the layers of satin around her legs. "I did it for this spectacular dress. And your mother."

Blake cocked an eyebrow. "My mother?"

Bridget pointed to the table where Bette and Clyde sat talking to her parents. "Did you see her beaming from the front row? She didn't stop smiling the entire ceremony."

He spun her to the right and reeled her back into his chest. "Your eyes were supposed to be on me, TNR."

"They were, Blakey. Mostly," she added with a grin. "But I didn't want to miss a single moment of this day, so I might have looked away from you. Once or twice. Just for a few seconds."

"That's what photos are for," he said, pulling a frown that she knew was one hundred percent for show. He and Bette had been working to repair their relationship, and while there had been a few bumps along the road, her happiness was very important to Blake.

"How about I don't take my eyes off you for the next two weeks?"

Storyhill had a two-month break between concerts, and Bridget trusted the Flames staff to keep everything running smoothly in her absence. Okay, let's be serious. She'd probably —definitely—check in occasionally from their honeymoon in Santorini.

"Sounds like a deal." He kissed her on the forehead. "Have I told you recently how much I love you, Bridget Hayes?"

She smiled. "Not in the last five minutes."

"Well, I do. More than I thought possible."

"I love you too, Blake Kelly."

A finger tapped on her shoulder. "May I cut in? DJ's orders."

Bridget laughed. "Far be it from us to defy the DJ." She stepped from Blake's arms into her father's.

Bridget watched over Charles' shoulder as Blake extended a hand to his mother, who waited at the edge of the dance floor. They'd decided that a father-daughter dance was a little antiquated and it'd be much better to have a child-parent dance . . . or whatever it should be called. They never came up with a name for it. Blake had applauded when she finally said, "It doesn't need a label. Let's just do it." Well, he applauded *after* he teased, "But if it doesn't have a label, how will you slot it into the evening's agenda?"

"You happy, Sugarplum?" Charles Hayes asked, pulling Bridget's attention from her husband and mother-in-law.

"More than I ever thought possible," she said, repeating Blake's words. Adopting Destiny, coaching youth sports, marrying Blake, they'd all led her to the same conclusion: to get life's best rewards, you had to take some risks.

Grabbing a drink at the bar, Blake watched Clyde spin Bridget around the dance floor. His grandfather, his mother, his brothers, his new in-laws, his beautiful bride, the family he'd craved for so long, all in one room. Grateful wasn't a big enough word.

He grabbed a second beer from the bartender, walked to a table tucked into the corner, and set the drink down in front of his best man.

Nick took a long drag from the glass. "If memory serves, I predicted that you'd be next."

Blake shook his head, his eyes flashing back to the woman in white currently laughing with his grandfather. "And I still can't quite believe it."

"She's an amazing woman," Nick said, lifting his glass. "Even if she is—"

"Related to Andrew," they said in unison and laughed.

Nick's smile quickly faded, and he spun the glass in his hand, bringing the beer's foamy head to the brim. Blake studied his face. They'd been sitting at a table like this one, each nursing a beer, when they decided to start Storyhill. Friends before that, brothers since. Nearly fifteen years later, Blake easily read Nick's moods. Smiles and laughter came easily to Nick, but so did worry and melancholy. Tonight's expression was something Blake hadn't seen before.

"Where's Henry?" he asked, wondering if Nick was worried about his son.

Nick drummed his fingers against the glass. "His grandmother picked him up after the ceremony."

"So, you're free to dance," Blake said, biting his bottom lip and shimmying his shoulders, trying to perk up his friend's mood.

"Not really feeling it tonight."

Blake raised an eyebrow. "When have you ever turned down an opportunity to prove that a guy might look like Paul Bunyan, but he can still bust a move?" He poked a playful finger into Nick's shoulder.

Nick's eyes flashed to his, immediately falling back to the table. "Kirsten finally signed the divorce papers."

Blake's smile fell and he squeezed Nick's shoulder. "When?"

"A courier delivered them on Tuesday."

"Why didn't you say anything?"

"This is your wedding, brother. No room for talk of divorce here."

"I'm so sorry, man. I know it's been a long time coming, but that doesn't make it any easier."

Nick ran a hand through his short hair. "She didn't even ask for any kind of custody. It's like she's washed her hands of both of us. I get marriages not working out, but walking away from your own kid? Who does that?"

A barbed arrow punctured Blake's heart. "My dad," he breathed out before he could stop himself.

Nick's head popped up. "I'm sorry, B. I wasn't thinking . . ."

"It's okay. Really," he added when Nick's expression fell further. "It took me a long time to get there, but I realized that if someone doesn't want to be a parent, it's not a good idea to force them. Kids feel that stuff. No one wants to feel like an obligation or a burden."

Nick nodded. "I've been trying to convince myself that it'd harder for Henry if she suddenly reappeared in his life after all this time."

Blake pulled his phone from his pocket and typed in a quick three-word text. Three men in various parts of the room reached into their pockets and, seconds later, scanned the room. Blake gave a small wave and they walked toward him and Nick.

Matt, Joe, and Andrew pulled up chairs. Nick looked from Blake to the other men, his forehead wrinkling in confusion.

"Blake sent the Bat-Signal," Andrew said, answering Nick's silent question. "What's up?"

"Family meeting," Blake said, gesturing to Nick.

Nick cleared his throat and relayed the story to the three men, while Blake sent an additional text. Grace met his gaze and nodded. She wound through the tables, speaking in turn to

Avery, Julia, and Bridget. Moments later, the women ringed the men's circle of chairs.

Now, it was a true family meeting.

Grace wrapped her arms around Nick's shoulders. "We're all aunties, and Henry is one of our own. We'll all make sure he never forgets that."

"Even when he wants to," Avery added with a soft laugh.

Blake stood from his chair and slid an arm around Bridget's waist. "I am the luckiest man alive," he whispered in her ear.

"*We're* the luckiest people alive," she whispered back, placing a light kiss on his cheek. "We get to chase our dreams and take risks knowing we have each other and these people at our backs."

He kissed her temple, his gaze traveling over the assembled group. "Bring on the adventures, TNR, bring 'em on."

ABOUT THE AUTHOR

Annmarie Boyle is a connoisseur of yoga pants, Sharpies, and fancy coffee drinks.

She loves to create stories about strong, smart, and sexy women tackling some of life's biggest issues—while finding their happily-ever-after along the way. Throw in a lot of laughter and a fabulous supporting cast of characters and you've got the stories she both loves to write and read.

She enjoys traveling the world but spends most of her time in a sleepy Midwestern town overlooking a lazy river with her husband, who, after 20+ years, still makes her believe in happily-ever-afters.

To sign up for Annmarie's latest news, new release notifications, and priority access to bonus material, visit her website and subscribe to her monthly newsletter.

Also connect at:

instagram.com/annmarieboyleauthor

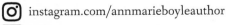

facebook.com/annmarieboyleauthor

bookbub.com/profile/annmarie-boyle

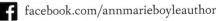

ACKNOWLEDGMENTS

.

Thank you for reading Bridget and Blake's story! I'm so thankful for each and every reader who takes time from their busy lives to slip into the Storyhill world for a little while.

Thanks to my editor Jolene Perry who patiently edited this book, not once, but twice. It's been a hard year for this writer (along with so many others) and I'm so appreciative of your kinds words and hanging in there with me.

To Niomi, Tricia, and Emily, my steadfast proofreaders, I take these books to print only after they have passed under your watchful eyes. The world (okay, just this book) would have an excess of periods, missed words, and commas in wrong places without you! Thank you for your time and attention! As has become my habit, I'm thanking you the only way I know how—with a character named after you inside this book!

To all the book bloggers and bookstagrammers, I appreciate all the advance love you've given this book (and the other Storyhill books)!

And finally, to Emilie at RatetheRomance, I'm sending a big virtual hug for suggesting (when I was stumped) several possible names for Blake's favorite charity — Woof Watchers is the perfect name name!

Made in the USA
Columbia, SC
07 August 2022